First Tango In Paris 2

"The Conclusion"

By

Emma Styles

COPYRIGHT

AUTHOR'S NOTE:

DEDICATED TO:

PREFACE:

Chapter One: The Big Four "0"

Chapter Two: An Exquisite Appetiser

Chapter Three: Into The Unknown

Chapter Four: The Grand Event

Chapter Five: Discovering Charlotte

Chapter Six: A Bejewelled Friday

Chapter Seven: Much Admired

Chapter Eight: Planning and Scheming

Chapter Nine: A Dutch Indulgence

Chapter Ten: Paradise In The Paradise

Chapter Eleven: Fun4Two

Chapter Twelve: The Rise Of Cougar

Chapter Thirteen: London Awakens (Slowly)

Chapter Fourteen: Good Penny – Bad Penny!

Chapter Fifteen: Unexpected Glamour

Chapter Sixteen: Relight My Fire (Les Pompiers)

Chapter Seventeen: Planning, Plotting & Playing

Chapter Eighteen: Online Assignations

Chapter Nineteen: Miami Beckoned

Chapter Twenty: Mandingo Overload

Chapter Twenty-One: London Awakens 2

Chapter Twenty-Two: Marbella Madness

Chapter Twenty-Three: Moulded In His Image

Chapter Twenty-Four: Moon City

Chapter Twenty-Five: A Monumental Event

Chapter Twenty-Six: Showboating!

Chapter Twenty-Seven: The Rise & Rise Of Social Media

Chapter Twenty-Eight: Post NOTW

Chapter Twenty-Nine: The Accidental Exhibitionist

Chapter Thirty: Beach Life

Chapter Thirty-One: Cabopino Playa

Chapter Thirty-Two: A Staring Role

Chapter Thirty-Three: First Tango - The Upshot

Chapter Thirty-Four: Mentoring Karen

Chapter Thirty-Five: A Soiree With A Difference

Chapter Thirty-Six: Paul's Point Of View

Chapter Thirty-Seven: The Exuberance Of Youth

Chapter Thirty-Eight: Paris v London

Chapter Thirty-Nine: A Late Entry

Chapter Forty: In Summary

Chapter Forty-One: And In Conclusion

COPYRIGHT

©Emma Styles. 2016

Emma Styles asserts the moral right to be identified as the author of this work.

emmajstyles@gmail.com

AUTHOR'S NOTE:

This book is a work of memoir. It is a wholly true story based on my best recollections of various events in my life. Where indicated, the names and identifying characteristics of certain people mentioned in the book have been changed in order to protect their privacy. In some instances, I rearranged and/or compressed events and time periods in service of the narrative, and I recreated dialogue to match my best recollection of those exchanges.

"EROTIC FACT IS ALWAYS BETTER THAN FICTION"

Current Favourite Quote

"Nymphomaniac: a woman as obsessed with sex as an average man". Mignon McLaughlin

Revealingly Honest & Explicitly Written Erotica

"My Journey From Kitten To Cougar"

DEDICATED TO:

My ever understanding husband Paul, who as always gives me his blessing and complete support.

All the great people I have encountered along the way. Especially all of you the readers, who made this possible by reading "First Tango 1" and giving me the confidence to continue writing. Your Emails and feedback are a great source of inspiration. Enjoy!

Also from this Author:

"*First Tango In Paris*" an Amazon #1Bestseller & the bestselling Novella "*Distracted*"

Multiple 5 Star Reviews on Amazon and Across Multiple Book Sites.

Available For All eReader Devices.

PREFACE:

Many of you will know that after the totally unexpected and overwhelming success of my initial book of memoir "First Tango In Paris" that I decamped to Southern Spain to write this *"The Conclusion"*, however, once again a great many of you will be aware that as a result of a completely unforeseen Skype call from Antonia that my plans were completely scuppered. Thankfully, all was not lost, and as a result of her extended visit, and our rather risqué adventures together in the sun, my second book was written and published on Amazon (*Distracted*).

So, armed once again with all my notes, diaries and my trusty Macbook Pro I returned home to Kew, where I now sit glued to the keyboard with the sole intention of finally bringing you up to date with my journey from "First Tango 1" all the way through to this *"The Conclusion"*.

In the following chapters you will once again meet many of the original characters from the first book, and many new ones that were corrupted along the way! I have included several of my further adventures in **Paris**; however, in the "Noughties" I spread my wings to also enjoy the delights of **Amsterdam, London** and beyond. As a treat there is also a segment written by Paul, expressing his point of view and one of his own personal highlights described in explicit detail.

As the book journeys through to its present day *"Conclusion"* I detail comprehensively my experiences in the swinging scene in **London** and across England and its massive explosion in popularity after the demise of "The News Of The World" and its titillating exposé culture.

I also widely document as how the explosion of the Internet during this period was a major factor in cultivating the booming swinging scene in the United Kingdom today. How the small niche websites of the early days have now mushroomed into enormously popular swingers meeting places and a massive knowledge resource, with all genres catered for. From vanilla to the extreme, it's all a click away.

As a guide to help you along in your quest for excitement I have added a chapter titled "**In Summary**" at the end of the book, where I index and give a brief synopsis of some of the finer swinging establishments that London and the U.K has to offer at the present time. A small directory of decadence!

So please just pick up where we left off in the first book, and enjoy the adventures with me in this the concluding book, as always I look forward to all your emails and hearing about how the books helped you on in your own "special journey".

As usual please take the time to *Google* the places and locations mentioned, even better search and visit them on *"Google street view"*. Many readers have emailed me saying they did just this in planning their own trips, and that it added to the excitement enormously!

Chapter One: The Big Four "0"

It was March in the early "Noughties" (vanity prevents me from being too specific!) and I was fast approaching a milestone in any woman's life, the big 4 zero, the psychologically fearsome fortieth year on this planet. I had been ignoring it for several months, simply pretending to myself that it was just another birthday, but then that little voice inside my head, yes, the voice of insecurity was constantly there to remind me.

Around a month before the fateful day, Paul told me to keep my dairy free for the entire birthday weekend as we were going to celebrate the occasion in "style". I guessed, in no small part due to the many furtive and whispered phone calls that had been occurring of late that Yves would have a major hand in the planning of the event. Over the years Paul and Yves (Le Général) had established a strong bond and a firm respectful friendship. At this point Yves was approaching his mid seventies, Paul saw him as the elder statesman and trusted him explicitly to look after my wellbeing, as on many occasions over the years he loaned me to him as his muse and sexual plaything. Something as you know I wholeheartedly throw myself into with total abandon and enjoyment.

All I was permitted to know was that the celebrations would be taking place in, yes; you guessed it, my favourite city on the planet Paris! The place where it all began, way back in the early nineties.

The children were at this stage both away at school so we planned for them to be home for the weekend prior so we could all be together for a family birthday meal. Paul's parents would also be visiting from France for the occasion. As the date drew closer, I admit to getting my usual tingling feeling of excitement whenever a visit (of which there had now been so many) to Paris was on the horizon. The mere mention of the city still sends a tingle down my spine.

Chapter Two: An Exquisite Appetiser

With only a small roll on case packed, as I still kept many of my clothes at the Paris apartment that I'd been using as a base over the years whilst running the successful on-line business, which, as many of you will know we sold and now still flourished under the umbrella of the large American Corporation that we'd sold out to.

We travelled on the Friday, first class on my transport of choice, Eurostar, which always adds a frisson of excitement to the approaching delights of Paris. It's so relaxing yet so exhilarating!

That feeling deep in my core intensified substantially the closer we got to the Gare Du Nord, the starting point of a great many of my sexual dalliances, both with Paul and as a fully liberated solo female, who was entirely in charge of her sexual needs, and fed them copiously at will, all with the full approval of her encouraging husband. Over the years the level of trust between us has never waivered, and this simply adds to the excitement of it all.

As normal Yves sent a car to pick us up at the Station. Bruno his long time driver had recently retired and had been replaced by a very charming young man called Marc, who swiftly as the occasion warranted delivered us to the most sumptuous and elegant hotel "Le Meurice", which is directly in front the Tuileries Garden and a few steps away from Le Louvre, it's a perfect hotel in a impeccable location. The Belle Etoile Suite was at our disposal for three nights courtesy of Yves, complete with inclusive Spa treatments of my choice as a birthday gift. We soon made short shrift of the complimentary bottle of iced Krug and the platter of fresh strawberries and raspberries waiting in the room for us.

As my party was arranged for the following evening we'd arranged to meet Yves, and a few of his close friends at eight in the hotel bar for drinks prior to dinner at a close by restaurant that had recently been opened to much acclaim from the local food snobs. In the meantime Paul and I took a stroll to a nearby lingerie shop that over the years had become a favourite of mine, to do a bit of retail therapy. I bought several new pairs of La Perla hold-ups and a selection of very tiny lace panties of varying colours.

It was as always a pleasure to be in the company of Yves and his friends, who were your typical suave older Frenchman; they flirted outrageously with me over dinner, much to Paul's delight and encouragement. During coffee and brandies there was a lot of seat swapping going on, with the men taking turns in sitting beside me and chatting, whilst discreetly giving my ever responsive clitoris some much welcomed attention. I was wearing a three quarter length figure hugging silk dress which had cried out to be worn without panties, so I was very accessible to their inquisitive fingers. It was a huge challenge not to make any obvious noises during my several mini orgasms and alert the fellow diners as to what was happening. Great fun, enjoyed by all involved. As everyone was saying their goodnights Yves slipped me a small envelope with that familiar glint in his eyes, one I'd become accustomed to over the years and knew it was "trouble". Trouble of the kind that always appealed to my decadent nature.

Returning to the hotel and retiring to the suite for a customary night cap of Jack Daniels my mind started to race when reading the note that Yves had given me, it was simply an address and time early the following afternoon and it stipulated "go alone". I sipped my drink with my thoughts going into overdrive as to what Yves had planned for me prior to my party. I was intrigued and excited but soon drifted off in the huge comfortable bed whilst Paul finished his drink out on the terrace, with its fantastic views of the Eiffel Tower, all lit up in its magnificent glory. An inspiring, if not phallic symbol, proudly proclaiming all that's erotic about Paris and its people.

Chapter Three: Into The Unknown

After a very leisurely breakfast served to us on the aforementioned terrace in the warm Parisian sunshine it was time to shower and get ready for what lay ahead of me at midday. It was a struggle to take off the huge fluffy cotton robe, but the walk in wet room shower rapidly hit all the right spots. I was unsure as to what to wear, as I had no idea whatsoever what Yves had planned, so simplicity seemed the best way forward. I had not had a chance to go to the apartment so was limited in choice, so jeans, heels and a light cashmere V-neck sweater in vivid yellow were chosen.

Paul had arranged to meet some old friends from the music industry for lunchtime drinks, so we left the hotel together, but with totally different agenda's, I had an inkling mine may turn out to be a bit fruitier.

The concierge immediately walked me to the taxi that had been prearranged for me. I handed the driver Yves's note with my destination, but he was obviously already briefed as he nodded and instantly drove off. I was still completely in the dark as to what to expect, but starting to get very excited, with an intense fizz starting to emanate through my body as I was being driven through the bustling streets. Within twenty minutes we were pulling up outside an elegant looking five-story townhouse on the Avenue Hoche, a stone's throw from the ever frantic Arc de Triomphe and its world renowned round about.

The driver had been taken care of in advance, but I still slipped him a fifty euro note, extravagant, but excusable, as I was now approaching the plateau of my quick and instant mini climaxes, which over the years I'd learned to control, it was like second nature to me.

I climbed the steps to the large solid oak entrance and tentatively rang the buzzer whilst looking directly up into the security camera. Within seconds a very attractive middle-aged lady, elegantly attired in a black trouser suite, opened it. She introduced herself as Inès and smiled as she saw what I was wearing and said, "you really don't know why you're here, do you? She lead me in to the grand marbled foyer whilst telling me that the other lady guest had already arrived, and that we would join her for a drink, where she'd then explain to both of us the etiquette of her new, but very much in demand "Club Privé".

I followed her down the staircase to the basement area passing a room with large closed double doors, from which was emanating voices, laughter and the tell tale clinking of champagne flutes. There were several more doors and passageways until we eventually arrived at a wood panelled snug room where I was given a glass of Gosset Grand Rosé Champagne and introduced to Valérie, the other lady guest, who was here for her own special occasion.

Inès proceeded to explain about her little establishment, and what it catered for. The club was called "*la langue ludique*" which roughly translated meant the "playful tongue". I was now totally captivated and intrigued, she had my full attention. The club was open four evenings a week and afternoons were reserved just for private bookings. The concept was as the name suggests a place for gentlemen who were connoisseurs of pleasing a lady with solely their tongues and for ladies who relished various gentlemen feasting on them. She explained that there would be no penetrative sex, and the gentlemen remained dressed at all times. Their sole purpose was to worship our womanhood and give pleasure to the lady. The men would then return home to their wives and mistresses, and according to Inès they then performed with a fervour that left their own partners gasping and totally satisfied. She told us there were ten gents waiting with eager and expertly talented tongues, and that they would pleasure us in turn, each being allotted ten minutes to show off their unique skills. Both Valérie and I grinned at each other, and she said, "I hope they have big appetites".

We both followed Inès to our own individual pleasure rooms. Inside there was a small en suite bathroom complete with shower and bidet, enabling me to have a quick shower and check everything was in pristine order and ready to be presented to the "gourmands" who would shortly be taking care of me. The main room itself was very elegantly decorated with a small bar area to one side, and central to the room was a large winged leather recliner which had been subtly adapted to include padded supports for ones legs, which were strategically placed higher than the arm rests, ensuring everything was open and fully accessible. Also to one side there was a padded massage table whose legs had been totally removed and it was set about eighteen inches off the floor on solid wooden supports. Strategically placed on a small table beside the chair rested a cut glass tumbler, small ice bucket, a bottle of Jack Daniels, and to my complete surprise a brand new bottle of my current popper of choice "Rush Extra Strength". I had a good idea who'd arranged these little extra treats; attention to detail is always the key in these pre-arranged indulgences.

Having showered and moisturised my entire body with the gorgeous Chanel No.5 body velvet I slipped my heels back on, feeling totally decadent as I poured myself a snifter of JD and took a small hit of amyl before settling myself into the chair ready for my first visitor of the afternoon. The poppers began to wash through my body as I was positioning my legs comfortably in the supports, soon I began to feel that tell tale pre climax heat taking over my body and my vagina begin to throb sensually, I adore this initial sensation. I love the feel when my labia start to swell and part as if they have a mind of their own and those first small rivulets of my juices start to flow out of me.

No sooner had I got comfortably positioned when there was a knock on the door and an elegant looking older gent entered, and introduced himself whilst his eyes appraised me, with a smile he walked over and swiftly knelt in front of me, taking a good minute to scrutinise my excited vagina. I started to tremble as he gently blew on me before beginning to tenderly circle my anus with his wondrously coarse tongue, probing, licking and flicking it with great finesse. The constant murmurings of approval from him encouraged me to allow myself a small, brief but powerful orgasm, much to his joy as a small jet of my ejaculate splashed onto his forehead. He was spurred on by this and upped his tempo taking each of my engorged labia into his mouth in turn, softly sucking and chewing on them. I was in ecstasy when he looked up into my eyes and pleaded with me to feed him. I didn't need asking twice, I took a big hit of my poppers as I stared into his expectant eyes, within seconds a surge shuddered through my core unleashing a powerful torrent of my essence directly into his willing and very eager mouth. As he finished licking his lips and mopping his face with his handkerchief a discreet light flashed on and off signalling his allotted time was sadly at an end. With typical French courteousness he kissed the back of my hand and left the room. I knew I had two or three minutes to have a little sip of my drink and compose myself before the arrival of the next "gourmand" of the female sex.

The subsequent gent was a very attractive guy in his early forties with a very cheeky smile who didn't waste any time in assuming his position, and began feasting on me like a man who'd not eaten for days, he was lapping and slurping on me so enthusiastically

I just felt I should reward his endeavours with a full blown climax for him to drink, by now I was well into the theme of the afternoon and was flowing and squirting at will. It continued in the same theme until gent number five who simply wanted to admire my womanhood at close quarters whilst I pleasured myself with my fingers, he was very vocal and appreciative as I peeled back my clit hood, fully exposing it for his close inspection as I began to gently stroke it into his mouth, gripping it tenderly between thumb and forefinger like a tiny penis, gradually increasing the tempo until I let go a large potent climax, which gushed from me in a powerful arc, jetting over his head and making loud splashing sounds as it hit the marble floor. He gently applauded me and swiftly backed out of the room, smiling at me in appreciation of his time spent worshipping my yoni.

    The time flew by, and my final aficionado of all things oral entered the room. He introduced himself and immediately went and laid prostrate on the low-level massage table. I followed his lead and went over to join him, standing above him with my legs either side of the table, allowing him a good view of what was shortly going to be his to devour. I began to lower myself slowly and teasingly until I was perfectly positioned, squatting an inch above his face offering him the choice of my anus or my fully gaped vagina to taste and suckle on. As I suspected his tongue worked skilfully on both, he was vocally encouraging me to open myself as wide as possible for him as I was flooding his mouth with my warm sweet ejaculate. He was valiantly struggling to swallow all of it with copious amounts running down his cheeks soaking the collar of his shirt. It was over all too soon, and both Valérie and myself met up again in the Gentlemen's room behind the large double doors for a social drink before our respective taxis arrived. I thanked Inès for a wonderful fun filled erotic few hours and promised that I'd return in the very near future, which is exactly what I did. It was a truly wonderful way for a girl to spend a few hours in Paris.

    Totally relaxed and chilled I returned to the hotel to enjoy a session in the spa in preparation for the evening's main event!

Chapter Four: The Grand Event

Upon entering the room I could see Paul had been busy, not only meeting friends as planned, but had also taken in a large amount of retail therapy, judging by the amount of various shopping bags strewn around. My actual birthday was the following Monday, so I excitedly anticipated a few of the bags were destined to be coming my way.

After taking a nice relaxing time in the spa, indulging in a good shoulder and neck massage, coupled with a few sessions in the steam room and Jacuzzi it was time to get ready for the evenings festivities.

The instructions Yves had given Paul had been that guest were to arrive in normal casual clothing as "Party" attire was all waiting for the guests at the venue and all that I was required to bring was a pair of heels and stocking or hold ups if desired. Still very intrigued, but most relieved that I brought to Paris with me a pair of very high platform black patent Louboutin heels, anticipating they may be needed at one stage or other.

Paul knew more of what the evening held in store but was being very secretive as to what he and Yves had organised, telling me it would spoil the surprise element if I knew too much. It was at this point I had a feeling Mike had also had a hand in the planning.

Our taxi picked us up promptly at nine o'clock and whisked us to the venue, which turned out to be a very old traditional small theatre in Le Marais district, which had recently been closed and was due for refurbishment. Yves as ever knew someone who knew someone and had arranged to have the run of the facility for the evening and had employed a team of theatrical set designers to transform and decorate it for the night's festivities.

We were dropped at the stage door to be immediately greeted by a rather large attractive black doorman, who told Paul that all guests (unbeknown to me) had arrived at eight o'clock and the party was underway and all that remained was for Paul and I to put on our party gear and make our "grand" entrance.

We were shown to the dressing rooms where it very quickly became evident it was a "white party", as there on the coat rail were our outfits, which can only be described as his and hers skimpy togas. We both quickly disrobed and helped each other into our costumes, it became apparent that the ladies toga covered only one breast and barely covered ones lady bits. Glancing in the full-length mirror I was pleased with the how the modern heels worked with the ancient Roman outfit. The effect would have even given Nero an erection; well it would have stopped him fiddling at the very least.

The first thing that struck me as I walked in was the décor, all the seats had been stripped out and replaced by several large tables all covered with an array of erotic finger style food, a large well stocked bar along the far wall, being attended by three barmen who were overdressed in full bartending attire. There were many tall tables and stools to relax, eat and chat. The most dramatic effect were the abundance of large white drapes everywhere, like giant sails, the mainly ultra violet lighting made everything look serene. The stage area was completely closed off by a large curtain and only accessible from the side and hidden behind on the actual stage the decorators had installed many inflatable couches and a large bouncy castle. It later resembled a giant adult playpen once the evening got into full swing. Also on the upper level the private boxes had been made into small private playrooms.

There were half a dozen extremely well buffed waiters dressed very inappropriately in brilliant white boxers and bizarrely, motorcycle boots, wandering around making sure everyone was well taken care of on the drinks front.

So many familiar faces were present both from London and my Parisian circle of playmates, also a fair smattering of new faces. We both grabbed a glass of Champagne and split up to mingle and reacquaint ourselves with friends past and present. First though I went in search of Yves to thank him for arranging such a great venue, I found him ensconced in one of the boxes with a French couple I'd met previously, he was happily watching the merriment and debauchery unfolding below. From his vantage point in the box he could see both the main area and behind onto the stage. He was in his element, and it was always a great pleasure for me to see the naughty twinkle in his eyes.

After a brief chat I went to mingle in earnest, and was delighted to very quickly bump into Mike and Sarah, who were over from London, probably our longest serving sparring partners in the world of decadent pleasure. His slender "digits" looked as playful as ever and Sarah looked her usual horny self. Then to my great surprise Thierry was present, not only present but with his gorgeous son Laurent, yes that Laurent, the boy I'd taught how to pleasure a woman many years ago at my home in Kew, I'd seen him several times since and there was always an under current of lust lurking in both our minds.

The evening had a very laid back hedonistic atmosphere with the DJ playing just the right blend of current music mixed with some chilled jazz.

Antonia was also in attendance, and as always I could tell she was eyeing up her prey and making mental notes of who she would have a play with over the next few hours. Her appetite never failed to impress both Paul and myself, and as she was in deep conversation with two very attractive friends of an old business acquaintance from the website days I knew she'd soon be toga-less so to speak.

Eventually after plenty of sumptuous food, some excellent cocktails coupled with lots of birthday wishes midnight came around, then suddenly from the backstage area a giant, and when I say giant I mean mammoth birthday cake was wheeled in with much fanfare, then with a well timed explosion of crackers and fizzing indoor fireworks three of my favourite Parisian Fire fighters burst out from within, all oiled up and glistening, wearing only their overalls, rolled down and tied at the waist, a sight to behold, a sight that judging by the response had made every lady present very moist, or as Paul would say "wetter than an otters pocket".

The shenanigans had already started and there was much activity and gasps of pleasure coming from the stage area. I decided it was time for some birthday treats for myself and along with my three oily firemen we followed the tell tale sounds of debauchery. Soon I realised the centre of attention was Antonia and Sarah completely oiled and being pleasured by a multitude of men, erections proudly being offered for use. Very rapidly my toga was removed by one of my "pompiers" leaving me just in my heels ready to be also oiled up in readiness for some heavy prolonged sexual combat. As ever I go into these situations with total commitment, with the mind-set of aiming to be the last one standing…. so to speak. In short order I was being lathered in a beautiful scented body oil by a multitude of eager and most skilled hands, with several ensuring that every little nook and cranny was taken care of before being unceremoniously thrown into the affray on the wobbling adult bouncy castle, I was instantly joined by the three firemen, who immediately set about putting me through my paces. I was promptly fed two large well-oiled pulsating erections, and I was left gasping in delight as one entered me forcefully from behind in one powerful lunge. They began to work me literally like a well-oiled machine, yet all the time using every ounce of their balancing skills not to be tumbled off the heavily undulating surface. Both Antonia and Sarah gave me the customary thumbs up and pointed over to the swing, where Paul and a guy I didn't recognize were taking turns in penetrating a rather attractive caramel skinned lady, who it later turned out was the owner of a knew adult play club that was going to be opening in a few months time, much more on this later. The waiters by this stage had their work cut out, not only replenishing drinks, but distributing condoms of every shape, size and flavour.

    Occasionally out of the corner of my eye I caught Yves watching me approvingly and telepathically egging me on to even greater sexual athletics with these most virile men, every time I climaxed and unleashed a torrent of fluid over my enamoured suitors he nodded approvingly. There was much sexual activity on every corner of this stage, but I was giving total concentration to the task at hand, which to put it bluntly was to drain every last drop of semen from these guys. I was in no mood to submit, I was going to conquer the three of them at all cost. I had reached the point where I became vocal, instructing them forcefully to use every orifice hard and without mercy. I was being triple penetrated, every opening stuffed full with hard French meat, I was as they say "airtight". I recall gushing and erupting with such intensity even Sarah and Antonia who'd seen it all before stopped to watch and encouraged the guys to show me no compassion. I sensed my crammed sphincter and vagina begin to tighten simultaneously and they began to rhythmically milk the men behind and under me, whilst my tongue went to work on the guy in front, darting and flicking over the large glistening mushroom shaped dome of his meaty weapon. It all seemed to lapse into slow motion as I felt them begin to flood me with copious amounts of their hot sweet semen. My entire body was shaking violently as a massive orgasm ripped through me, drawing every last drop of cum from the men. To murmured gasps and polite quiet applause we collapsed in a hot sticky slippery mass of exhausted flesh on the still bobbing bouncy castle. Waves of pleasure swept through me as I relaxed into a post orgasm state of tranquillity, a feeling that is beyond explanation. Thankfully there was a waiter on hand with a very welcome glass of champagne, complimenting me on my vigorous performance, which judging by the beast that was straining at the front of his boxers had the desired effect. Being in a very playful and mischievous mood I reach forward to place my glass back on the tray, immediately freeing the monster, without further ado I knelt in front of him and whilst locking eyes on a mesmerised Yves who was looking on from his box began to fellate the beast in the most pornographic fashion I could muster. Encouraged by Yves's gentle approving nod I continued my ministrations until the waiters' thighs began to flex and tighten as a huge torrent of sperm erupted from him, arcing over my head, filling my mouth and splashing off my cheeks, it was like he'd been saving up all his life for this one moment of epic release, even after thirty seconds it was still flowing from him, admittedly in successively smaller jets, but still a gargantuan amount from one man. I glanced over and winked at Antonia who was watching slack jawed in amazement at the spectacle.

Now I really needed some more fuel on board and tidied up as best as I could and went to grab a few nibbles and a long cool drink. It was a good opportunity whilst perched on one of the high stools to catch up with a few of the guests whom I had not had the opportunity to chat with during the evening. It was during this time that I got to know the stunning lady who had earlier been entertaining Paul and Mike amongst others.

She was called Charlotte or Charlie as she preferred to be called. We hit it off immediately, and she soon suggested we met for a drink before I went back to London in a more tranquil environment.

With this in mind I decided with Paul's blessing that I'd stay on in Paris for a few extra days and relocate to the apartment, my home from home in Paris on Rue Marbeuf. Thankfully, over the years I'd built up a fine collection of clothes both formal and casual that remained ready and available for my various visits, both business and pleasure.

After saying farewells to old friends, and a few new ones that had been made throughout the evening, Paul and I retired exhausted to the hotel courtesy of Marc, who'd already taken Yves home, and who had been thoughtfully placed at our disposal.

Chapter Five: Discovering Charlotte

After a leisurely Sunday just wondering around the streets and taking a long lunch at the wonderful *Les Deux Magots* in Saint Germain, where we ate a wonderful selection of smoked meats and a gorgeous platter of seasonal vegetables, along with a sumptuous bottle of Chateau Recougne, all enjoyed outside watching the world go by, a perfect way to spend a few hours in the warm Parisian springtime. I highly recommend a visit here if you're ever in the area, you'll certainly not regret it.

As Paul was travelling back alone due to my change of plans, we spent the evening together in the hotel bar relaxing, and him constantly reminding me to be careful when sitting down or getting up, as I was now forty and the body was now in decline! Cheeky toad, lots of life and mischief in the old girl yet I quietly thought to myself. As I'd go on to prove over the forthcoming eventful few days.

No sooner had I'd seen Paul off in the taxi than Marc arrived to drive me to the apartment so as I could get myself organized. There was a lovely welcome note with a vase of colourful flowers from Yves suggesting lunch, which I readily accepted.

It was during this lunch at one of the private dining rooms at Yves old military school (yes that infamous establishment from the first book) that Yves went on to brief me regarding all things Charlotte and how he thought that we were a perfect match for one another. He explained that she was the eldest daughter of a wealthy couple from Marseille, her mother was French and her Father was of Algerian origin. That explained her stunning caramel complexion; she was thirty-seven and fresh out of a long term relationship. The family had made their fortune in saffron, exporting it all over the world.

She'd been making waves on the social scene over the last few months since moving to Paris, being seen at all the right parties and many of the wrong ones also. I was certainly looking forward to meeting her the following day.

Over coffees and brandy Yves requested that I keep Friday afternoon and evening free and be prepared to catch an afternoon Eurostar instead of one in the early morning. As always I nodded my acceptance, which always made his eyes sparkle more than usual and admittedly made me moist in anticipation of the unknown.

The following day I met Charlotte for a late Brunch at The Westin Paris – Vendôme in The Tuileries Bar, where we both indulged in some café and a selection of crêpes. At her request we spoke in English as she was in her words "brushing up her language skills" she was pretty fluent by any ones standard. We ended up being there most of the afternoon telling each other our potted life stories. She was very interested in my knowledge of the Parisian club scene, particularly the "Swinging Clubs" and how she could improve upon them. She already had the premises and was currently busy researching various ideas for the décor and themes. Which is where I think I became an invaluable source of information to her over the coming months. At my suggestion as she'd never been to an afternoon club Parisian style we settled our bill and killed two birds with one stone as they say.

We jumped in a cab and were shortly on Île Saint-Louis outside my club of clubs "*L'Escapade*" (now renamed "*Le Taken*" with hospitable new owners Isa and Alain).

After much birthday hugs and kisses from my old friends Amanda and Costas I introduced Charlie. She was all eyes as we descended that oh so familiar stone staircase to the bar for a customary glass of Champagne. Being a Tuesday it was fairly quiet which was a good thing as I could show Charlie around without stumbling over amorous couplings. She was quite intrigued when I explained that select single males were warmly welcomed, as she'd only ever attended the strictly adhered to "couples only" clubs such as "*Le Deux Plus Deux*" and "*Chris et Manu 2*", the mere mention of Chris et Manu takes me right back to my first ever foray into the world of swinging all those years ago.

I could tell she loved the ambience of the club and it's general classic décor with a strong undercurrent of sensuality radiating from every corner. Amanda told us that there was a private party the following evening and said we'd be both more than welcome to come if we hade no other plans, well Charlie nearly bit her hand off, suggesting we dined together early evening, then get ready at my apartment before the revelry. I found myself quickly agreeing and ordered a Jack Daniels for us both.

We took a taxi back to the apartment, and over a mid evening Chinese take out we brain stormed ideas for her club. I must admit she was focused, and already had a good idea in her head as to what her club would be and most definitely the calibre of clientele she was going to be catering for. This lady had set the bar very high and the more we talked the more convinced I became that she'd succeed. We decided to meet up the following morning and she'd give me a tour of the premises she'd secured on a long lease through a family friend for her venture. Once she'd left I poured myself a nice JD with a chunk of ice and FaceTimed Paul for our usual catch up on events.

After taking coffee, and my by now rare St Moritz menthol cigarette at the much frequented bar opposite the apartment it was time to meet Charlie, who was picking me up in her car as the building was located south of the River Seine in the 6th arrondissement near Le Jardin du Luxembourg. It was approximately a twenty-minute drive in her zippy BMW Z3.

The proposed club was situated in a courtyard off a very elegant and quiet street. It encompassed the entire basement area of a large building that housed several individual companies office suites, mainly in the world of fine art and it had until quite recently had been a Jazz Club and restaurant. Upon entering there was a reception area and a large zone used as a coatroom and general secure area for customers items. Through reception off to the left was the main clubroom which comprised of a large area with a long bar down one side and a large stage area at the front. There were stairs up to another area and a balcony looking down on to the main club area. Though more intriguing to me was the area at the rear that lead through a small passage to several more rooms of varying sizes, eight to be precise. These later became individually themed rooms or "libertine salons" as the French refer to them. It was astounding how similar our ideas were at this stage, when compared to the resultant outcome and completed design.

It was going to take some work and fairly deep pockets to achieve her goals, but it was something that I was firmly excited by, and I looked forward to helping her in any way I could. Also, on a selfish side it gave me a good excuse to have a few trips over, under the guise of a "business trip", as since selling the online business reasons to visit on a frequent basis had declined.

We left and wandered the local area and shortly found a wonderful traditional brasserie called *Le Nemrod*, the kind of place where the locals hang out for a morning coffee and a chat while standing by the bar, or where people linger at terrace tables smoking cigarettes, having a drink and people-watching. We shared a large house salad and a chilled bottle of Sancerre and after much thrashing around of ideas regarding the interior design of the club it was time to drop me off back at the apartment as I needed a nap (must be because I was now forty and a few days). She was going to pick me up three hours later at eight and as arranged we'd get into our club attire after eating.

After pottering around for a while I managed to get forty winks before running myself a nice warm bath to start my long standing habitual preparation for the evening ahead.

Charlie turned up promptly at eight, complete with a small roller case, which she left in the hallway for later. We'd decided on a tried and trusted place that I'd been to several on occasions, and only a five minute walk from the apartment. "*Le Relais de l'Entrecote*" the name gives away the house specialty, which we both indulged in, cooked to perfection with a secret sauce and beautiful home cut fries. However, the highlights for me are the desserts, which are outstandingly indulgent. I went for one named Vacherin Summer; a superb creation with meringues, ice cream with vanilla and raspberry sorbet all covered with a raspberry coulis and whipped cream, decadent but so addictive.

We were back to the apartment by ten to change and be ready in time for the taxi I'd ordered for ten-thirty.

I showed her to one of the spare bedrooms to change and went to get my own glad rags on, which tonight was going to be simple and effective, a very form fitting Hervé Léger little black dress that I accompanied with a skimpy lace pair of my new La Perla panties and sheer black hold-ups. The high platform Louboutins finished the look, apart from an application of my trusty Chanel Rouge Allure Velvet Lipstick. I arranged my small clutch bag with a new fresh vial of poppers and a few other essentials to see me through the evening. I poured us both a small JD on ice on cue just as Charlie appeared looking resplendent and positively oozing a "come eat me" look, draped in an exquisite turquoise silk wrap dress split from the knee to hip and a pair of strappy heeled sandals. After a few minutes just as we finished our drinks the intercom rang and we descended to get the taxi. We were both beginning to get an adrenalin rush as we got closer to the club, especially as I'd recounted a few stories of some of my previous evenings exploits there over the years to her.

Amanda as usual greeted us at the door after checking on her CCTV screen. She was her usual hyper bubbly self and took our coats and told us that people had already started to arrive and that the lady whose party this was in honour of was due along with her husband any time soon as they'd just rung to say they'd left their hotel. So

Charlie and I descended "my" stairway to heaven and we put a little extra wiggle in the hips, much to the appreciation of the gents watching our entrance from the bar below. Immediately a young man who was on drinks patrol for the evening proffered us a glass of pink Champagne, which we most gratefully accepted. We were both rapidly enveloped by a swarm of elegant men, all vying for our individual attention. I could see Charlie enjoyed this attention as much as I myself relished it, never failed in bringing on a degree of moistness. Once I'd settled into the situation I sensed it was going to be a most entertaining evening, there were a few other ladies in attendance, but there was certainly an overload of swarthy single males. The ratio of roughly four to one was perfect for me, and by past experience always resulted in a truly decadent scenario resulting in much debauched behaviour.

The evening's special guest had arrived, which turned out to be a very elegant older lady of around sixty accompanied by her much younger husband. I later found out from Costas that they had attended the club on several occasions recently, as the lady in question enjoyed the attention of many men whilst her husband looked on and orchestrated her pleasure. Apparently, her first husband had passed on several years previously and on the rebound had fallen head first into the arms of a young Parisian, who catered to all of her whims and fantasies (most of a decadent sexual nature).

Very swiftly she retired to the large backroom boudoir whilst her beau selected several men to join him in entertaining her. From the sounds of ecstasy radiating from that area the lady was certainly receiving the attention she desired.

Charlotte and myself were being entertained by a group of gents at the bar; however, we both soon gravitated towards the dance floor, where to the encouragement of the men we proceeded to engage in some very inappropriate and flirtatious dancing. Charlie certainly had all the moves and was showing them off to full effect. The hedonistic and overtly sexual atmosphere took hold and we both began to get more and more outrageous in our gyrations, so much so I took her by the hand and lead her swiftly into my room of choice adjacent to the dance floor. Instantly the expectant men began to discreetly follow us.

The experienced young waiter appeared like magic with fresh drinks as we began to provocatively tease the watching gents. I love looking into the individual men's eyes as I suggestively caress myself, showing more and more of myself as the sexual tension increases, it was heightened even more so as Charlie was swiftly following my lead and was rapidly morphing into a prodigious partner in crime. We both stood up releasing our breasts and inviting the men to play with them, several of them were more than eager to suck on our erect nipples. Numerous men were already openly stroking and proudly showing off their solid erections. The thing I love about Frenchmen is their total lack of reserve or modesty, presenting themselves with full authority and total confidence in their physical and sexual prowess. Soon both of us were fully disrobed and our near naked bodies being vocally appreciated by the men. I was already highly aroused and this was accelerated rapidly up to the next level as a younger guy stepped forward through the group and knelt in front of me, staring passionately up at me as he very slowly and erotically stroked my nylon clad legs prior to peeling my panties off. At this point I lost track of Charlie and concentrated on my own pleasure, swiftly reaching for my clutch and taking a big hit of my poppers. Whilst placing them handily on the drinks table for future use. As the heat swept up through my body I was bent over and felt two guys spread my bottom, holding me wide open for the gent on his knees to worship. I shuddered with delight as I felt his tongue tentatively probing my rectum while an anonymous hand deftly manipulated my engorged clitoris. I was building very nicely to a series of wet mini orgasms, much to the delight of the guys; out of the corner of my eye I glimpsed Charlie getting similar treatment, and responding with equal desire. By now I was starting to get very busy, proud throbbing erections of all shapes but most importantly my favourite size…large and numerous extra large were on display and presented for my choosing! Several men had completely undressed, which prompted others to follow suit. I knelt astride the corner couch inviting the nearest man to penetrate me, looking wantonly over my shoulder I watched as he skilfully began to feed my eager vagina with his girth, I experienced that wonderful feeling when my labia starts to be stretched and eased open by a girthy cock. I soon enveloped this most welcome intruder with my welcoming pussy lips. Simultaneously two angry pulsing erections were offered to my mouth, both stroking them across my cheeks, automatically by muscle memory my mouth and jaw opened to take their endowments in turn, darting my tongue over their large mushroom like helmets while gently teasing their scrotums with my fingers. I was in my element, taking occasional hits of amyl and unleashing mini torrents of ejaculate as these anonymous men pleasured both themselves and me. I was fully at a level of total climactic lust inviting the men to use me, vocally urging them to pound me without mercy. I was also enjoying the additional accompaniment of Charlie's moaning upon reaching her own frequent climaxes. The level of noise and intense activity tempted one of the other ladies present to join us; a welcome addition, as by this stage there was probably Charlie and myself central in a scrum of ten or more rampant men. The new lady took no time in getting stuck into the ruckus, immediately straddling a gent who'd been patiently awaiting an opportunity to avail himself upon us. Shortly, I left the proceedings, hastily slipping into my dress and headed to the bar for a welcome drinks break. I also took the opportunity to sneak a much desired menthol cigarette, which never fails to enhance my Jack Daniels moment. I was in total awe of the lady whose party it was, as she hadn't yet taken a break, and by all accounts was still having the time of her life in the back room, and was using and discarding men with consummate ease. She was definitely one very adventurous lady, but so typically French.

    Refreshed and revitalised I decided to have one last round of pleasure for the evening and sauntered off to a quiet area of the club, hoping that the distinguished gentleman who I winked at in passing took the hint and followed. I got settled in one of the large comfortable sofa chairs and slipped my dress up, slightly exposing myself in hope and anticipation. Within a time frame that was long enough for him to not look desperate, but swiftly enough for him to appear charmed by my unsubtle invitation he appeared by the arched stone entrance. No words were needed as I took the bull by the horns and slid my dress up further, spreading my legs wide. He smiled enchantingly as he approached, whilst I deftly butterflied my heavy engorged labia for him, he took the hint and strongly grasped the back of my thighs as he knelt in front of me getting in position to give me the benefit of his tongue. Immediately, I realised this man was a true expert, a "gourmand", he very delicately unleashed my erect clitoris from its hiding place and began to gently nibble and suckle on it, swiftly I reached for my amyl and discreetly took a hit. I was delighted when he reached up to take it from me, taking a good sniff himself, into both his nostrils. As it began to have its usual lust enhancing effect on me he slid his forefinger expertly deep into my anus, my well trained muscle immediately gripping it and welcoming it inside. His teeth gently nibbling my lips felt sensational and it shortly brought me to a shuddering crescendo with my juices flooding his very willing and eager mouth. Once I had regained my composure I grasped the moment to repay the compliment, kneeling in front of him lustfully, smiling up at him as he released his erect member for me to feast on. It was just the perfect size to devour whole, only gagging slightly as I eased him deep into my throat, holding him still momentarily, allowing the relevant muscles to get accustomed to the intruder. I locked eyes with him and gently slapped his thigh indicating that I wanted him to take the initiative. He swiftly took hold of my hair, adeptly knotting it in his hand and withdrew his penis, completely teasing me with it, rubbing it over my face before slowly working it into my mouth again. I eagerly accepted it as he began to slowly and passionately fuck my mouth. He began to build the intensity and rhythm, making me gag and gurgle in helpless pleasure, and as he began to unload his hot sweet semen down my throat I felt my own juices erupt vigorously from within me. He came heavily, testing me to the limit in my quest not to allow any of him to be wasted. My mouth and throat were worked over time drinking every last drop his sweet cum. It was a most pleasurable encounter, the type that sticks in ones memory. By way of a thank you as I returned the bar area a fresh Jack Daniels was presented to a most grateful me. Charlie soon appeared looking well satisfied by here dalliances over the course of the evening and savoured a glass of wine before our taxi arrived.

At my insistence she stayed the night at the apartment, and we both discussed the evening and her thoughts and ideas of how to incorporate certain elements into her club. We talked well into the early hours, accompanied by a lovely smooth brandy. We'd certainly bonded, and I was beyond pleased when she proposed that I should work with her and assist her on a consultancy basis. We swapped emails and I agreed to draw up some plans once back in London of how I saw the clubs interior design and she'd do likewise. We arranged to meet and compare the results the following month.

After a late breakfast at the bar opposite we said our goodbyes, but happy and excited as we both sensed that this was the start of a great new friendship.

Chapter Six: A Bejewelled Friday

After a relaxing Thursday Yves rang, informing me that Marc would be collecting me the following afternoon in preparation for one of his intriguing evenings, where as customary I took on the role of his "muse and plaything", a role I'd always taken on with full commitment and total trust. These occasions will always remain with me, and are some of the most decadent moments I've ever had the fortune to participate in. From that very first evening all those years ago at "Le Roi René" in Ville d'Avray on the outskirts of Paris, they have always been both mentally and sexually stimulating, always challenging, pushing my boundaries, and all in a completely safe and respectful environment. What more could a girl wish for.

After a very languid lazy breakfast in a newish establishment a short walk from the apartment called *"GranCaffè Convivium"*, where I sat outside indulging in too many of their fine pastries with several large espresso's. A great place to chill out and people watch.

Dressed casually as instructed in a five button light cotton coat dress and heels I climbed into the back of the Mercedes that Marc used and excitedly daydreamed as to what was planned for me as he whisked me through the bustling Parisian streets towards my destination. After about thirty minutes we arrived at a suburb called Neuilly sur Seine and a shop that specialised in body art and design, an upmarket tattoo and piercing boutique called Abraxas. I was very hesitant upon entering, as the last thing on my mind was any thing remotely associated with tattoos or body piercing. The receptionist swiftly put my mind at ease, and quickly introduced me to a charming man called Michel who was their resident in house jewellery designer and had been given strict instructions by Yves, which quickly alleviated any concerns I had.

It was around the time when female body decoration was becoming fashionable, complimenting their very artistic designs many were also getting nipple piercings, and full genital adornment for the brave. I was intrigued and aroused at the thought, but needles were most definitely not my thing, however in true Yves style he'd unearthed a more than acceptable solution. The in house specialist Michel had been at the forefront in the design of elegant temporary body jewellery of the clip on and cleverly moulded styles. I was here for a fitting, and to select something decadent from the various designs to wear that evening. Excitedly accepting the offer of a relaxing glass of chilled Chablis he showed me through to one of the private studios. It was a fully equipped room whose centrepiece was what resembled a very comfortable dental chair surrounded by viewing mirrors. He opened a large case and showed me a few of the designs that he'd brought for me to try. I told him that I'd be guided by his expertise. He instructed me to get undressed totally, and to make myself comfortable in the chair whilst he went and refreshed my wine.

    Once he returned he suggested we start with my nipples and proceeded to spray them with a light mist of fragrant oil, giving them each a gentle tweak in turn, which had the desired effect of instantly getting them erect. He then picked out several differing designs and tried them one by one, until I eventually settled on a set, each one made from a pair of delicate one inch 18ct gold chains with a ruby attached to each. The fitting clip was a gold moulded loop, which slid down over the top and sides of an erect nipple; they looked stunning and felt unbelievably sensual. It had a matching adornment for the vagina, same clasp in principle, instead of nipple it slid down and over the sides of the clitoral hood, gripping the clitoris with delicate authority. It was a wonderful feeling having this man fitting it; it was all I could do not to cum all over his deft hands. He complimented me on my meaty labia, which at this stage were well engorged and he then selected a pair that actually clipped on to the lips. As a finishing touch he produced a crystal butt plug, whose end was encrusted in many small reflective semi precious stones, gently inserting it into my anus encouraging me to admire the look in the mirror. It was simply sensational and most erotic. He asked my permission and took a few digital pictures for his portfolio. It was over all too soon, but I took advantage of another glass of wine whilst my new decadent items were wrapped for me.

    Marc was waiting outside, ready to drive me back to the apartment, where as a long established ritual I took a long slow soak in the tub with a nice glass of white wine letting my mind wander, allowing erotic thoughts to stimulate me.

    Marc the drive had passed along a note from Yves with an outline of the evening's itinerary, albeit brief it told me the outfit I'd be wearing, or in this case lack of.

Chapter Seven: Much Admired

In my typical custom I spent a considerable time allowing my body to absorb the liberal application of my favoured Chanel No.5 Body Velvet moisturising cream, every nook and cranny treated with care and attention it deserved.

As Yves had requested, I was to wear my beautiful new black silk Valentino evening dress, that he'd thoughtfully left hanging in the wardrobe as a little birthday gift. I was to wear it with no underwear or stockings, simply the elegant gown and a complimenting pair of heels. As ever on such occasions I wore my Gold Cartier "Tank Francaise" and Eternity bracelet. As requested my new body jewellry was taking pride of place, nestling conveniently inside my clutch bag.

None the wiser as to my destination, I climbed in to the rear of the Mercedes, chivalrously helped by Marc. It turned out to be a very short drive, as no sooner than I'd got in Marc was helping me out again and walking me to the entrance of a Gentleman's Private Dining Club situated on Avenue George V, just a short stroll from the Arc de Triumphe. The very official doorman greeted me and consulted his note pad before opening the very secure looking door allowing me entrance into the small yet elegant foyer, where my coat was taken.

I was then taken to the internal lift and accompanied to the ninth and final floor of the building, once again as the lift doors opened a rather official looking gentleman greeted me and checked me off his discreet note pad. It was only much later did it become clear as to why all this security was taking place, it was simply that since it's inception back in 1908 only a handful of females had ever crossed its hallowed threshold. This only happened upon the behest of people with great power and influence. I was later told a few stories involving one or two famous French Presidents who'd organized such events, however, my lips are sealed, likewise not actually naming the establishment, as long may it thrive. I just hope the tradition continues and a few more ladies such as myself are privileged enough to be invited.

I followed the man along a corridor lined with portraits of France's good and great from the past, the atmosphere was one of opulence and distinct privilege. Steeped in history and I felt it a great honour to just be in the building itself. It gave you an overwhelming feeling that these walls most certainly had eyes and ears and were watching my every move. Shortly, I was shown to an anti room where Yves was waiting to greet me, he silently appraised me for several moments before quietly whispering to me "vous êtes tout simplement divine, tres magnifique". Taking my hand he lead me into the room, a room devoid of any other female guests. I was alone amongst a small group of distinguished gentlemen. All elegantly attired in full evening dress. Enough to make any lady aroused, and me being me, highly aroused was the result. Whilst sipping on my flute of Champagne Yves introduced me individually to the five gentlemen, whilst at the same time as explaining that they were all meeting their wives shortly for a night at the ballet and were in need of some entertainment of a much different kind prior to their evening. I was to be their "entertainment. Yves outlined his wishes, and after indulging in another Champagne to unleash the exhibitionist in me further the official gentleman came and escorted me to the lift. I watched intrigued as he used a key to override the lift buttons and pressed a hash tag key on the panel, which deposited us swiftly into the bowels of the building.

 I was shown into a locked room that was obviously once used as a wine cellar, the ancient stonewalls gave it an ambiance of a large prison cell. Discreetly placed in the shadows were six armchairs, and in central to the room was a raised crimson velvet plinth. A 360 degree white curtain, adding to the sensuality of the room, concealed it. The entire room was dark with just a subtle spotlight illuminating the plinth. As Yves requested I quickly slipped out of my gown and proceeded to adorn my nipples and vagina with my new erotic jewellery. The effect immediately triggered a series of small wet climaxes, resulting in my thighs glistening with my juices. The door opened and the official gent informed me that the guests would be along in a few minutes. I just had time to take a massive hit of my poppers before placing my self provocatively on the plinth behind the curtain. I was now at a very heightened state and the slightest touch or even a look would trigger a massive orgasm, I love this state and ensure when it occurs I abandon myself to the moment, gaining maximum pleasure.

 I heard the door open and the discreet murmuring of the men as they settled into the armchairs. As the curtain rose fully exposing me to the men an appreciative quiet applause accompanied by some most explicit verbal utterances ensued. I began to play, stroking my thighs, holding my breasts together provocatively showing off the chains that were snuggly gripping my bullet like nipples. The murmurings from the gents hidden in the shadows sipping their cognacs was gaining in sexual vulgarity the more I played.

    The appreciation escalated substantially as I began to beguilingly spread my legs allowing them an unhindered view of my jewel-adorned gaping vagina. My labia were fully engorged and open, its juices shimmering on my thighs. I went into total overdrive as I unpeeled my clitoris and began to manipulate it provocatively for the watchers gratification. I built my self to a crescendo, holding back the flood, bringing myself to the edge on several occasions before unleashing a gargantuan torrent of ejaculate in several powerful arcing jets. As the fluids deluged from me the gents gasped loudly in appreciation, which only spurred me on further. I was pleased to hear Yves guests thanking him in very complimentary terms for inviting and allowing them the privilege of what they'd witnessed. I reached for my Champagne and took a well deserved gulp, just as I'd finished it was my turn to gasp as the door opened and "Mr. Official" lead in two absolutely huge naked black men. I was staggered at the sight. They were glistening, as their skin had been coated in a thin layer of oil, neither carried any excess body fat, simply six foot six torso's of pure muscle. My eyes were quickly drawn to two colossal shining mahogany erections. They were fiercely pointing my way, pulsating and angry. Ready to inflict some serious pleasure upon my enthusiastic body. They approached me and stood either side of the plinth appraising what they had to work on, slowly stroking their manhood's to full erection. They gestured to me to turn side on and kneel on the plinth, which I did with zest. The room was deathly silent as the anticipation of what was about to transpire rose. I soon felt a long tongue flash across my buttocks, quickly spreading them and plunging into my anus; I was in ecstasy as he worked it skilfully. I gratefully with relish accepted the enormous penis, which was being proffered to my mouth. I lewdly commenced darting my tongue up and down its immense length and encircling its colossal head, salivating on it profusely. I had to use all my effort and skill to take this monster into my mouth; my lips were taught, stretched to the extreme. Simultaneously the ripped giant behind me sheathed himself with one of the *préservatifs* that had been discreetly brought in, and swiftly began to nudge his rock-solid spear of joy into me, my vagina welcoming him blissfully. My labia instinctively wrapped themselves around him, my muscle memory kicked in gripping him as he worked his vast penis fully into me. Then clutching my hips he commenced to rhythmically drill into me with ferocious power. I was working overtime and on full autopilot as these two monstrous men worked me viciously from both ends. I was beginning to climax uncontrollably as they swapped positions, taking turns in using both my vagina and mouth. I was being well and truly tested, being penetrated in every imaginable position. I was being stretched like never before and adoring every single moment. Matching these men as best I could. Finally, after a long bout of merciless, power fucking I was lifted from the plinth and was knelt on a cushion directly in front of the six armchairs, really close up and personal as they both began to feed me their gargantuan meat. I was going crazy with lust as they both used my mouth for their own gratification. Like a well-drilled double act they began to tense and quiver, and in unison their immense erections began to jerk and flex powerfully as they both began to climax. Huge powerful hot torrents of semen ejaculated forcefully into my eager mouth, flooding the back of my throat. I was being completely deluged in their ejaculate, gulping and gagging, endeavouring to drink every last drop from them. Eventually their orgasms subsided and they departed leaving one very battered, cum covered but fulfilled lady, slumped back on the plinth, exhausted and in dire need of a much-deserved drink.

Yves along with his guests departed, but not before each and every one bowed slightly whilst placing a kiss on the back of my hand and quietly complimenting me on my dexterity and enthusiasm regarding all things amatory.

Finally Yves embraced me and said his goodbyes and that he'd be in touch. Marc drove me back to the apartment where I immediately undressed and threw on my jeans and a pastel pink cashmere Ralph Lauren crew neck sweater and as it was still only ten-thirty strolled back up the road to where I'd taken breakfast earlier in the day.

It was alive and bustling and as it was a warm evening I sat outside and ordered a chilled bottle of Sancerre whilst perusing the menu. I relaxed into my first few sips with one of my infrequent St Moritz menthol cigarettes, divine bliss! My exertions during the last twelve hours ensured a very hearty appetite and the mixed green salad and bowl of steaming muscles in a fiery tomato based sauce went a long way to satisfying. Leaving just enough room for a dessert of triple chocolate cheesecake and an espresso. A quite exquisite end to a fun day filled with total decadent over indulgence.

Chapter Eight: Planning and Scheming

Back in West London life continued at its normal hectic pace. Paul was now travelling back and forth to New York in his recently acquired role as track procurement consultant for a film and TV company. He was thoroughly enjoying working freelance on projects that he personally approved. His role involved the acquisition of music that blended and fitted various scripts and screenplays the company had currently in post and pre production.

Over the following twelve months there were several quick visits to Paris to catch up, and go over plans and ideas with Charlie regarding the club. She at this stage had the majority of permissions and licenses in place (these had taken much longer than she'd anticipated) and was almost in a position to begin the interior work.

During this period a Swingers Club in Holland that had been open for several years, *"Fun4Two"* was starting to make waves and was fast gaining a reputation as the adult version of Disneyland. During one of my frequent Skype calls with Charlie she suggested we visit the club together to see what all the fuss was about, and maybe incorporate any of their ideas we'd not thought of into her final design. It was agreed that she'd take care of the accommodation, and we'd stay for five days, visiting the club in question and exploring any others.

We agreed a suitable date. As I would be flying from Heathrow to Schiphol and she by train From Paris direct to Amsterdam Centraal Railway Station we'd arranged meet up at the accommodation she'd arranged for our brief "recon mission".

Chapter Nine: A Dutch Indulgence

After a very pleasant hop across the North Sea by plane and a swift taxi into the centre of Amsterdam we met up as arranged. I was delighted that she'd opted for a holiday apartment rather than a touristy hotel.

She'd in fact booked a stunning 2 bedroom designer apartment situated over 3 floors, overlooking one of the main canals in the heart of the trendy 9 street area, just around the corner from the Royal Palace, Flower Market, Dam and the Jordaan.

We spent the initial afternoon taking in the atmosphere and stopping off at several bars along the canals for lubrication. We did one of the tourists "must see" attractions and wandered through the De Wallen or De Walletjes district as its known locally; yes the famous Red Light District. There were all manner of sights on offer in the windows that ran along both sides of the network of alleys and canals. It most definitely caters for every conceivable human fetish and kink, all available at a price. I must be honest that during the day it's a very depressing sight, but comes alive after dark with all the neon signs and the hustlers out in force trying to entice you into the various live sex shows. The traditional image that Amsterdam had been infamous for over the decades was still thriving, and much in evidence, however, over the previous couple of years it was gaining a reputation as a go to destination for swinging couples and many clubs had sprung up and were gaining very positive reviews. One in particular that we had on the agenda for the following evening was to become a very big favourite of mine to this very day. It's called *"Club Paradise"* and is located at Schaafstraat 26 in North Amsterdam. It's a converted unit on an industrial estate, and from the outside looks horrendous, but what a pleasant surprise once you enter.

The first night we dined in a very authentic Indian called Koh-i-Noor. It was very close by on Westermarkt 29, quite small inside and we had to take a drink at a nearby bar, as there was a forty-five minute wait for a table, always a good sign. The food was exquisite and I'd highly recommend it, in fact I've been back several times, the Fish Tikka Tandoori is the food of the gods and the cheese nan bread is a must. I advise you reserve for the evening, as it gets full quickly such is its popularity.

After dinner we sampled the aforementioned Red Light District after dark, and we were both amazed at the transformation. It was alive and buzzing, crowds of people thronging the bars along the various canals; the atmosphere was electric, totally different from the daylight hours. It wasn't long before we stumbled upon a tremendous bar called *'t Smalle*, which is situated beside a canal with a bustling outside seating area, and great cosy candle lit tables inside. They specialize in Belgian beers, of which we sampled a few. Sitting at an adjacent table were two Swedish couples that quickly struck up conversation with us. They proved to be very knowledgeable, as they had been visiting Amsterdam and sampling the various burgeoning swingers clubs frequently over the previous eighteen months.

Once we explained the reason for our visit they opened up, furnishing us with an overload of information of the good, bad and ugly of their Amsterdam experiences. It was during this exchange that it quickly became apparent that we'd both overlooked a problem that needed to be addressed quickly. Basically our club of choice for the Saturday evening and the prime reason for our visit, *"Fun4Two"* had a very strict policy of couples only, no single people of either sex. It appeared even single ladies would not be allowed entry, as this would upset the equilibrium of the evening. After much debate and head banging via a very expensive mobile phone call to Paul, who was in New York but about to board a flight back to Heathrow the following morning and our old friend and fun sharer Mike, it was sorted. Sarah most graciously agreed to loan out her husband for the evening. Several hours later I had both of them booked on a flight into Schiphol mid morning Saturday. In the meantime we had some exploration of our own to indulge in.

After breakfast on the Thursday and up on recommendations from several reviews from people that I'd read on a site suggesting things to do whilst in Amsterdam we spent the afternoon at the most amazing health spa I'd ever visited. *"Sauna Deco"* located centrally on Herengracht 115 is just the most beautiful and relaxing environment you could wish for and the best twenty euros you'll ever spend. I urge you to look it up online and see for yourself. We both also paid for a sublime massage to compliment the various sauna and steam rooms. The facilities and décor are among the best you'll ever find anywhere. Very elegant and incredibly tranquil, oases of calm in the centre of this most vibrant capitol city.

Chapter Ten: Paradise In The Paradise

Neither of us had much of an idea as to what to expect from our first ever foray into the Dutch swinging scene, and at that time the club we were visiting didn't have a website (today it has an excellent and most informative site in several languages) so we were going in blind, sometimes this turns out to be the most exciting and rewarding way to do it. As in fact this was most definitely the case here.

Unlike what we were both used to in Paris things begin a lot earlier, where as French clubs don't tend to get busy until midnight in Amsterdam they start filling up around nine to nine-thirty. There are several other distinct differences, which became apparent over the next few days and frequent visits.

We fuelled ourselves at a busy little Thai eatery close to the apartment and after much deliberation we both decided to wear LBD's, skimpy panties, hold-ups and heels after both going through the body moisturizing rituals. Conveniently there was a taxi rank within a two minute walk, so at nine o'clock we were on our way, within fifteen or so minutes we were pulling up outside this as previously mentioned rather drab looking industrial unit, the driver winked wishing us a pleasant and fruitful evening.

We entered to a small reception where we were each given a key to a locker in the mixed changing and shower area, hesitantly we looked at each other, fortunately the man on the desk saw our confusion and spoke good English. He explained that it was required that ladies were either in just lingerie or totally naked with one of the provided towels to wear if and when needed, also for the men towel or boxers were the norm. This is totally alien to how the majority of the Parisian clubs operate. There is a distinct line in Paris between elegant clubs and swinger's saunas. But here in Amsterdam many of the venues combined the two.

We both at this stage just removed our dresses and stowed them in the lockers, wrapping a towel around ourselves we braced ourselves and went in search of the bar area. Which turned out to be a wonderful U shaped mahogany bar with many stools around it and every drink under the sun available. Over a glass of wine we struck up conversation with one of the attractive girls tending the bar, she went on to explain that it was always very busy on a Thursday evening as the theme was "Gang Bang Night", and many couples attended where the wives enjoyed being the centre of attention. It was certainly a United Nations of the swinging world with many different nationalities, all making new friends in a very hedonistic environment. The central bar room was spacious, with a dance floor and a large "group fun" bed being prominent, many smaller open rooms were situated around it. Together we followed the people who were appearing and disappearing back past the locker rooms and up a dimly lit passage. Initially we came to another shower area with two saunas, one hot the other nuclear hot, also a steam room that was very popular. Moving further along there was a staircase up to another level where there was another sauna and a large swimming pool that was busy with many couples intermingling in and out of the water. We then climbed up another small staircase that opened to yet another large orgy area and access to the outdoor play area on the roof, which was popular when the Northern European weather permitted. I have had several pleasurable liaisons up there over the years.

During our meanderings we became aware that several men were following us around albeit discreetly. It was a most non-threatening environment with every one friendly and out to enjoy and evening of grown up debauchery, Charlie and myself included. Once we'd got the lay of the land so to speak we made our way back to the main bar to enjoy something a bit stronger than wine.

Sitting at the bar, Jack Daniels in hand we soon became the object of a group of men all vying for our attention and endeavouring to find out as much about us, and what had brought us to the club. Basically anything to give them a signal that we were there to play, we both played along and as always fully enjoyed all the attention.

As different men of varying languages were entertaining us and constantly having our drinks refreshed, Charlie and I inevitably got detached from one another and with a knowing look that we had each others back we began to do our own thing. By this stage I was feeling positively frisky, what with the Jack Daniels and a serious amount of outrageous flirting I decided to go for a solo wander and see what transpired.

Firstly, I returned to the changing room and took off my hold-ups and panties and popped them in the locker, leaving just my heels on and the towel. I immediately headed to the steam room as they have always had a big effect on me; I think it the not knowing what's lurking inside that hot misty tiled room. Hanging my towel on a peg outside I ventured in, moving very slowly so as not to make a fool of myself by bumping into something or even worse tripping over. Quite quickly my eyes became accustomed to the dim lighting and I soon found myself perch on a warm, wet marble bench, my ears also became accustomed to the sounds, from the giggling and intermittent moans I realised that there was at least one other female present. The fun for me is that until you are right next to someone all you can see is shapes and absorb the sounds. I was seated at the far end, away from the door and could just about make out when it opened and people left or new people came in. I was getting to experience my tell tale shiver stir within me and a wave of anticipation course from my head to my toes. Shortly I sensed two bodies sitting either side of me, subtly looking out the corner of my eye I discovered it was two males, which made my excitement levels spike. With no words spoken the man to my left chanced his arm and inconspicuously placed his hand where it just touched my thigh, when I didn't move away he very discreetly started to delicately stroke his fingers up and down, I encouragingly moved my thigh that extra millimetre closer, giving him a positive signal to continue. Soon the gent on my right began exactly the same thing. Now with a total devil may care attitude I relaxed into the scenario that was slowly unfolding. The two men quietly and adeptly caressed my thighs moving from the sides to the tops and slightly towards the insides, which encouraged me to allow them over the next few minutes to be parted, until eventually I had a leg propped over each of their thighs. It was a sensational feeling of total overwhelming decadence to have these two anonymous hands exploring my achingly wet gaping vagina, tweaking and pinching my swollen labia, taking turns to manipulate my clitoris, they were both ensuring that I was enjoying the experience. They were saying things in a language that I didn't quite understand, but definitely got the gist of and made my feelings known with my soft guttural feline mewling, which spurred them on further. I noticed that another man had appeared and I could just about make out that he was knelt in front of me watching the two guys working at my vagina, from which my juices were now flowing freely. I bucked and writhed as two fingers entered me delicately and proceeded with great dexterity to immediately locate my G-spot. This did it for me, they could sense I was about to erupt; they skilfully began to edge me, bringing me close then backing off. They continued in this way for what felt like an eternity until I could take it no more and vocally begged them to let me cum. This made them up the tempo another notch until I was completely overwhelmed, my body taking over and erupting into a crescendo of pure ecstasy, I unleashed torrent after torrent of ejaculate, virtually drenching the man knelt in front of me, he was staring intently at my pulsating and gushing vagina, hypnotised by the power of my orgasm. It seemed to be that an unstoppable dam had been breached; eventually as the squirting began to recede the men decreased their manipulations back to gentle featherlike caresses. It was a truly erotic fifteen minutes that will live with me forever. As if to prove my point, I'm sat here getting aroused simply writing about it!

I graciously thanked the men and fumbled my way out kicking off my heels and plunging my body under a lukewarm shower to cool me down a bit before getting a much need long drink back at the bar. Even the shower was erotic as two men were openly watching me whilst they enticingly stroked their erections. I just smiled encouragingly as I towelled myself dry and slipped back into my heels, cheekily giving each one a gentle stroke before I wandered off. I watched a young couple enter the steam room and just hoped she'd get as much intimate attention as I did.

Back at the bar I was pleased to see Charlie having some fun on the large orgy bed, busy enjoying herself within a mass of writhing bodies. It was nice to regain some energy just watching all the action whilst enjoying a drink, with no pressure to perform. It's always a good feeling just relaxing after an intense orgasm and secure in the knowledge there would be more to come and all conducted at my pace.

I soon got talking to a young blonde guy from Denmark who was living in Amsterdam for a year working as an art restorer at the world famous Rijksmuseum, coincidently Charlie and I had planned to visit the following day. He gave me a good insight as to the best time to go to avoid the crowds and what to see. During the conversation he told me this was his fifth visit and that he enjoyed it, as there was always a good mix of people who were always polite, friendly and above all respectful of the ladies. He also explained something that I was unsure of, which was the price, saying that unlike the tourist traps in the Red light District where single men could be fleeced paying exorbitant prices for watered down drinks, here a single guy paid sixty euros which included entrance and four drinks, an even better deal for single females all they paid was twenty five euros and all drinks were included. Also on some evenings they lay on a free buffet. Obviously check their website for current events and prices. I've always found it tremendous value for outrageous fun with top-notch facilities at your disposal. Soon he began to make sexual overtures and flirted overtly, especially as at this stage my towel was just discreetly laying across my lap, several times he praised my erect nipples as he brushed the back of his hand across them, causing them to stiffen even further. Glancing down discreetly I could tell there was something most tempting lurking beneath his towel, I could sense it stirring. He was surprised that I hadn't taken a peek in the very popular dark room. I explained that I was totally un aware that it existed, and was sure Charlie and I had fully explored the club, oh how wrong I was, as this area of the club went on to become a real magnet for me, especially on my future solo visits.

After a brief description of the room my curiosity was piqued, and when he suggested he should be my chaperone and guide I positively leapt at the chance. I did however tease him a little by insisting on having another small drink and a menthol St Moritz beforehand, this seemed to set him on edge, and increased the sexual tension and anticipation up another notch.

Eventually, I followed him back towards the reception area where there was a narrow dark passageway that both Charlie and I had completely overlooked on our tour. I was completely stunned when it opened up into a huge dark room with several individual rooms of varying sizes build along its perimeters; these rooms all had clear, thick Perspex walls enabling couples, triples, groups or simply a single female to play and exhibit themselves locked inside, to an often packed audience outside on the other side of the glass. My eyes were quickly drawn to one of the smaller Perspex rooms, which featured six strategically placed glory holes. I watched absorbed as a curvaceous middle-aged lady who was inside hungrily pleasing many members that were being offered to her through the holes. A well-groomed gentleman of around sixty, and who was either the husband or lover was orchestrating proceedings from the side and watching in wrapt delight as she devoured everything presented to her, her face was continually awash with sperm, an awesome spectacle. This room is as popular now, as it was on that very first visit. Also in the middle of the main room there is a gorgeous fully leather padded "bondage horse" with leather buckled restraining straps. A low wattage blue light giving a very sensual effect dimly illuminates it from above. This had a lasting effect, and when I showed Charlie a while later she wholeheartedly agreed that she must have one in her club.

All the while my new Danish friend was becoming increasingly well acquainted with my bottom, his hand gently stroking my cheeks and frequently running a finger tantalisingly down its groove, lingering teasingly on my anus. Encouragingly I would push backwards onto him, firmly indicating my approval. Glancing down I'd noticed his most impressive erection had broken free from its confines under the towel and was throbbing intensely as it proudly announced its presence. We moved closer to the "bondage horse" to watch as a man began to harness his female partner over it face down, legs pulled forward and buckled, her derriere was naturally pushed up and spread open naturally by her body position. Shortly, at the invitation of her partner several men began to play with her, her partner was vocally coaching both her and the men. It was a most intensely erotic spectacle as the group of men began in turn to use her mouth, vagina and rectum in unison. She was completely overcome by pleasure, moaning loudly as wave after wave of raw pleasure swept through her. After observing this most decadent of displays while being sensuously played with I needed more, much more. Spotting an opportunity I lead him by his penis to one of the smaller rooms which had become vacant, it was as I was entering the room I realised that my hand could barely close around him, such was its girth, a massive tremor ripped through me causing me to climax wetly without warning, much to his amusement. Once inside the room with the door shut he removed his towel and much to my complete delight I noticed he was wearing an all enhancing cock and ball ring combination, and that he was completely waxed smooth. The effect of this ensemble made his penis look oddly but beautifully solid and too big for his body. The sight of it just made me even hornier. Grasping this bull by his horn I sunk to my knees in complete adoration of his weapon and slowly began my cock worshipping ritual, leaning back on my haunches and simply marvelling at its size and power before beginning to work on it with my tongue. I could both sense and see a crowd gathering to watch what was starting to evolve. This attention spurred my exhibitionistic streak to come rushing to the fore, playing to the crowd, drooling over his shaft like a true porn star. I was in full flow when I noticed Charlie giving me a cheeky wink and the global thumbs up sign of approval.

I gripped his thighs with both hands as my jaw muscles relaxed to accommodate him, we established firm eye contact as he began to slowly feed me more and more of himself. I was in total ecstasy as he placed his hands either side of my head as he established his rhythm, like a metronome his hips moved back and forth working my mouth and throat feverishly. Pure exquisite face fucking! My thighs were trembling and my knees shook as I began to unleash a series of rapid intense orgasms, one after another they arrived with a wave of heat from my inner core. I gasped as he stood me up and positioned me against the glass wall facing the crowd of voyeuristic men, my arms outstretched above my head and my breasts squashed firmly against the Perspex. I shuddered with pure desire as I felt his erection begin to stretch me open, entering my sodden vagina with great panache. Gripping my hips he rode me from behind as I watched the mass of men in front stroking their erections in appreciation, so close, yet out of reach, separated by a solid wall of glass. I savoured every moment he was inside me, arching my back, thrusting myself backwards firmly impaling myself on him. My juices were flowing from me continually, soaking both of us. Several of the watchers sensing the end was close, I can only assume by his facial expression, were openly ejaculating. A truly decadent sight, several began to silently applaud as he began to unload his seed into my eager throbbing vagina. He remained inside me for several minutes as I milked every drop from him as his erection subsided. Once we'd both recovered we left the room to many complimentary comments, and headed first to cool off in one of the shower areas and then to the bar for a much needed and well-deserved drink. Charlie joined us looking most pleased with her self, saying that she'd left a trail of devastation on the upper level.

 Compared to the Parisian clubs last orders for the bar were very early and the club was due to close at one a.m. The only night it stays open later is a Saturday, when it doesn't close until four, which is still early by French standards. So my advice is to arrive early and make the most of the club and its wonderful ambience, truly a must visit. Suitable for beginners and the more experienced swinger alike.

 We said our farewells and both excitedly discussed the club and our individual impressions of it during the short taxi ride back into the centre. We were both wired from the evening and found a vibrant bar and began to examine in detail what thoughts we'd come away with into the small hours.

 We did spend a good few hours at the wonderful Rijksmuseum, admiring the vast collection of Masterpieces on display, Rembrandt, Vermeer, Van Gogh to name a few. To take full advantage of what this museum offers I would definitely recommend you take advantage of the audio guide, it adds to your experience, especially if you are a first time visitor and makes the large museum manageable. On a sad personal note I never did bump into my Danish art restorer and female body pleaser ever again, but if you're reading this you know who you are and the pleasure was all mine. Get in touch!

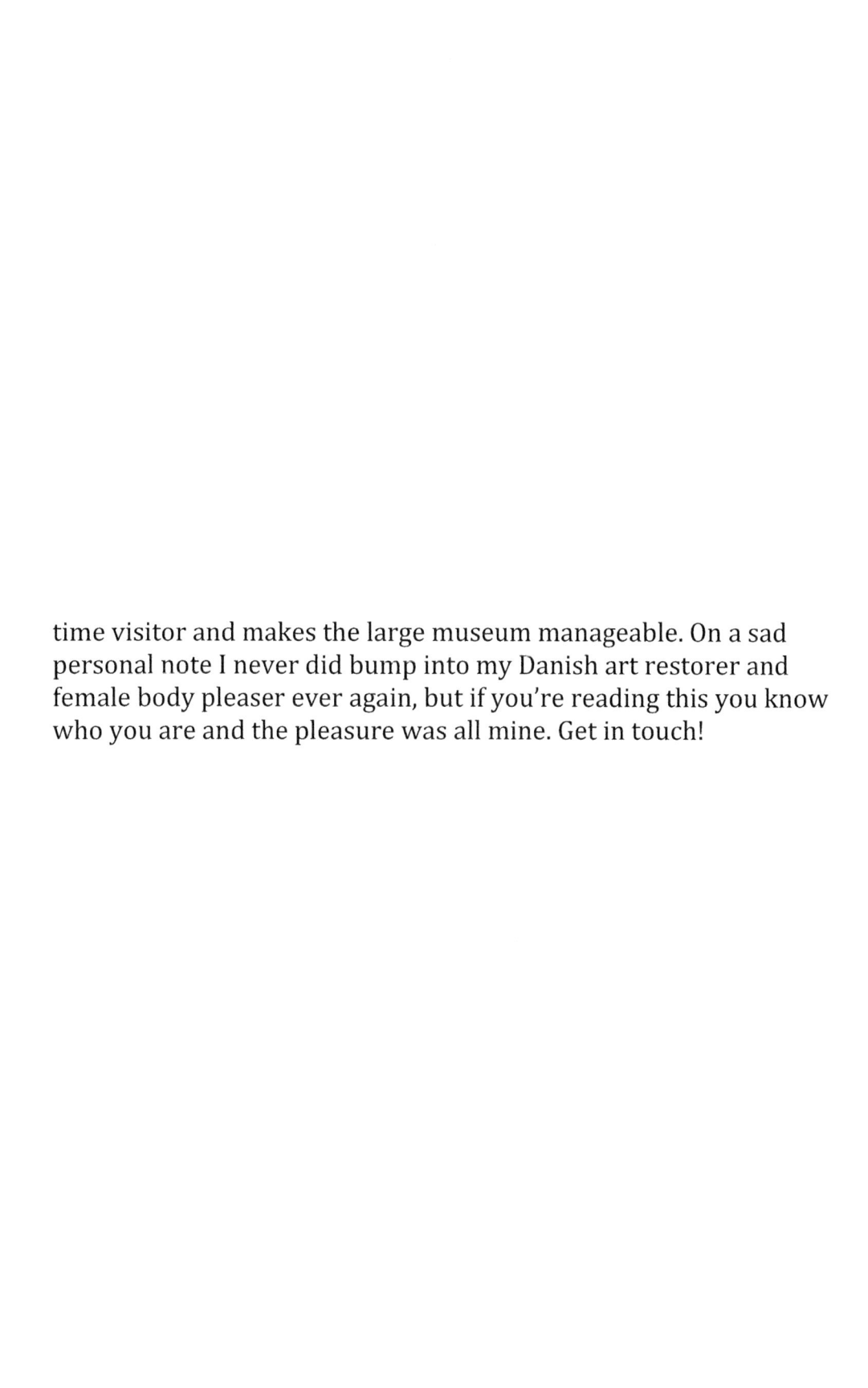

Chapter Eleven: Fun4Two

After a most relaxing but non eventful Friday evening, both having decided to give our used and battered bodies a day off and time to replenish the energy levels we awoke refreshed to a glorious warm and sunny Saturday morning with the cafes of Amsterdam in full swing. Strolling along a nearby canal we parked ourselves outside one that looked popular and took an unhurried breakfast whilst waiting for Paul and Mike to arrive from London. Paul had sent me a text letting me know that everything was on schedule and they would be arriving around lunchtime, giving Antonia and I a few hours to do some shopping.

We headed back toward the museum district; where luxury designer brand shopping is at its best and can compete with the best other European cities have to offer. The P.C. Hooftstraat is Amsterdam's most exclusive shopping street, featuring shops like Chanel, Louis Vuitton, DKNY, Mulberry, Ralph Lauren to name a few. We also paid a visit to the famous Dam Square and discovered the delights of De Bijenkorf, one of Amsterdam's best department stores, very much along the lines of Harvey Nichols. When it comes to shopping in Amsterdam there is so much on offer, I would certainly buy a guidebook. Do not miss the Singel flower market, which is by far one of Amsterdam's most colourful attractions, all the shops and stalls are located inside a row of floating barges, many locals refer to it as the "floating market". There are plenty of bars and cafes in the area to while away a good few hours. In all honesty there is so much to do and see in Amsterdam that like myself I can guarantee you'll catch the bug and return time after time. I have never been stuck for some form of entertaining distraction on my frequent visits.

On the way back to the apartment I paid a fleeting visit to one of the numerous sex shops in the area and stocked up on a selection of my much loved poppers. The manager was most surprised, and was most generous when it came to a bulk discount. I ended up buying fifty bottles across several different brands, Rush Extra, Bang, Pure Gold etc. I was going to donate quite a few to friends in London, as at that time it was almost impossible to buy and if you did strike it lucky it was at least five or six times the price.

Due to a slight delay Paul and Mike didn't arrive until mid afternoon, having been in constant touch via text we arrived back at the apartment with our various bags of shopping a few minutes before they pulled up in the cab. Paul and Charlie obviously new each other from their dalliances in Paris and both her and Mike vaguely recognised each other, saying the evening was a bit of a blur. We immediately headed out and found a pleasant canal side bar where we planned our evening. As we didn't want to take any chances we rang ahead and had them put our names on the reservation list (the club is now so popular its mandatory to book for Friday and Saturday evenings). The club is located in a small village called Moordrecht near the town of Gouda, which is approximately forty minutes south of Amsterdam, with this in mind we booked a private taxi to take us there, being given assurance that we'd have no problem getting back, as the club had several local firms that were always on call for them.

    The taxi was booked for nine so we decided to sample some traditional Dutch cuisine, and on a recommendation we went to Haesje Claes close by on Spuistraat 275, it dated back to 1520 but don't worry its kept abreast of the times! It has many dining rooms set over this original group of nine cottages. They live by the restaurants motto, which is "Van Kaantjes tot Kaviaar" which roughly translated means "From Pork Crackling to Caviar" … Something to suit everyone! Many of the main dishes are hearty stew like concoctions; I personally had slow cooked beef in old grandma's style with red cabbage, mashed potatoes and apple compote. It's well worth a visit and reasonably priced. But as well as being traditional it is also a very popular tourist destination, we were lucky to get a table and we were dining early!

    The boys made sure they wore classy boxers under their trousers and polo shirt combo's, whilst Charlie and I went for our tried and tested LBD's, which are perfect for any eventuality. We'd both bought some very expensive yet elegantly skimpy panties by Aubade and complimentary hold-ups, both topping our ensembles off with high strappy Jimmy Choo's. The pre booked car turned up at nine on the dot, thankfully was a nice roomy 7 Series BMW.

    When we arrived at the club it was already packed, having checked in at reception and produced all the relevant documents needed to get our temporary membership (see their very comprehensive website) we found the large bar area complete with numerous bar staff and to make life a little easier we ordered a bottle of house champagne, which was brought to the table we'd luckily nabbed just as two couples were leaving to explore this vast themed club.

The club is actually an old converted Dutch farmhouse and is built on land reclaimed from the sea. The part of the building, which is now the main club, it was used in the past to house the cows, keeping them warm during the winter months.

It felt very different to the Parisian clubs that the four of us were used to in a great many ways, the main one being the strict club rule that at exactly ten-thirty the DJ plays a very unsubtle song titled "Get your clothes off Now" which is the sign for everybody to traipse off to the large changing room areas, grab a locker and do exactly as the song says. Men have to wear boxers and ladies lingerie. We did find this most bizarre and to be honest very clinical and a tad off putting. To me the elegance, mystery and anticipation that creates a heady sexual atmosphere is destroyed by this regimented theme. However, it does put all the couples on a level playing field. The lack of select single men was also definitely a big blow for me and the many ladies that thrive on being the centre of attention in a group of males, whether it be just flirting at the bar or taking it further to the full on decadent sexual pleasure stage.

The club can hold around one hundred and forty couples comfortable and once the fun gets underway in the plethora of themed rooms the main bar/dance area thins out and the claustrophobic feeling eases.

There are two very distinct parts to the club, a dry side that houses a mini Red Light area upstairs with many different themes in each room. Its great to go up and explore, it really is like an adult maze. I counted at least fifteen open playrooms up there, along with a few private lockable rooms.

On the very top level they have an area called "The Orgy Loft"; there is a small ladder leading up to a large dimly lit room located under the slanted roof of the house. The ceiling is very low, hence you need to crawl on your hands and knees to get around, when I ventured up there it was heaving with bodies everywhere enjoying themselves in the completely anonymous surroundings.

Crossing a bridge back down on level one you enter the "wet area", or as it's commonly referred to as "The Spa area": A very impressive area of the club, it has showers, a sauna and a giant Jacuzzi that fits at least eight couples comfortably sitting inside or on the edge. Many frisky party people were having lots of fun, although notices tell you that sex is not allowed in the pool itself. There was a lot of enthusiastic under water fondling going on. There was also a small intimate bar up a set of stairs that overlooked the fun. It's paradise for those of a voyeuristic inclination.

Outside: On Sunday afternoons (during summer and when the weather permits) the garden is accessible, which has a large pool where they host naked pool parties.

Apparently they have opened a Tantric temple, and several people we know who have been many times have reported that this has rapidly developed into the clubs most exotic zone. You are requested to keep silent in the area itself and it has several large cushioned platforms on which you can lie down. It apparently has a very esoteric feel to it, and there are lotions and oils available that you can use for massages. Two of our close friends said that the quietness of the room is a bit ghostlike, as all you can hear is the muffled whimpering of the many other people in there engaged in slippery fun and frolics.

One of the rooms in the Red Light area that the four of us did make use of along with another couple was the mini replica sex theatre. It had its own mini stage complete with a large bed and a few rows of theatre seats for the audience. A spotlight illuminated the bed and you were encouraged to put on a performance, stage your own production as it were. From the audience reaction people liked our particular presentation that evening. The highlight of the act was when Mike (le digit) had Charlie and the other lady knelt facing the audience whilst he furiously plesured them with his legendary skilled fingers, working both of them like a master puppeteer until they were unable to hold back any longer, both uttering a low guttural cry they embarked on a series of powerful gushing orgasms. Soaking the enthusiastic couples in the front row, everyone quietly applauded the exhibition. Mike was, as always beaming with pride as he dried his sopping hands, as I've said before his finger work alone is something every woman should experience (an extra addition to your bucket list ladies!). He was doubly delighted when an attractive younger couple approached him and requested a personal consultation! We left him to it and made our way back to the bar for a round of Jack Daniels on ice. Another good idea the club implements is that they have a set price per couple and that is all inclusive of drinks, buffet and towels. No hidden extras whatsoever. Always nice to relax in the knowledge that no hidden surprises would ruin your evening. You pay on entrance and then play and party till four in the morning or when ever you can't take anymore.

It's a perfect club for everyone who enjoys and feels more comfortable in a couple's only environment. On this particular evening the couples ranged from early twenties to late fifties, with everyone mixing well together.

We did achieve what we set out to do and came away with lots of ideas, which Charlie would later modify and incorporate into her club, albeit with a certain degree of fine-tuning.

As promised a local taxi was ordered and appeared within minutes to whisk us back to the apartment. I distinctly remember everyone dozing all the way back.

We actually left the club around two (it was still in full swing) and I remember we were all ensconced by three back in Amsterdam in a late night pancake house getting stuck into various flavours, all topped of with a large brandy. It was a great way to end the evening. One, which I've repeated on my frequent visits to Amsterdam and the Paradise club and the awesome *"Showboat"* just north of Amsterdam at Zaandijk (much more regarding this amazing venue later).

Chapter Twelve: The Rise Of Cougar

Daily life continued back at the house in Kew where I spent a vast amount of time designing and redesigning my vision of how the interior of Charlie's club should look. The swinging club scene in Paris was now becoming very competitive, with more and more venues opening, giving people more choice and enabling them to be more selective. So she had to get it right in every way or it would end up being just another club. It simply had to stand out from the crowd in every way.

One memorable interlude during this period was when out of the blue an email pinged into my inbox from "young" Laurent, who I'd not seen or heard from since my fortieth birthday. He was coming to London for a few days with several of his team mates from the amateur rugby club he played for down in South West France, incidentally not a million miles away from Paul parents. They were coming over to attend the Six Nations Rugby match between England and France. There was going to be seven of them arriving on the Thursday prior to the game and they'd be staying at the Chelsea Harbour Hotel. He was wondering if I was free for dinner on the Friday? This immediately brought a smile to my face and that certain inner glow burst forth as the memories of our time spent together during that long hot summer came flooding back. The time spent at the request of his father, teaching his eighteen-year-old son in the art of pleasuring a woman are some of my fondest memories. However, the boy I trained all those years ago would now be twenty-seven and a man of the world. I couldn't respond to his email quickly enough. I checked with Paul first as always and had his full blessing to go. The children would not be home that weekend so I had nothing to keep me from going.

What initially was just going to be drinks and dinner together soon escalated into something more substantial, and over the coming few days I arranged for both Sarah and Antonia to join the party. It wasn't difficult to persuade either of them, as they'd both met Laurent, and Sarah had even played on several occasions with his father Thierry. The very thought of what the evening may hold in store made me shudder with expectant delight. The three of us, a thirty seven year old, me an early forties and Sarah approaching late forties let loose for the evening amongst seven fit Frenchmen, all in their mid twenties to early thirties. Cougar time, total devastation was on the cards and that is exactly what occurred.

The three of us met up in Kew for lunch at my local, the Coach and Horses on Kew Green and over a chilled bottle of Pouilly-Fumé Sauvignon Blanc we discussed how to approach the evening. Both had brought their most elegant yet enticing evening out fits with them, as we'd arranged to get ready at mine and I had a taxi booked for seven thirty.

Back at the house we began our individual rituals for the impending evening. Accompanied by a soupcon of vino we moisturised lavishly, and hair and make up took on theatrical like preparations. It was like our late teens being revisited. I had picked out a very elegant black and silver Roberto Cavalli short cocktail dress with matching evening heels, both recent purchases from Liberty on Regent Street. Audaciously I decided to go commando as it always added an extra frisson of exhilaration and devilment to the occasion. Sarah and Antonia were similarly attired, however Antonia was wearing a stunningly eye catching lace thong by La Perla. One last look in the mirror and we were on our way to Chelsea. The atmosphere in the taxi was electric, lots of laughter and knowing looks.

The driver dropped us right outside the door, and there waiting to greet us was Laurent, looking deliciously edible in chinos and pastel blue Ralph Lauren button collar oxford shirt. Kisses all round and many admiring glances as he escorted us to meet his group who were all eagerly awaiting our arrival in the Harbour Bar. As the flamboyantly French introductions were made I could sense simply by the looks and enthusiastic kisses that Laurent had regaled them with what this married English lady had taught him in his teenage years. I must admit a distinct lustful feeling swept over me as I discreetly appraised these young French men, I could tell Antonia and Sarah were equally impressed.

Thoughtfully there was a welcome bottle of Laurent-Perrier Champagne on ice ready for us. A most pleasant way to start the evening. They'd booked a table at the hotels Chelsea Riverside Brasserie with its spectacular views over Chelsea Harbour Marina. Everyone was beginning to bond and very quickly a definite undercurrent of sexual tension became evident. The anticipation was building nicely. To make things easier Laurent ordered a selection of their traditional thin and crust pizzas with several different salads and side orders that were dotted around the table. It was very casual and most tasty, no airs or graces necessary, just lots of innuendo and good-humoured banter. The wine kept flowing until everyone was well fed, they do take some feeding these young French rugby players. Not just food as we were soon to find out.

This hotel consists solely of suites; between them they'd booked the huge King Penthouse Suite, along with the Abingdon and Kensington Suites, very conveniently all on the same floor. We all excitedly jumped into the first available lift and headed directly to the top floor.

Everyone quickly decided that the King Penthouse was ideal, the perfect environment for the ten of us to continue the party in more private surroundings. The suite was perfect for the occasion, it consisted of two bedrooms, both with King size beds. The master bedroom includes a dressing area, a large screen television, a private sauna and an en-suite bathroom with an infinity spa bath and a double walk-in shower. The second bedroom also has a large screen television and its own en-suite bathroom. The spacious living area of the suite has yet another large screen television and a Bose sound system, as well as a separate guest washroom. The most exquisite space to play in. After much discussion Sarah had written down every ones drink requirements and rang down to room service. Most pleasing to my ears was when I heard her ordering a bottle of Jack Daniels. Whilst waiting for the drinks to arrive everybody went on to the terrace and marvelled at the panoramic views of the stunning London skyline and its night-time lights. Once the drinks arrived things accelerated quite rapidly as the room lighting was dimmed and some chill out music was played on the sound system. Antonia was busy teasing three of the guys by seductively raising her dress slightly, giving them a tantalising peek at her La Perla panties, which I knew would not remain in place for too much longer. I began to play up to Laurent and another man, as when asked I just shrugged and told them it was an oversight, and I'd simply forgotten to wear any panties. They both nearly choked when I discreetly lifted the front of my dress, briefly showing them my freshly waxed and very wet pussy. Sarah was occupied with the two other men and was flirting outrageously, all very touchy feely, the men in turn were playing their part and were soon helping her step out of her dress, revealing her magnificent breasts and bullet like erect nipples. She never misses an opportunity to flaunt them.

Before going any further I excused myself and sauntered out on to the terrace for a quick St Moritz in preparation for some extreme physical exertion. Whilst leaning on the terrace railings a gent, who I knew by this stage was called Francois joined me and happily accepted a cigarette. In typical French style his hand mischievously found its way onto my bottom for a cheeky, but most enjoyable fondle, in my typical English way I actively encouraged him with a provocative wiggle. Taking this as a green light his hand travelled underneath my dress and slipped between my already parted thighs. I moaned softly as he explored my wetness, at this stage he was unaware of my fluency in French, and this turned me on hugely as I understood every single one of his lecherous utterances. Finishing our cigarettes he gave me the most erotic full on kiss, pressing his obvious erection that was straining at his trousers into my groin. Slowly I reached down and playfully stroked him through the material that was desperately struggling to retain him. Quicker than I could catch my breath, and with an artistry that belied his age he unpeeled my dress from my body and placed it like a winners trophy over his shoulder. His hand darted between my quivering thighs; instantaneously his fingers found my clitoris and gently teased it out to play. I was putty in his powerful and sexually poetic hands, he manipulated my vagina with total expertise and he looked a bit disappointed when I briefly broke away from him to grab my clutch bag. He thought I wanted to slow things down a bit and have another cigarette break, but his eyes lit up as I produced a fresh, unopened bottle of Amsterdam's finest poppers. I resumed the position and frantically opened the bottle and took a huge hit in both nostrils. The effect was almost instant, my core began to rapidly inflame and every nerve ending started to tingle, I sensed my orgasm rapidly approaching, gripping his broad shoulders and bending my knees slightly I unleashed a deluge of my holy water over his hand, soaking his wrist and splashing noisily on the terracotta terrace floor. The look of amazement and sheer bewilderment on his face was a joy to see. He was intrigued, never before sampling the delights of what insane and intense pleasure amyl will bring. I handed the bottle to him as I squatted on my haunches and commenced freeing him from his trousers. His erection sprang forth impressively, throbbing angrily in front of me, he groaned softly as I began to run my tongue up and down his length, circling its pulsating purple head, nibbling him gently. I leant back slightly with my mouth open inviting him to feed me and by golly did he feed me, inch after inch of solid manhood entered my mouth, filling me, stretching me, working me fervently. I was salivating uncontrollably over him, alternately sucking and licking at him, what really blew his mind was just as I sensed his orgasm was approaching I told him to take a hit of my poppers. I mentally counted to ten, but only reached five before his thighs began to quake violently, his eye balls rolled back into his head as he began to ejaculate uncontrollably, it was spraying everywhere in large powerful jets, it was like an out of control garden hose. His entire body seemed to go into shock and he was rigid, statue like for a good three minutes as the last of his semen flowed copiously from him, dripping warmly onto my outstretched tongue, I remained in this position still having my own mini gushes whilst scooping up the big pools of semen from my breasts, eating it off my fingers like a depraved forty something! Quite fitting really.

We both had another menthol cigarette whilst basking in the after glow of the evening's first bout of orgasms, with many more on the horizon.

We were greeted by a scene from a Roman orgy as we re-entered the room, Sarah was slumped back on the sofa as one guy lapped at her swollen vagina, another two were knelt precariously either side of her as she sucked noisily on them. Whilst Francois fixed me a drink I went to the bathroom to freshen up and pop on a bit of lipstick. On the way I back popped my head in to the master bedroom to be confronted by the delightful vision of Antonia energetically riding on a rather meaty looking French penis, while Laurent and Guy were watching intently, erections in hand, ready to step in at any given moment. I knew from experience the three of them had their hands full with Antonia, having seen her in full flow in Paris, outlasting a group of the most experienced and revered swordsmen France had to offer. She had left them drained and in virtual tears, demanding more as they threw in the white towel. She, to this very day lays the blame for her wanton behaviour firmly at my door. As if?

Having taken a much-needed five-minute Jack Daniels break it was back into the fray as Guy and another hunk took me to the other bedroom. Clutching my bottle of poppers I detoured briefly, and let a grateful Antonia take a hit. Once in the room the two young guys were lying side by side on the bed offering me their erections, a nice position to be in, as I am an avid believer that a lady should always have a choice. Kneeling in between them I sampled each one in turn with my mouth, my tongue flicking rapidly over them. They grinned as I sat up pointing at their erections and played a little game of eeny meeny miny moe catch a Frenchman by his… Who cared who won as I took turns in straddling their solid thighs and lowering my eager vagina on to each of them in turn, using all my skill and not least a vast amount of thigh muscle control. My powerful and well trained vagina gripped and milked them zealously, sometimes slow and gently and other times slamming down hard and fast. At one stage whilst I was fully impaled on Guy and feeding my nipples to his friend we took a large group hit on my poppers, this took the whole scenario to another level. I instantly began coming hard and squirted copiously all over Guy, which he adored, every zone of my body was on fire, my nipples felt like they were going to explode, my clitoris throbbed with pure unadulterated pleasure. The scenario was further enriched by the flamboyant screams and ecstatic whimpers emanating from all the other rooms of the suite.

    There was a lot of intermingling from the get go, with each of us ladies being given total attention throughout. There were many memorable highlights, including briefly watching Sarah getting very naughty with four of the men in the infinity whirlpool bath whilst sipping on what appeared to be another glass of Champagne. On several occasions she had everyone in stitches as she told the men, or rather boys as she referred to them, "I'm old enough to be your mother". Whilst continuing to use them for her gratification.

    My personal highlight, or to be more accurate my own gold medal standard performance involved my protégé Laurent and Francois. We left the others and snuck off to the main room, where they both took turns in pleasing me orally. It was sublime; having two young twenty something fit Frenchmen fighting over my very wet and willing vagina was unsurpassable. They had me in all sorts of trouble; I was in a high state of orgasm throughout their eager feasting. Eventually I climbed on top of a very aroused Francois, lowering myself slowly on to him, once he was fully inside me I twitched uncontrollably as Laurent's accomplished hands parted my buttocks and he gently began to work his erection slowly into my exposed rectum. It was a pretty tight fit, but once they were both snuggly accommodated inside my willing orifices they commenced building a rhythmic tempo, thrusting into me with supreme dexterity. I had a really intense out of body experience, looking down from above watching them plundering both my vagina and anus in perfect harmony, a joyous feeling; I wanted to scream with lust. I came with incredible force as I felt them both begin to climax, filling me with copious amounts of their hot, sweet semen. My muscles milked them for all they were worth, draining every last delicious drop from their rock solid young members. Their youthful cocks remained inside me until they were completely limp and empty, even then I was loathe to let them withdraw from me. Given half a chance I would have kept them solidly clasped inside me until their penis's recovered and awoke from their brief slumber and were ready to ferociously pound me again. I had certainly taught Laurent well all those years ago. Touchingly they carried me through to the wet room, where under the powerful hydro jet shower they both soaped and cleansed my aching body. I felt like an empress with her two young slaves, most decadent, but such wicked fun.

    The evening ended with room service bringing a huge platter of bacon sandwiches and a most welcome steaming pot of coffee. The perfect end to an unforgettable evening. Three **"Cougars"** most definitely tamed their "*Cubs*" on this occasion. A most enjoyable and filth filled soiree was enjoyed by all.

Chapter Thirteen: London Awakens (Slowly)

The following months flew by. Since selling my interest in the online company a few years previously the American Corporation consulted me less and less, they had exhausted all the knowledge that I could furnish them with. Also, with Paul working away in the States, frequently at this stage and the children away at school I often found myself twiddling my thumbs, not exactly bored, but in dire need of something fresh to occupy me. I was grateful to have a role in the planning of Charlie's impending new club venture, but needed something closer to home and to be more involved on a daily basis.

Eventually, after a chance meeting with a couple that we'd met fleetingly at several private house parties over the years in and around London a seed of an idea was planted. Paul and I arranged to meet them for lunch and listen to their proposition to see if there was any common ground for us to be involved and work with them.

It was a most interesting lunch meeting, and they'd both certainly done their homework.

David and Penny at that time were a couple in their late thirties, successful and wealthy. Having sold their niche market greetings card company two years previous, they had found themselves struggling to fill their days and had come up with an idea that they both wanted to pursue, but needed help and advice in the planning and more crucially the marketing aspect of it.

With some of the money from the sale of their company they'd bought a large secluded home in Hertfordshire, it came complete with a large out building adjacent to an all weather swimming pool. The property was set in several acres of land with no neighbours to speak of. To access the house you have to drive a good half a mile along a private road then once the large electric wrought iron gates had been opened remotely a further long secluded driveway awaits. It was very discreet and it seemed from their description perfect for what they had in mind. In a nutshell they wanted to turn the outbuilding into a sophisticated adult party venue. They had our full attention, and as soon as we explained our experiences so far in the swinging world it was evident that we were a good combination. They'd been swinging for several years, but were totally disillusioned by the London scene, or what little there was outside small private gatherings. London and the rest of the U.K was a lifetime behind what other European capitals had to offer. It was still very much in the grip of the deep entrenched "News of The World" mentality, where anything remotely classed as swinging was labelled perverted, and the old suburban wife swapping exposés reared up on the front pages. I still laugh at the get out clause they trotted out time after time, "Our reporters made their excuses and left, and we've passed on our findings to the authorities". Excuse my language, but what total "wankers".

The few attempts at doing an adult themed club were always marred by the locations and the organiser, who invariably was just in it for a quick buck. It was still very much the tacky French Maids get up for the ladies and cardigan and slippers for the men, complete with the obligatory buffet of stale sausage rolls and warm cans of Fosters lager. No sophistication or style was evident at the few we briefly attended. For us it was always in the front door, one look and straight out the back door. But thankfully we'd learnt our lesson early and avoided them at all costs.

They in turn were intrigued by Paris and its delights and wanted to tag along on our/my next visit, which incidentally wasn't that far off, as I'd arranged to visit Charlie and finally settle on her clubs interior design, but more importantly visit Yves who'd been taken ill and was currently convalescing in a private clinic near Versailles, fifteen minutes west of Paris.

Paul and I accepted the invitation to visit their home the following weekend and to see and discuss their plans and ideas face to face.

As we'd arranged we met them at a very old traditional pub drink in the quaint village of Bulbourne called the "Grand Junction Arms" for a lunchtime drink. It has a lovely large beer where we all indulged in a pint of cider before following them to their home ten minutes away.

As instructed we followed behind them and after a few miles took a left turn up a very narrow road marked private, it was just wide enough for two cars, although two 4X4's would be a tight squeeze. Shortly we arrived at a tall imposing set of ornate wrought iron gates that had begun to open courtesy of David's security fob. We then continued along a sweeping driveway to the main house, adjacent to it was a fairly substantial fenced area that had been laid to gravel, which later became the guests' secure parking area.

We followed them to the rear of the house, where the main large imposing out building was situated, along with a couple of smaller ones. They had already been semi renovated, structurally sound, but needed a fair amount of work to the interiors to create what was needed to achieve their objectives.

David became most animated when I suggested Penny tagged along with me to Paris, where she could see the work in progress at Charlie's venue and maybe include a visit to *L'Escapade* and *Quai 17*, "purely business" I exclaimed with a knowing look to Paul, who simply raised his eye brows as if reading my mind. David gave Penny his full consent; he was in fact quite adamant that she should go and return with plenty of ideas (and a few naughty new experiences). I did promise not to lead her astray, but I had my fingers firmly crossed. I could sense her excitement, as it was very evident from our conversations so far that they'd only dabbled at the events they'd previously attended, but were both totally committed to jumping in with both feet, so to speak. A while later when we were alone together she expressed a firm desire to visit the *"Paradise Club"* in Amsterdam, I smiled at her and said "little steps, bit by bit". I sensed a real kindred spirit and was certainly looking forward to her joining me in Paris for a few days.

It was also around this time that Paul treated me to my first Macbook Laptop, it was white, it was beautiful, and he'd bought us both one on a recent business trip to New York. I was the envy of our friends. To this day I still love Apple products. In fact I'm writing this on a late 2015 Macbook Pro. I don't know how I'd survive without it and my trusty iPad. Call me weird but one of the things I do when I visit any major town or city I check out where the local Apple store is and spend a good few hours perusing the products on display, nuts I know!

I felt our meeting and bourgeoning friendship with David and Penny was going to result in a very positive and fruitful partnership. We both had very similar aims in bringing a socially acceptable chic and classy swinging lifestyle scene to the U.K, London in particular. It took a lot of time and effort, but over the coming months and years London and a vast many towns and cities up and down the U.K began come to the party, albeit slowly.

Chapter Fourteen: Good Penny – Bad Penny!

Subsequently after several excited Skype calls with Penny the day arrived for our "business" trip to Paris. As arranged David picked me up, and kindly dropped Penny and I off at the train terminal. We took a mid morning Eurostar to the Gare Du Nord; it was Tuesday so the first Class section was very quiet, in fact only six other people were in our carriage. Penny didn't pause for breath the entire journey; it was a full on interrogation. Over a bottle of white wine I tried to answer her multitude of questions, the more glimpses of what Paris had to offer the more excitable she became. I felt that this going to be a tiring, but fun filled few days, this certainly turned out to be the case. She was like a child let loose in a sweet shop, she was determined to make the most of it, sample everything on offer. She reminded me of myself all those years ago when Paul and I took our first tentative steps in to this hedonistic, decadent world of pleasure.

I'd arranged with Marc to pick us up at the station, but not to tell Yves, as I wanted it to be a surprise visit. Sadly during the journey to the apartment Marc briefly told me the full extent of Yves's illness, and that he hoped my surprise visit would perk him up, I certainly hoped this would be the case. I arranged for him to pick me up the following morning at eleven so as not do interrupt the clinics visiting schedule.

After showing a dumbstruck Penny around the apartment (she was still in shock as I'd not told her that I had a driver at my beck and call) we went for a drink opposite. She positively skipped across Rue Marbeuf to the bar that over the years had become my local, and often first port of call. After the customary greetings from the ever present friendly faces we had a nice bottle of chilled wine, it always has a powerful effect and relaxes me instantly back into the Parisian way of things. I was nicely chilled, however Penny was wound up like a clock, wanting to do everything at once. Eventually she began to ease into the situation, savouring her new temporary surroundings.

I'd arranged to meet Charlie and visit the club to see all the recent developments, and then the three of us would go out to dinner, somewhere special and typically Parisian, in honour of Penny's visit.

Promptly at seven she was downstairs buzzing on the intercom, we met her at the door and I made the introductions. Her sporty Z3 BMW was totally unsuitable having only two seats, so she'd borrowed a friends more appropriate Renault Clio. We jumped in and zipped through the busy Paris traffic and were soon pulling up close to her club.

I was shocked at how different it looked from the last time I'd visited, work was well under way. The first thing I noticed was the fully completed reception area, which had been given a total make over, it was warm and inviting but still remained very functional.

The main area had been gutted, but the raised stage and bar remained, there were a couple of VIP seating area's being installed.

Most pleasing to me was that she'd firmly taken on board my ideas for the plethora of rooms behind the main area. Several were already well underway in design and décor, but all areas had printed room names and layout firmly pinned at its entrance. The eventual design and layout pretty much remains today as it was back then.

Charlie opened the club a few months later with great fanfare, plenty of word of mouth and selected adverts on relevant websites and hard copy magazines, including "Pariscope", the little Parisian what's on guide that helped Paul and I on our way back in the day. It all ensured the grand opening was jam packed with the bold and beautiful from the Parisian scene. Sadly, Paul and I couldn't attend as planned due to a last minute emergency, Paul's mother had taken a fall in their local village in South West France and had shattered her hip, and was quite poorly for several weeks. We dropped everything to go and help Paul's father, who was understandably upset and worried. However, Paul and I did have a very pleasant flying visit to the club our way back to London, better late than never.

The club was an instant success, and Charlie was overjoyed at the reputation it had gained in such a small space of time, especially as there was now plenty of competition and a wide choice for the Parisian party people to choose from. Charlie quite clearly had got it right and the regular unique themed evenings, that were always well executed with great attention to the detail proved popular and always ensured the club was at full capacity.

Both Charlie and the club went from strength to strength, however, after a couple of years she decided to sell up, as the 24/7 stress of owning and running a club on this scale was taking its toll on her. The change over to new ownership was seamless, and the club continued as *"L'Overside"*; it's still to this day one of the best and most popular swingers venues in Paris. The Greek themed room was a particular favourite of mine; it houses a huge hexagonal bed as its centrepiece with large comfortable sofas all around. Each time I attended this room it was always jam packed with seriously attractive people all fully intent on enjoying each other. First time couples, as well as the more experienced swing club connoisseur can most definitely enjoy this club. The swinging devotee will appreciate the large mosaic room, with its two huge beds and mirrored walls and ceiling. It's perfect for the narcissistic exhibitionists amongst us. I do on occasion include myself in this category. Also, for the more initiated the club allows single males, usually on a Sunday and Wednesday, but do check the website. I strongly recommend if you get a chance that you treat yourselves, and enjoy a night in this most elegant of clubs.

Back into the Clio, Charlie navigated her way back across the river to the restaurant I'd suggested, for two reasons, firstly it was in the same street as the apartment, and secondly Charlie could park the car securely in the reserved underground car park space and enjoy a drink or two without any worry. I'd eaten there twice previously and had loved its food, décor and total ambience. It's called *"La Fermette Marbeuf"*. Its really a must visit, its Art Nouveau decor is listed as an historical monument, in particular its magnificent glass roof designed in 1898 by Hubert and Martineau. It has great class and history.

The food is extraordinary, out of this world even. On each occasion I've always ordered as a starter the exquisite Blue Lobster Bisque, followed on this occasion by Normandy beef fillet, with dauphine potatoes and peppercorn sauce. The flavours will truly assault your palette, leaving you with just enough room for their stunning Tahitian vanilla crème brûlée. It really is up there with the finest dining experiences I've ever had the pleasure to enjoy. After coffee and a nice smooth French cognac, much to Penny's chagrin we called it a night, and being a Tuesday most clubs would be very quiet anyway. We wandered back to the apartment to take a Jack Daniels and an early ish night, promising Penny I'd fully impart some of the decadence that Paris had to offer after a good nights rest, and that I'd be all hers after my visit to Yves. She fully accepted that this was for the best, as it had already been a long day and she'd not gotten much sleep the night before, she said her head was full of erotic thoughts of what this solo trip may deliver. I fully appreciated how she felt; I'd been there.

Marc collected me as planned, and it didn't take long to reach the private clinic, which was in a small village just outside Versailles called Chaville. It was set in very well tendered grounds and seemed very tranquil. Marc came in with me and introduced me to the receptionist as we signed the visitors' register. Yves was sitting in a pleasant sunroom; he looked frail, but was most pleased to see me. He'd had a slight stroke, so his speech was slightly slurred, but that little twinkle was still present in his eyes, if a little dimmed by the sadness of his current situation. I spent a good few hours updating him with all that had been going on recently in my life. He was fascinated when I told him about Penny, and he made me promise to treat her to the delights of Paris, as only I knew how. He was just annoyed and frustrated not be able to join us for an adventure, or at least arrange one of his special evenings for us. I left him smiling with the promise of another visit soon. He instructed Marc to keep an eye on me and to be available as and when needed. Before leaving I managed to have a word with one of the resident Doctors who explained that Yves was getting the best care possible, but his "Joie de vivre" had caught up with him and we must accept his advancing years were also a major factor.

Marc dropped me off outside the apartment at around three o'clock; Jenny was waiting patiently at the bar for me. She ordered me a much-needed glass of wine as I crossed the road. She'd been exploring the local area and had done a bit of shopping; she'd found a local lingerie shop and had severely dented her credit card. She was now impatient to explore some of the more erotic aspects of Paris. With this in mind I'd decided that for her first club visit I'd take her to the ever popular *"Quai 17"*, which over the years has gone from strength to strength, always coming up with new ideas and wild themed nights. At this time Wednesday nights was "La Nuit du Masque". I explained the plan and suggested we jumped in a taxi and went to a fantastic warehouse that I'd previously discovered that specialised in selling theatrical costumes online, but always welcomed visitors after three in the afternoon (they have a very comprehensive website, which is also in English). They have possibly the best range of masks I've ever witnessed. They are called "Theatr'Hall" and are based out in West Paris, close to Gare de Lyon. Once there we both had a good rummage around, with Penny getting more and more turned on by it all. We ended up buying two very elegant, ornate and flamboyantly decorated Colombina eye masks each. We then headed off by taxi to the "Demonia" Fetish store, where we both ended up with an outrageously revealing party dress each. She was overwhelmed by the shop, which has become a Parisian institution over the years. Whilst taking a small café and cognac at a nearby bar she was so aroused by the thought of what the night had in store she was squirming in her seat, much to my amusement.

By this stage it was approaching six thirty so we decided to head back and get an early supper before getting ready to go out. We kept it simple and had a great steak and chips, side salad and vino at "my" bar opposite the apartment; always delivers great food and drink at very reasonable prices, especially for this chic area of Paris.

Once we'd refuelled we got started with my well established prepping and pampering routine prior to a club night. Penny followed my lead, and as she was moisturising I had my first glimpse of her naked body in all its glory. Very toned and lean, with a very pert pair of breasts, and just a very narrow strip of pubic hair on display. Quite gorgeous to be honest, very tempting. Once we squeezed ourselves in to our very small, clinging, body contoured black party dresses we stepped into our very high platforms. The very nature of the revealing cut out panels and slits on the dresses meant no panties were required. As per my normal routine a little nip of Jack Daniels was taken along with a St Moritz for me whilst we waited for the taxi to arrive, we could of used Marc, but I didn't want to take advantage, also a girls got to keep an air of mystery about here whereabouts.

We arrived at around eleven o'clock, and the place was already fairly busy, and as we were two single females entry was free (this is still the case on a Tues/Weds/Thurs). Handing our coats in at reception we donned our masks, enhancing the mysteriousness of these two unaccompanied ladies and their agendas.

I lead the way to the bar area, which as many of you'll know already is situated adjacent to the dance floor. Alain the head barman recognised me instantaneously, even with the mask, and in French told me that he'd recognise my legs anywhere. We drew many looks from the other customers as we took up our positions on the bar stools. A rough head count told me that already in attendance were around thirty couples and around sixty hand selected men. They have a very strict door policy regarding single males. Have a read of their etiquette and dress code at their website, where you can also see the current prices and what the future evening themes are going to be.

The prominently purple and crimson décor is set off beautifully by discreet use of ultra violet lighting, which I feel always creates an air of naughtiness, and it makes even the pastiest individual look tanned. On this particular evening there were some seriously attractive people there ready to play. Everyone looked most decadent in his or her chosen masks. I ordered us both a "Coupe de Champagne" to begin with, telling Penny, who was quivering in delight to "just relax, pretend you've been to this kind of club many times and to go with the flow". Several men made pleasant and engaging conversation with us, often with me translating for Penny. This was a real hoot, as when she asked what the guy had asked, it gave me carte blanche to make up anything I wished, and a few times I did, causing much raucous laughter. The club was pretty much full by midnight and the dance floor was in full swing. A totally decadent mood was palpable and the sexual tension was building, all enhanced by the masks and the complete feeling of anonymity they give you.

Alain freshened our drinks and reserved our stools, as I felt the time was right to give Penny a guided tour of the clubs erotic playrooms. Then, if as I suspected would be the case, that she was comfortable and confident I would let her off the leash to explore and play alone, unsupervised by me.

Her astonishment was audible, and her eyes were darting everywhere as I firstly showed her the cinema room, complete with its two rows of comfortable theatre seats and the cushioned play area set off discreetly to one side. There were already two masked gents pleasuring a lady whilst her husband watched both her performance along with that of the actress on the large screen. Penny's eyes were out on stops, we both giggled when she whispered in my ear "I think I'm going to cum if we stay in here any longer, I've never been anywhere quite like this". To which I replied, "you ain't seen nothing yet". The small fetish room with its St Andrews Cross and padded restraining bench got her juices flowing even further, she firmly gripped on to my arm for support as we watched a lady noisily feasting on the erect penis of a young man whom she'd secured firmly to the cross, her husband watched on approvingly whilst holding her mask for her as she indulged on her prey. Most thoughtful of him!

It would be an understatement to say that the glory hole area blew her mind, she just couldn't take it all in, her head was spinning. We headed back to our drinks just so she could cool off for a moment and compose herself. Things were really starting to gear up a notch as several groups were in various states of undress and playing enthusiastically on the many sofas. There were two particular men whose masks were quite extraordinary, black metal and leather with a small white plumage of feathers on one edge. I'd noticed them earlier, but unless someone actually makes conversation directly it's difficult to tell if they are looking at you, let alone smiling. The whole masked theme gives a distinctive air of anonymity. This always adds to my level of excitement and I had the distinct feeling Penny felt the same.

Penny was champing at the bit, her level of anticipation and expectation growing rapidly as I pointed the two men out to her. I suggested she have a little wander, as I had a gut feeling they were sizing her up, and I fully expected them to follow her. Without hesitation she seductively slid off the bar stool and made her way hesitantly up the three inviting steps to the play areas, taking the top step with a very exaggerated hip wiggle. Sure enough they placed their drinks on a table, and discreetly followed her within a minute. I smiled inwardly and decided to give it a few minutes, and if she didn't come rushing back in a state of shock then I'd follow in a while just to keep a watchful eye.

I took full advantage of the situation accepting a cigarette from a gent and we flirted outrageously for a while until I felt it was appropriate to go and check on Penny's progress.

I casually meandered my way throughout the various play areas in my search, however, I eventually heard her before I saw her. Talk about hitting the ground running, she was taking pride of place, knelt on a small bed that was surrounded on three sides by metal bars. She had removed her dress and was just in her heels and was busy, greedily sucking on the plethora of hard throbbing cock that was being offered to her through the bars. One of the men was on all fours at the side of the bed voraciously eating her pussy, her firm bottom pushing back onto his enthusiastic mouth. She was moaning loudly as she slurped and salivated on all the available erect men present, giving each a good amount of tongue work. It wasn't long before I felt a gentle brush of fingertips on my bare shoulder and another brushing the back of my thigh. I quickly realised the hands were unrelated, and glancing left and right identified the two individuals responsible for the tingling feeling rapidly shooting through my nerve endings and making my vagina begin to pulsate. It's these initial moments that I crave, the unknown, the anonymity and the total wanton feeling of lust.

I parted my legs an inch or two as my slutty dress was rolled up to my waist, exposing more of me, giving the fingers an unfettered and most welcoming entrée. My breasts were rapidly freed and more anonymous hands began to tweak and fondle my erect nipples. Many hands were certainly making light work on my responsive body, my core was buzzing with an intense heat. Penny uttered an audible gasp of delight as a man positioned himself behind her and slowly penetrated her. As I watched her being used by the men I was getting seriously wet from the all the skilled gents that were encircling me. Soon a selection of large erect cocks were being unleashed and proffered to me, as always in these scenarios I take full advantage of the situation, feeding hungrily on strangers cocks. As I leant forward to suck on a rather thick manhood I myself was swiftly penetrated from behind, with one powerful thrust was all it took for me to let rip an explosive jet of my juices, completely drenching his heavy, loaded balls. It had swiftly descended into a scene of total debauchery. The sound of Penny getting fucked hard and fast by a succession of men spurred me on to get more and more lewd in my own actions, whilst vocally; in both a mix of French and English I directed the activity. At one stage there were a dozen men working feverishly on our every sexual whim and pleasure, resulting in much interest from all the other party players nearby.

 I subtly pretended to throw in the towel and rescued Penny at an appropriate time, whispering to her "always leave them wanting more, time for a break", she nodded gratefully and recovered the piece of material that was somehow called a dress and we skedaddled back to the bar for much needed refreshment. It was during this time out that a very elegant lady in her early sixties approached me, and sweetly asked me if I'd help her and her husband fulfil a longstanding fantasy, she explained it was their fortieth wedding anniversary. I was intrigued and listened, and instantly agreed to what turned out to be a very straightforward request and a most enjoyable thirty minute interlude.

 I left Penny at the bar and went with the lady and her husband to a small private room that featured a padded "love seat" (there's a picture on the website) where as per her request I reclined back in the chair, pulling my dress up above my hips exposing my already wet and heavily engorged labia. Her husband stood to one side as she assumed her position on the floor on all fours. She was quivering as she tentatively leaned forward for her first ever taste of another woman. Her husband was transfixed as she began to use her tongue on me, gently exploring and savouring the places that it had never ever been before. I simply lay back and let this elegant older French lady indulge herself on me, whilst her speechless husband looked on approvingly. As she began to circle my anus with her tongue the entire decadence of the situation hit me full on resulting in a colossal orgasm erupting from deep within me. Great rivers of fluid rushed from me drenching her entire face. She was at first taken aback, but rapidly recomposed herself and began to drink from me with a lustful flourish, savouring every last drop, pleading with me for more. Eventually, after several more thirst quenching orgasms three very satisfied and fulfilled people returned to the bar as if nothing had ever happened, the tell tale smiles hidden by our masks. Incredibly decadent but so much fun.

    With a fresh drink courtesy of Alain waiting for me on the bar I arranged for him to send over a drink to the anniversary couple, as a combined thank you and congratulations. Penny was still completely charged and was ready for round two. I told her to feel free to wander and have fun, as I was going to chill for a while. She didn't need telling twice, she was off, her tight compact bottom seductively wiggling as she disappeared along to the fun zone.

    Several men chatted to me, all trying to entice me to join them for a play; one chap in particular who was there alone was most persistent and piqued my interest, he eventually persuaded me to join him in the cinema room. We never actually made it, as there was a bit of a crowd trying to get in; apparently there was an insatiable English lady inside putting on a "performance incroyable". I did chuckle to myself; Penny had taken to this, like as they say "a duck to water".

    All was not lost as we ended up in one of the other play rooms, again having my pussy devoured whilst witnessing a young girl who was performing some incredible acrobatics on a very appreciative man, who every so often would reach across and stroke my nipples. I just lay back as my pussy pulsated and expressed its gratitude in its own special way, much to the delight of this hungry guy. Then, unexpectedly the acrobatic girl motioned to swap with her, I nodded in agreement and as she dismounted the man he swiftly rolled on a fresh condom and invited me to climb on board. Once firmly in position I began to rhythmically milk him with my powerful gripping muscles. It was a perfectly sized erection to ride and I soaked him several times during our intense animalistic fucking. After a period in this position I think he sensed my thighs were tiring and I needed a change of position. Swiftly without withdrawing he turned me on to my back and instantly began to pound into me relentlessly, his forehead was dripping in perspiration, and he had the look of an angry bull as he mercilessly drilled my saturated vagina. I was in mid climax with ejaculate erupting from me as he began to growl like a wounded bear, pulling out and ripping the condom off. In one rapid movement he climbed up over my legs to straddle my chest, and almost instantly began to unload warm torrents of his cum over my breasts, he was producing copious amounts of semen, for a change it was me being drenched and it did it feel good. Once his orgasm subsided he very gently helped me off the bed and lead me to the bath/shower room for a much needed clean up. A most charming and unexpected encounter.

 A very happy, but exhausted looking Penny eventually returned to the bar and proceeded to talk in her rapid over excited style, not even taking a breath, this was one very contented women. When I eventually managed to get a word in, I asked her how she felt, she grinned when she gave me her one word answer, "empowered". I smiled, reflecting, and remembering that was just how I felt on my first real awakening in the hedonistic Parisian nightlife.

 We both had a small brandy whilst we were waiting for our taxi and said our goodnights to people, many of whom had by now removed their masks. It was great fun looking at every ones faces, knowing everybody was thinking alike. Wondering if...?

 Once back at the apartment I crashed on the sofa with a St Moritz, and relaxed whilst Penny continued chatting away at full steam. She was wired; she'd sleep well, eventually!

Chapter Fifteen: Unexpected Glamour

Thursday morning, well according to my diary never happened, it seems we both slept through it. Eventually we managed to get some fresh air and took a very late breakfast at the bar opposite. Penny was complaining that she ached in places she didn't even know could ache. She was hooked, exclaiming that it had been simply the best Wednesday night of her life, and now she wanted more she left it down to me to arrange another evening of debauchery. She was intent on cramming as much pleasure and fun as she possibly could into our short Parisian trip.

We discussed the club and how her and David could incorporate certain elements into the design of their outbuilding. It was certainly big enough, and had massive potential.

Penny was in full agreement when I suggested that we have an evening of pure elegance, with a level of depravity thrown firmly into the mix. With this in mind I gave Amanda at *"L'Escapade"* a call and let her know that I'd be coming that evening and would be bringing a very excitable friend. Amanda promised to make a few calls from her special black book, and have a few of the most popular gentlemen in attendance.

We headed off to one of my favourite stores *"The Galeries Lafayette"*, where I've spent a small fortune over the years. We both indulged ourselves in a pair of high strappy black Sandro evening shoes and some stunningly sheer, black Le Bourget hold ups.

We stopped for a drink at a bar that Paul and I had discovered on our first ever visit. It was exactly as I remembered it, an old fashioned "bar à vins" (wine bar to you and me). Its called "Le Rubis". We sat at the traditional zinc counter and savoured a large glass of Beaujolais. It still exudes that old French charm; it's got a very hospitable atmosphere, the café chairs and tables are worn but shiny from years of use. It was lovely to return somewhere that held fond memories and had not changed one bit over the years. As we chatted we agreed that she'd borrow one of my elegant but risqué gowns for the soiree, promising that she'd look after it with her life.

There was a wonderful surprise waiting when we returned to the apartment, not only were there several vases of fresh flowers and a wonderful bottle of "Laurent Perrier" Cuvee Rose Champagne chilling in an ice bucket, but a note from Yves saying he'd arranged a little fun for us for the following evening and instructions on time and attire. This, as always got my juices flowing, Penny bless her almost went into total meltdown. I was touched that Yves had taken the time considering his situation to even contemplate organising a little soiree for Penny and myself.

We'd bought a cooked chicken locally and enjoyed the simplicity of eating it with warm crusty bread and a mixed salad. It gave us both the time to relax and chat before getting ready to throw ourselves into the fray once more. Also we both took the opportunity to check in with our other halves via Skype.

We had lots of girly fun trying to pick which outfits we'd wear, finally settling on Penny wearing my long black silk Chanel evening gown with the high thigh split, she looked simply "fabulous" as Coco would have said. I picked my equally elegant yet risqué Balenciaga gown. We'd also both decided we'd be overdressed if we wore any panties.

As a treat, and a bit of nostalgia for me I ordered the taxi to drop us off on Rue Daunou, as I wanted her to experience a cocktail or two and the unique ambiance of Harrys Bar. We certainly caused a few heads to turn as we wandered in, taking a stool at the well worn polished mahogany bar. We both indulged in a Zombie (Cognac, Fresh cream, Honey), followed by a single shot of Jack Daniels, which gave us both a very pleasant warm tingle, perfect appetisers for our next destination.

Arriving at the club Amanda as ever was there to greet me in her usual flamboyant style, complimenting us both on our appearance. I'd primed Penny as to the staircase and to be careful, hold on tightly to the bannister and to play to the audience, who'd be watching in expectant admiration from below as we descended to the bar. Lions to the slaughter, some may say!

We were greeted by a sea of suave gentlemen, who as one raised their glasses our way as we hit the stairs. I felt Penny tremble slightly, and she immediately steadied herself on the balustrade. A very similar sensation overcame me, I have never not been effected by this descent, always sends my insides in to turmoil, like a swarm of butterflies in flight. Waiting for us was Costas, with two welcoming flutes of Champagne in his outstretched arms. The atmosphere was intense; there were three other couples that were in the lounge area deep in conversation. Penny and I were most definitely the centre of attention, these gents were most certainly hand picked from Amanda's "best of the best" list. Introductions were made with many accompanying kisses and deft discreet touches. By natural selection Penny was rapidly engaged by the men who spoke a little English, which was a relief as I had my hands full with a group of rather divine men, all vying for my individual attention. I explained that it was Penny's first time, and that I was her chaperone and guide, and to treat her like a lady, I said this with a cheeky wink. Amanda joined us briefly, and I was grateful as she personally gave Penny a quick guided tour of the play areas. This saved me from the obvious perils that would ensue if the two of us ventured through the red velvet drapes at this early stage. A bit of teasing and flirting at the bar was needed before anything more of a sexual nature developed.

Penny reappeared at the bar with a most decadent and alluring look on her face, and was once again quickly surrounded by several admiring suitors. She was now becoming at ease with the situation and was playing up to the men with total ease. She adored the attention, holding court with aplomb, belying her limited experience.

Suddenly, Amanda appeared three steps down beckoning me with a frantic look on her face. We met half way on the stairs, and in a panicked voice she explained that there was a famous American actress in reception with a much younger companion, and neither of them spoke any French, and would I speak to them, primarily to check that they knew where they were and in the correct venue. I followed her to the reception area to be confronted by the smiling couple. I had to do a double check, and I almost choked when I realised who it was, for reasons of discretion I won't name her, but I knew that she'd fit right in as she'd gained much notoriety by going commando in one of her earlier films. With this in mind I'll just refer to her as "the actress". Her young escort was very smartly dressed and she was wearing a very slinky, figure hugging short cocktail dress, a dress that screamed, "I'm here to play". I introduced myself and explained the club and its "raison d'être", and in her sensual American drawl responded with " fabulous just lead the way".

Chaos ensued as we descended, heads turned, necks craned, audible gasps were heard above the music. It was surreal, as her entrance captivated a stunned group of revellers. Decorum was resumed as I swiftly grabbed them a glass of Champagne from Costas. She had no airs or graces, she purely out for a good time. I took them to the lounge area where we chatted for a while; she was totally intrigued as I gave her a potted synopsis of my own personal Parisian experiences. She was all ears and her companion busily scribbled down several of the recommendations that I suggested. She was particularly interested in the *"la langue ludique"*, and I promised I'd call Inès on her behalf the following day and for her to expect a call from her. She went on to explain that a young French actor she'd recently worked with in Hollywood had recommended this particular club to her, and if she did visit she'd be well looked after and discretion was assured. Whilst her young companion went and arranged some more drinks I gave her a quick tour of the club and explained which areas were the best for certain activities. She especially like the look and feel of my favoured room with the prison like grilled entrance door. We stayed for a few moments at her insistence watching two couples playing in the large orgy room with several of the selected men in attendance. What became oddly apparent was that we were left totally alone, it seemed that the men were very reticent and were a bit in awe of who she was, basically nervous of making any kind of overt approach. They were holding back watching in discreet expectation; she wistfully explained that this was the usual response, and it drove her insane. Between us we hatched a cunning plan. I beckoned Penny over and made the introductions, explaining the situation and that we needed her to be a bit of a diversionary tactic, running a bit of interference for us.

As we'd arranged Penny and the younger man who ironically was called David left us and wandered off to the lounge/play area adjacent to the main orgy room, as hoped for in my little ruse they were swiftly followed by several of the gents from the bar. The effect of this was that the bar area had thinned out substantially, leaving just eight or so men, and one couple who were taking a relaxing breather from their personal playtime.

On my cue the "actress" and I made our way to my favourite room, yes the one with the lockable doors and prison bars. She indicated that she was more than happy to follow my lead, as she was comfortable that I was more conversant with the general etiquette. Very soon several, sensual swarthy French men appeared loitering very unsubtly close by, hoping to witness some action or just catch a glimpse of this most famous actress in the flesh, quite literally. We both reclined suggestively on the large sofa and began to slowly caress each other, she soon relaxed and eased gracefully into the scenario. Quicker than I'd ever experienced before a huge sense of anticipation reverberated from the other side of the door, the men had now increased in number and were watching in silent admiration as we slowly and provocatively undressed each other, delicately I took her dress and hung it on a peg along with mine. We both stood naked in our heels, we smiled knowingly to each other and teasingly remained just out of reach of any arms and hands that were already tentatively sneaking through the bars .We began explore each other with increasing intimacy. Her figure was even better in the flesh than what I recalled from several of her films. She stood at my shoulder as I moved forward and turned to face the door, legs apart and hands above my head gripping the bars. Eager hands shot through instantly and fought over each other to play with me, I stood there quivering in ecstasy as fingers penetrated me playfully, teasing my clitoris and stretching my glistening labia open. Fingers and thumbs manipulated my nipples; I sensed her breathing very heavily behind me, her warm breathe on my ear and neck, her own hand gently playing with herself, she was on the verge of her first orgasm as she watched the men intimately working on me. I held myself in check and rapidly swapped places with her. She came immediately as the first hand made contact with her. She was on another plane, revelling in all the attentive, probing fingers that were pleasuring her body. She was thrusting back and fore in a hypnotic orgasmic rhythm as the men played with her. I couldn't resist the temptation and dropped to my knees behind her and parted the exquisite cheeks of her bottom, and much to the audible delight of everyone began to probe her anus with my tongue. This resulted in a cataclysmic shuddering climax roaring deep from within her, rewarding me with a warm sweet mouthful of her juices. It was very apparent that she was heavily into this particular scenario, and we took it in turns several times to pleasure each other in this position. Both releasing several wet climaxes'. Eventually we collapsed back into the couch, and one of the watching men courteously brought us a refreshing glass of Champagne. During this small break in the proceedings she remarked she needed "some wood", confused momentarily by this Americanism I responded with "no you need Coq", with a brief explanation as to my little play on words.

When we'd quenched our thirsts a little I took her at her word and told her to point out whose "wood" she fancied sampling. I beckoned the initial two gents to join us, and promptly unlocked the door for them to enter and to be of service. They both immediately undressed and set about pleasing her with typical French flair and finesse, taking turns in feeding her from both ends. This lady was in full flow, climaxing in rapid succession, demanding that her admirers fuck her ever harder and faster. I lay back gently working on my clitoris as the crowd at the door pleaded to be allowed in to join the decadent scene. I was definitely in my devil may care attitude and reached into my clutch bag, retrieving my poppers and indulging in a huge hit, which within a few seconds resulted in the guys at the door getting a good soaking, much to their approval. She held her hand out and growled at me "give me some", this spurred her on even further. She demanded more "wood", so I quickly admitted two fresh men to feed her insatiable appetite. I stood watching from the door as a young man penetrated me from behind through the bars. Brusquely I felt him unload into his condom, and another eager gent instantly replaced him. At the same time I was gorging on a most impressive erection, attached to one of the first gents I'd initially allowed in, he winked at me and cheekily gave me a double thumbs up as he fucked my mouth with long powerful thrusts. The evening had begun with a surprise turn of events, and had now descended into a complete hedonists dream scene. I glanced over my shoulder where the voracious "actress" was continuing to put on an Oscar worthy performance. The heady aroma of sex was emanating from every corner of the club; I could occasionally hear Penny whine loudly with sexual gratification from another room, I'd recognise that high pitched mewling orgasmic screech anywhere! Eventually, after a while things reached their natural ending and two very satisfied ladies retired to the bathroom to dress and make themselves presentable once more.

 On the way back to the bar to take a nightcap I caught the eye of a very busy Penny, who was busy enjoying all the undivided amorous attentions she was receiving within the middle of a group of considerate men, I gave her a "see you at the bar in ten" sign.

 Finally it was time to leave, Amanda had organised taxis for us. After much hugging and thanking to all involved a very happy and exhausted "A Lister" departed with her young companion into the Parisian night. I often think of this evening and how very surreal it was. As a side note the actress in question did contact Inès and apparently did sample the delights of "*la langue ludique*". Sadly I wasn't a witness to this.

 Once again "L'Escapade" had delivered its certain "*je ne sais quoi*", it simply never fails.

Chapter Sixteen: Relight My Fire (Les Pompiers)

Friday morning arrived faster than we'd both expected, due mainly to Penny and myself discussing the previous evenings events over a soothing brandy well into the early hours, before finally hitting the hay.

We had no plans for the day, just the surprise evening ahead courtesy of Yves. So we decided on a lazy lunch, followed by some serious relaxing and pampering.

I made a quick call and reserved a few hours at a wonderful beauty spa I'd visited several times previously and had always come away totally fresh and rejuvenated. It's called *"Aquamoon"* and is situated on the famous Place Vendôme in the 1st arrondissement.

It's a truly extraordinary place, an absolute gem. I'd booked us a variety of treatments and delights from the many available. It was three hours of pure self-indulgence. It consisted of relaxing in the sauna, steam room and gentle exercise in the pools, followed by something they call "velvet care", which is a hydrating body scrub and full aromatic oil massage. We both also indulged in a luxury manicure and pedicure. Wonderful service, and they provide a mind boggling range of treatments, if you visit their website you'll see what I mean. You name it and I guarantee they do it. An oasis of calm and elegance right in the heart of Paris. What more could a girl ask for?

We stopped off during the fifteen-minute stroll back to the apartment at a small bar for a glass of wine and a Menthol St Moritz for me. Well, we deserved it having been vice free for several hours!

Once back at the apartment I checked on the instructions for the evening, which was split into two distinct themes. Dining followed by Debauchery. Marc, who was scheduled to collect us for the first part at eight sharp, would drive us to both locations.

Yves had Marc reserve us a table, at what he knew from previous visits was my favourite eatery in the city.

"Bofinger" in the Bastille district of Paris. Historic and full of atmosphere. Its the oldest surviving brasserie in Paris, the perfectly preserved restaurant is a museum of Belle Epoque decor. In the

centre of the main dining room is a magnificent stained glass ceiling and although the food is excellent, especially the oysters, half the fun of dining here is watching the spectacle going on around you: waiters yelling "chaud devant" to clear a path as they balance gigantic seafood platters on their trained arms; a diva making a grand entrance after a performance at the nearby Bastille opera house; and the occasional mishap when a "garcon" bumps into one of his colleagues, plates and glasses crash everywhere and diners stop for a moment to applaud the disaster. It really is an institution that delivers time after time. It never fails to delight.

The maître d' greeted us warmly and immediately whisked us to a wonderfully laid up table in a booth, with the ever comfortable black leather bench seating. Penny was particularly enamoured by the large cart outside the entrance with its bed of ice decorated by a vast variety of wonderful fresh seafood, hence our eventual choices.

The menus were delivered at the same time as a wonderful bottle of Perrier-Jouet Blason Rose Champage in a very ornate ice bucket. As we both loved seafood we started with a simply divine Crayfish bisque with crusty of bread. But for the main course I ordered my favourite, something I'd indulged in on a few occasions over the years. "The Royal Bofinger", which consisted of, 1 American lobster, 4 langoustines, 1 crab, 4 prawns, 18 assorted oysters, brown shrimps, shellfish. All presented on a bed of ice upon a large double level stainless steel platter. Several photos ensued as she fully intended to return at some stage with David, as he himself was a lover of all things seafood. To complete this feast we shared a large plate of Jivara chocolate cream cake with bourbon vanilla whipped cream, amarena cherry sorbet, simply outstanding. There was just time to take a coffee and cognac before Marc collected us to return to the apartment to prepare for the distinctly erotic second part of our evening.

Penny was at this stage still completely in the dark regarding the planned debauched finale to the evening. She was overcome with excitement when I presented her with my long leather coat, complete with its mink collar. As per the instruction I retrieved Yves's late wife's floor length fur coat from the wardrobe at the same time. Yves just adored it on the few memorable occasions I've worn it out in his company. It seemed to really push all the right buttons for him; I never questioned it, as it always seemed a very private and personal thing between him and the memory of his long departed consort.

Penny got extremely excited as she read the instructions that we were to only wear the coats and the highest platform heels at our disposal. She found it outrageously erotic as we slipped into our coats and our very slutty footwear. I'd loaned her a pair of mine that had been lurking in the wardrobe for a year or two, they were neon pink with platform and a six-inch heel. They were a present from Yves, but were a tad too tight for me, but luckily they fitted Penny a treat. We had a quick shot of Jack Daniels to start the buzz and were ready to leave just as Marc had sent a text letting me know that he was just pulling up outside.

Once Marc had turned onto the sweeping road that ran along the Seine my suspicions were confirmed as to the final destination. I shuddered at the memories of my first visit back in the late nineties. I'd still not told Penny what I suspected was in store for us, but as we drove past the Pont Neuf I felt I should reveal to her the full extent of the treat that was only minutes away. She gripped my arm making me repeat it slowly, I laughed and went on to explain the scenario to her again, and that these men were the crème de la crème of French Fire fighters, all army trained and as fit as they come (fit as a butchers dog as Paul would say). We both began to fidget a bit in pure anticipation and expectation of what depravity the next hour or so would yield. I had a damn good idea. We'd most certainly be well looked after in every respect, definitely pushed to the limits, but in a most welcome fashion. I got myself mentally prepared for this onslaught of testosterone-fuelled fun.

Marc had sent a text ahead, and as soon as we pulled up at the large old building another huge feeling of "déjà vu" swept over me. I remembered every moment of my first ever visit to this, the barracks and HQ of the special River Seine Fire Fighting unit. I was already experiencing a growing throb in my groin as I stepped out of the car to be greeted by the Brigades new commander, a tall distinguished looking man in his early sixties and resplendent in full uniform.

Marc introduced us and then smiled, telling us that he'd be on hand to collect us and return us to the apartment in one piece as and when required.

We followed the Commander inside the large main entrance, grinning at each other as he firmly bolted the door. We then followed him into the familiar anteroom where he offered us both a warming brandy to settle any nerves that this situation cause . Whilst sipping the smooth amber nectar he explained all was in readiness and his men were eagerly expecting us, and as per my prior visit a sixty-minute time slot was allotted.

Shortly he lead us along the most unforgettable corridor, passed familiar doors, and finally arrived at the small stone staircase that held a whole variety of memories for me, where he said "Ladies you know the way, go and enjoy my men". With a curt nod he swivelled on his heels and brusquely walked back along the corridor. I suspect he went up to the small discreet room with the cosy viewing gallery to watch the events unfold and keep a watchful eye on proceedings.

Penny was trembling with trepidation and excitement and firmly gripped my arm as we descended the stairway to pleasure. There were two quilted hangers outside the large wooden door, still resplendent with its familiar large antique knocker. Previously I'd secreted a vial of poppers in my coat pocket for just this kind of scenario, sneaky but essential. I swiftly unscrewed the top and we each took a huge hit. We removed our coats and hung them on the hangers, and both stood naked in just our heels, holding each other momentarily as the amyl took its overwhelming effect. My pussy was throbbing violently and a powerful wet climax erupted from me, the sound of my juices hitting the stone floor and decadently echoing around the stone walled passageway was astounding. Penny instantaneously followed suit with her own contribution. We composed ourselves as best we could as I gave the customary double rap of the knocker, we waited with legs trembling in pure lust to be ushered inside and to entertain and be entertained in a style that I excel.

The door was opened by a swarthy "*pompier*" provocatively wrapped in a bright white fluffy towel; he greeted us with "*Bonsoir mesdames, nous vous attendions*". The room was large, exactly as I remembered it, with lockers and several wooden benches. There was a lot of steam coming from the large open shower area, and through the mist I glimpsed several large men enjoying the hot jets of water pummelling their muscular torsos. Immediately a "three cheers" type of war cry was bellowed fervently by the dozen naked and semi naked young French fire fighters, which culminated with a loud whoop. It was now blatantly evident it was time for the games to commence. Penny looked at me with an expression, which firmly said, "let battle commence".

With that the men began removing their towels, revealing erections of all sizes, large, extra large and colossal. Proudly the majority were already sporting full-blown erections. I was placed on one bench and Penny on another as the men in rotation began to offer us their cocks to feast on, and feast we did, it was man meat overkill. Between Penny and myself it rapidly turned into feeding frenzy, we were noisily licking, slurping and sucking on any and every erection that we were offered, salivating heavily, whilst guzzling hungrily on them. There was so much solid young cock being presented to us, it was all a bit of a blur, it was difficult to see who belonged to what. My vagina was gaping wide, totally sodden with my juices and it flowed profusely as a series of mini orgasms hit my body, making me shudder from head to toe. The were some very unusual and animalistic sounds coming from Penny, as she in turn climaxed as her mouth was being stuffed full of hard pulsating cock. Talk about erection overload, it was the stuff of fantasy; being lived and acted out by a cast of skilled pleasure connoisseurs. I noticed out of the corner of my eye that a rather attractive man with the colossal penis was preparing for battle, and was strapping his mighty erection into a leather cock and ball harness. The effect was mind blowing; even several of his colleagues looked on in awe. When Penny saw what we were all looking at she just squealed, "OMG Emma what the fuck does he feed that on?" I couldn't help but laugh, but soon had another rampant cock between my lips silencing me. These men were good, in fact superb, and this was only the beginning.

I recall being lifted in the air by three strapping guys, one behind, with the other two either side of me, holding my thighs wide, showing off my gaping vagina and swollen labia to full effect. My inner thighs shimmered with my juices. Penny was lead across to me, and with much lewd vocal encouragement she was knelt in front of me instructing the men to position my vagina on her outstretched tongue. She proceeded to lick and suck at me with a wild passion, I could sense she'd done this before and more than once; she was thoroughly enjoying devouring my juices, that were now flowing from me like a river. Her tongue was greedily lapping at both my orifices, taking me to ever-higher plateaus of carnal pleasure. The men were thoroughly enjoying watching this intensely lewd girl on girl action; eventually she lay down on a bench and invited me to straddle her face in such a position that it enabled her to work her lizard like tongue deep into my sensitive anus. Much to everyone's delight I swiftly rewarded her with a massive torrent of my ejaculate directly into her eager mouth, she was gurgling loudly as she tried to drink it all, the excess running off her chin in profuse streams.

The men decided it was time to really put us through our paces, and we were both made to kneel side by side on a bench, our bottoms thrust in the air, our eager vaginas gaped open in wanton, needy expectation. We both gasped, as striding forward with a concentrated look on his face was the man with the gargantuan cock, harnessed, solidly erect and fully ready to inflict some serious damage on us. Firm hands spread both of our buttocks wide, holding us open for him to plunder his orifice of choice. I soon realised that I was to be the initial receptacle for this monster as I felt him place its massive tip at my entrance, slowly easing its way between my quivering labia. The sensation was indescribable as my vaginal muscles relaxed to accommodate both its length and colossal girth. I gasped loudly as he drove it in to me fully, right to the hilt, to stifle my moans two erections were simultaneously fed into my mouth. I took a severe and brutal pounding from behind until he withdrew, then in one fluid motion he sidestepped until he was at Penny's rear, ready to rearrange her internal organs in similar fashion. I stopped what I was doing and watched spellbound as he entered a whimpering Penny, his enthralled audience spurred him on as he drilled his immense manhood into Penny, hammering at her vagina, showing it no mercy. She was lost in the moment, screaming her approval, and desire for him to drill her into submission.

    He proceeded to alternate between servicing both our over eager and over stretched vaginas until he'd edged himself towards his own personal orgasm. He signalled his intention, and he was swiftly replaced by the wet, soapy men from the shower, who'd just joined the throng. They smiled, gave our bottoms a little friendly smack and skilfully entered us. Nippily Mr Gargantuan cock placed himself in front of us, proudly with hands on hips began flexing his monumental penis for us to worship. He soon wrapped his hand around its base and began to playfully slap our faces with it, rubbing it across our cheeks, cock whipping at its finest. He then held it still for both Penny and I to taste, we both used our tongues on his hugeness, licking him up and down, both taking our turns to nipple on its vast pulsating helmet. It quickly became apparent he was on the verge of climax as his thigh muscles tightened, his chest expanded, and he took a huge lung full of air before releasing a massive cascading deluge of his semen into our willing open mouths, both of us fighting over his cum, licking it of each others faces with decadent lust. It was pure guttural, lewd, filthy sex at its most depraved. It seemed that his eruption signalled a total free for all, these men began to work our bodies to extreme levels of pleasure, we were both being fucked hard, both our pussies, as well as our mouths were in overdrive trying to keep up with this unending onslaught of hard, young, throbbing cock. At one stage several men were taking turns in putting my anal muscles to the test, encouraging me to use them to maximum effect and milk their seed out of them, I didn't disappoint and came violently as they unloaded their cum deep in my anus, filling me to overflowing. Eventually, it must have been approaching the fifty-five minute mark when we were placed side by side on the benches, and the remaining men began to feverishly masturbate over our bodies, whilst encouraging us to lewdly work on our own vaginas with our fingers. It was an unadulterated joyous finale, with sperm being showered in copious quantities over our stomachs, breasts and faces. We were covered in their warm sweet sperm, both of us also enjoying our own wet climaxes throughout their copious outpourings. Penny lying there, covered head to toe in semen was a sight to behold; she looked possessed, in another world, one that I knew she'd revisit at the next available opportunity.

We were then taken in to the large wet room and hosed down with hot water, cleansing our used and aching bodies. Once we were dry we were escorted to the door and we departed to one final roaring "whoop" from the men. I felt I could have gone on for another round with these fit young men, given half a chance, and a Jack Daniels, obviously! Sadly that would have to wait for another day.

Marc was waiting for us as promised, and after thanking the Commander for the privilege and his hospitality we departed, not before he slipped me a small computer memory card to give to Yves. I was guessing he'd taken a few choice photographs of the event from his viewing room as a visual memento for Yves. A most fitting end to a most wonderful soiree.

Thanking Marc for being on hand and escorting us there and back we headed up to the apartment, where on the spur of the moment we chucked on jeans and a sweatshirt and skipped across the road to relax and discuss the evenings events over a large Jack Daniels and a much need St Moritz. The bar staff greeted us with a knowing smile, and once the drinks had been delivered to our table, several small plates of tasty morsels turned up for us to indulge in. Sliced bits of spicy sausage, ham, crusty bread, mini burgers, all so tasty and most welcomed, as we'd most definitely burnt off a few calories during the last hour or two. We giggled away like two teenagers who'd just had their first kiss at the school disco. She did have me in stitches when she recanted snippets of the evening's activities and said that it wouldn't have had the same erotic effect if it were in relation to "Blue Watch" at the Watford Fire Dept. Sorry lads.

Monsieur "Colossal" cock was revisited eighteen months later for a special assignment, which I might just dedicate a chapter to later on, it is seriously up for consideration.

Chapter Seventeen: Planning, Plotting & Playing

Over the next few weeks Penny and I were talking daily and swapping rough designs via email. Both her and David were getting itchy feet regarding their project and were eager to finalise the layout of the proposed party venue. We eventually agreed and set a firm date for all works to be finished. We were aiming to be ready within six months and be firmly in position to host their debut invitation only party. It was decided that it should be a "Valentines" masked theme.

During this period I made a couple of trips to Paris with Paul, primarily to visit Yves, who'd health had sadly declined. It was a despondent time and quite honestly partying whilst there didn't seem at all appropriate, considering his condition. Marc and Bruno, along with several of Yves's close confidantes were a tower of strength to me during this period.

After several months of internal building works David and Penny were ready to give us a guided tour of the "work in progress" venue, and it was agreed that our close friends Mike and Sarah would come along and give their valuable first impressions.

The first thing that leapt out at us was the very tropical themed covered walkway they'd installed, that lead through from the main venue to the covered swimming pool. They'd also partitioned off an area by the pool and fitted a changing room with secure lockers and a large shower area. They'd spent a small fortune on large exotic pot plants; with the colour scheme and décor it very much resembled a tropical beach paradise. Also, as an added temptation they'd also invested in a large twenty seater Jacuzzi that had a mind-boggling array of different under water lighting effects. This became quite obviously David's pride and joy, and at future events you'd always find him ensconced in there at the end of the soiree, grinning from ear to ear with a plastic flute over flowing with Champagne.

Many of my ideas from Amsterdam, coupled with what Penny had discovered with me in Paris were very much incorporated. Upon entering the main area from the parking zone you entered a large reception area with a small changing room and a separate zone for attendees belongings. All very secure and functional. Then once you entered the main room there was a lounge area with several comfortable sofas, leading on to a dance floor with a small raised plinth, complete with obligatory pole, for the more exhibitionistic ladies (and occasional gent). The long bar area was fitted with an array of fridges, as the licensing laws were so prohibitive it was decided early on that guests would bring their own alcoholic drinks, which would be name labelled and dispensed from the fridges as and when required.

Leading from this area was a small corridor with a variety of themed rooms on either side. Penny's own personal favourite was one that I'd designed based on our experiences at "*Quai 17* "in Paris. A beautifully engineered and constructed grope box and glory hole, which would go on to become a highly popular space with the guests, always a queue to experience the fun it exuded. There was a black metal spiral staircase leading up to the large loft area that was currently still under construction, but would go on to feature a large group area and what would eventually become one of the most popular installations. It featured a very large maze, lit with low level ultraviolet lighting and various fully black passageways. Many guests would when questioned as to the length of time they'd spent in there, always claimed innocently that they'd simply got lost! Yeah sure we believe you, not!

Mike and Sarah were most complimentary, but had one very fun idea that they'd enjoyed many years previously with us in Paris at the club "*Sas Association*" *(*now redesigned and reopened as a popular swingers sauna called "*Alina",* I've not visited but they do have a website). Paul and I quickly remembered the chill out area upstairs that featured thick glass viewing panels in the floor that looked directly into the playrooms below. Mike always loved to take a drink up there whilst watching Sarah playing below. Wild times. Penny and David loved the idea and they implemented this into the finished version of their venue.

We thought long and hard as how to market the initial event, we had to be careful as this was still before the demise of the "News of The World" and we didn't want to get foiled at the first hurdle and see David and Penny's pride and Joy fail due to bad press, let alone see all the money they'd invested disappear.

The initial party was almost three months away, so it was decided to make it an invitation only event. Between us we invited our close circle of like-minded friends, who in turn were asked to invite any similar people who they knew and could vouch for. Also everyone was required to bring along a form of photo identification and even sign a non-disclosure form. It was still that taboo in the U.K, seems crazy now, but true. We really did need to be discreet and take all the necessary precautions we could think of. There were several club nights already running throughout the country, however not one of them had a particularly good reputation. Our primary goal was recreating the elegance and sophistication of Paris on home soil. At least David and Penny had the courage of their convictions and had taken the plunge. It was a big financial risk; even though they could afford it nobody wanted them to fail. Over the coming months friends and acquaintances were contacted, and soon we had a list of around fifty confirmed couples along with several more who'd commit closer to the time if their schedules allowed. David and Penny sticklers for detail and were well on top of the project at all times. They fully expected all the works to be completed with a good month to spare, at which point we could begin to email everyone with comprehensive details.

There was one memorable experience during this period and it is more than worthy of a mention here at this stage in the book. It occurred during a particularly severe winters day, a week before Xmas. I'd been down Bristol for the day to drop off presents and have lunch with an old friend; I was godmother to her two year old daughter Amy. Paul and I had bought her a pink "my little pony" bike, which had to be hand delivered discreetly while she was at day nursery. So it only seemed right to have a gossip and a bite to eat.

I arrived in Clifton around twelve thirty and we secreted the bike in the attic, out of sight of inquisitive prying eyes. Then we walked the fifteen minutes to the Triangle at the top of Park Street and headed into Browns Restaurant. We had a drink at the bar whilst waiting for a table, as it was already packed with lunchtime diners escaping from the freezing temperatures outside. The atmosphere was jovial with many workers celebrating the up coming Xmas break. We had a good old catch up and chomped our way through a signature Browns burger each, one of the best burgers on the planet. After the food we took a coffee at the cosy lounge area by the bar before going to collect her little Amy. After having a little playtime with her and her Barbie doll collection it was soon five o'clock and time to head back to Kew.

It was already dark and the air had that feeling that threatened snow. No sooner had I hit the M32 out of Bristol than the skies opened and started to tip large flakes of the white stuff on to my windscreen. At that time I was driving a BMW X5 four-wheel drive so

I felt relatively safe and confident, however, as I turned onto the M4 eastbound towards London it started to come down heavily. I pressed on for a few miles, but it was becoming chaotic, blizzard like conditions that got more and more treacherous as the motorway climbed toward the Tormarton junction. I took the only sensible option at that stage and pulled off taking refuge in a picnic/parking area a few hundred yards along the A46 towards Bath. It was fairly deserted so I decided to wait it out, in hope that it was going to be a short-lived down pour. Soon a few other cars parked up, obviously with a similar notion in mind. Shortly a large truck without the long trailer part attached pulled in and parked up with its front end beside me. I lit a menthol cigarette and kept the engine running for warmth. It was an eerie scene, with the subdued lighting causing the various exhausts to appear like big drifting stacks of white smoke in the cold snowy air. I soon sensed the truck driver who'd put his interior light on looking down at me, I glanced up and we locked eyes fleetingly. He smiled, I quickly looked away and played with my phone as if I was texting, as well as sending out a clear message to him that people knew where I was, and that I wasn't stranded without any way to contact with the emergency services, if needed. A bit paranoid I know, but you can never be too careful. I really needn't have been concerned, after a few minutes my mind drifted towards all kinds of naughty scenarios to while away the time waiting. I subconsciously moved my hand discreetly under my skirt and onto my panties that were already getting damp. I quickly glanced up to see him fully absorbed watching me; he was no older than thirty and quite attractive in a beefy truck driver kind of way. My natural exhibitionistic streak came racing to the fore, I seductively unbuttoned my blouse until my bra and cleavage were very visible, and at the same time subtly slid my skirt up under my bottom so my panties were in full view. My doors were locked so my confidence levels grew along with my level of daring. As our eyes met again he firmly nodded his approval, mouthing for me to continue, this lone observer was beginning to push all the right buttons in my head, I was instantly wet and felt my vagina start its appreciating throb. I reached for the electric seat adjustment controls and lowered the position a good few inches, then unclasped my front fastening bra, instantly releasing my breasts, holding them both up for him to see, gradually playing with each in turn, tweaking and pulling at my erect nipples vigorously. I quickly began to spread my legs and pulled my panties to one side and started to slowly finger myself in a very exhibitionistic and provocative display, eventually wriggling out of them completely. By this time we had a solid and unwavering eye contact. He licked his lips most decadently every now and then as I began to feel that pre orgasm heat rising from my spine, shooting in spasms down to my toes and up to the top my head, making my skull tingle with a total erogenous pulsating delight.

After edging myself numerous times I took the bull by the horns and beckoned him over to me. He was out of his cab in a shot, putting on a quilted gilet as he climbed down. As he reached the car I let the electric window down and opened myself up, butterflying my labia for him as his hand tentatively reached in, I muttered hoarsely, "make me cum". He didn't hesitate and his fingers swiftly went to work on me, peeling my moist lips even further apart, gently fingering me as his thumb flicked my exposed clitoris. His other hand wrapped itself firmly around his erection and he began to pump it slowly. One hand pleasuring me, whilst the other working on himself. It wasn't long until we both came, with me soaking his wrist, and him spraying the door of my car with his cum. We both burst out laughing and grinned, he had such a nice way about him, that as we thanked each other for the pleasant interlude I offered him a cigarette whilst we waited for the weather to clear a bit, so we could both be on our way. It was very brief, very decadent but most memorable. It was a while later that I discovered that I was only a mile away from one of the U.K's most infamous dogging locations, Tog Hill (Google it).

Chapter Eighteen: Online Assignations

Having been in on the Internet from the early days of its inception to its current form, where its vast global reach dominates and effects many aspects of daily life. I have watched fascinated as it has grown and evolved. In the dark ages before Google steamrollered its way into out lives it was all very hit and miss in regard to swinging, and the majority of sites lacked any kind of structure and any that did function as you'd expect were all very American based. Obviously this was pretty hopeless for likeminded people to hook up, unless you had deep pocket and were prepared to travel vast distances.

After we'd sold the online company that I was heavily involved with, the up shot was that I was left with lots of free time to explore and play on the Internet on a daily basis. Around the mid "Noughties" a multitude of chancers had set up websites aimed at the ever expanding swinging life style in the U.K, the majority were in it for a quick buck and rapidly became defunct, as people soon realised they never delivered what they promised. You know the type I mean, the sites primarily aimed at men, featuring very alluring scantily clad ladies with a strap line that went something like "Betty in Hull is looking for daytime liaisons" JOIN NOW for details, any the many variations on this theme. Pretty much rip off's each and every one.

Thankfully, as they say, "cream always rises to the top" and out of this period two particular sites survived and prospered. They were set up by swingers for swingers, which has been a major factor in their rise to becoming the two predominant swingers online reference sites. Paul and I joined, both as a couple and I joined independently as a single married lady looking for adventure. I have travelled their journey from within as a member, regular user and contributor right up to this very day. Both *"Swinging Heaven"* and *"Fab Swingers"* have over a million active users and growing all the time, attracting new exciting members into the lifestyle. *"Fab Swingers"* is an invaluable resource, not only for meeting like-minded people, but also for useful information on all the clubs located across the U.K, customer reviews, addresses and all other relevant details can be found within the site. The great thing is that they are both firmly aimed at the U.K and are free to join and set up a profile, there are extra options available at a cost, such as being able to see the webcams in full screen instead of a small window, but these add-ons are very inexpensive. I personally have met some exceptional people both online and many in person at various times over the years. They both have very busy sections where you can promote a party, recommend a venue, or simply give feedback, whether positive or negative. It's a resource that I'd highly recommend to both couples and singles alike. Be warned though it's addictive and you could while away many hours surfing the site and chatting to people. I know this from personal experience, on many visits to their pages I've suddenly found I've lost a few hours engrossed in the site. Following links, seeing where they lead and generally exploring the new and exciting things they throw up.

It's entirely due to *"Fab Swingers"* that the following chapter is about to be written. Slightly out of sequence, but it just had to be included at this stage as it's still so fresh in my mind.

Chapter Nineteen: Miami Beckoned

As with a great many things in life events and circumstances develop most unexpectedly, sometime from a brief comment in a general conversation. This was exactly the case with this encounter.

I was having lunch one Wednesday in central London during April 2010 with Sarah; we always met up at least once a month for a general catch up and good old girly gossip. We'd arranged to meet in Harvey Nichols at the famous Fifth Floor Café and Terrace. I was early and took advantage of the warm sunny day and grabbed a table on the terrace, with its views across the elegant and outrageously expensive Knightsbridge rooftops. A gorgeous tall black waiter took my order of a chilled bottle of Sauvignon Blanc whilst I waited for her.

She arrived shortly, immediately taking a double glance at the waiter as he poured her a glass of wine. I smiled knowingly, as her love of all things black is legendary and is well documented in First Tango pt. 1, as many of you will recall. Bearing this in mind I proceeded to tell her in passing about *"Fab Swingers"* and how I'd read online that a club had been running for a year or so and was getting rave reviews. I told her I thought it would be right up her street. A lady named Helen had founded it, and it was aptly called BMFC (Blackmans Fan Club). It had grown at a rapid rate and was hosting parties at least twice a week at specially selected venues. The parties are specifically organised for females and couples who appreciate the extras that "Black" men bring to the table, and of course for the Black guys who enjoy being appreciated by these adoring decadent ladies from all spheres of life. Sarah's interest was most definitely piqued and I promised to email her the details that evening. We both ordered the wonderful steak salad with glass noodles and beansprouts, it was divine, but I could sense that Sarah's filthy mind was in overdrive. But who knew that from this briefest of conversations what would transpire several months later.

As I suspected Sarah acted on our conversation and my subsequent email in the only way she knew, immediately, and full on. It turned out that Mike had instantly registered them at *"Fab Swingers"* and went through all the news and reviews pertinent to "BMFC" and had attended their first party at one of the venues closest to their North London home. According to Mike the whole vibe was electric, the female was the queen bee and everything was geared around the ladies pleasure, just as it should be! At the second party they struck a more than just a sexual relationship with a suave black guy from the United States, Sarah named him "The Hammer". He was a hedge fund manager working for a few months nr Canary Wharf. They struck up a solid lasting friendship whilst he was in London, sharing many intimate evenings as a threesome and the occasional one on one afternoon delight for Sarah and her insatiable appetite for large black cock.

They'd made a firm arrangement that in celebration of Sarah's forthcoming fiftieth birthday in October that they'd spend a long weekend as his guests in Miami, and that he'd organise the kind of event that Sarah would never forget. As fate would have it four days prior to them flying off to Florida Mike broke his leg on the dry ski slope at Hemel Hempstead. They were both devastated as you'd expect, but after much soul searching and discussion Mike insisted she should still go and celebrate this landmark occasion in style and in the sunshine. This is where I came into the equation; they suggested that I used Mike ticket if Paul approved, giving me the role of being Sarah's companion and chaperone on the trip. Paul was excited by the thought, as he'd witnessed first hand on numerous occasions Sarah's love of the black member and thought I should go and look after her, and have some fun myself (he's so understanding of my needs!). He even offered to pay for the name change on the ticket, as long as I promised to take a few choice photos on my new iPhone for his later perusal. Well, that was an offer I couldn't refuse and I immediately agreed to go and look after Mike's interests. By the time everything was organised it was the Monday, and we were due to fly from Heathrow on the Wednesday, so it was all was rather rushed and last minute. Old summer clothing was dug out of winter storage and hastily packed. A few slinky dresses and a selection of shoes for all occasions were added to the case in a blur over the next thirty-six hours. Lots of packing and repacking took place until I called a halt when Paul suggested that if I needed something it would be easier just buy it whilst there. That calmed me down and I closed and secured the case for the final time.

We took a cab the short distance from Kew to Heathrow mid morning and excitedly checked in for the lunchtime Virgin Atlantic flight, which would whisk us from a dreary, wet London day to a warm sunny Miami. The flight was just under ten hours, scheduled to arrive late afternoon Florida time. We both stocked up on magazines before heading off to the Virgin Upper Class Clubhouse for a few complimentary glasses of bubbly and a light snack before boarding. We were tempted to have a pre flight massage but decided on another drink instead as you'd expect.

Arriving at Miami International at around six in the evening we were greeted by a very pleasant clear day with the temperature in the high seventies. As arranged "The Hammer" or Nathan as he preferred to be called in normal circumstances was there to collect us in a what can only be described as a tank. A gigantic, imposing black and chrome Hummer 4x4. Talk about bling. But it blended in well as these monstrous vehicles were everywhere and his was nothing out of the ordinary.

He lived a few miles south of Miami and a quick twenty minutes from the airport, in an area called Coconut Grove, where he had a large Spanish style villa set in exotic tropical splendour. The main house was large with a central marbled courtyard. There was a large entertaining area that lead out to the beautiful pool. Just visible on the other side of the pool, shaded by several tall palm trees was a guest bungalow, which was where I stayed. It had every conceivable thing needed, from a large stocked fridge to a divine en suite, complete with wet room and Jacuzzi bath. Outside, tethered between two palms was my very own hammock. It also had the much-needed air conditioning, which turned out to be a real godsend, as the weather was unusually hot and very humid for the time we were there. Sarah was to be staying in one of the four large bedroom suites in the main house.

After having the grand tour we relaxed around the pool with a most refreshing zesty margarita, made flamboyantly by Nathan before clambering back into his tank to drive to the restaurant he'd chosen for our first evening. This turned out to be a charming, funky place with oodles of atmosphere called "*Lulus in the Grove*". At Nathans insistence we started with possibly the most delicious drink I've ever had the good fortune to taste, a blood orange mojito, quite stunning visually, as well as being a taste bud sensation. We all followed this with the churrasco, a selection of marinated grilled meats with delicious chimichurri sauce. Leaving just enough room for a portion of their Nutella bread pudding, simply divine. Definitely got the thumbs up from me, well worth a visit if you're ever in the area. We all had coffees, and even with the excitement of the location and the cocktails my brain was telling me that it was four thirty a.m. back in London and I'd been up over twenty hours. So once back at the house I had a shot of Jack Daniels beside the pool and retired to the large comfortable bed in the cool bedroom of the bungalow. Whilst saying good night we arranged to meet early the next morning by the pool for coffee before heading off to have breakfast in the warm early morning sun and plan the day. Before climbing into bed, as always I took the opportunity to catch up with Paul via Skype, making him profoundly envious of first and foremost the weather, as it was late afternoon in London and cold and raining heavily. My description of the blood orange mojito finished him off!

The next morning bright and early we ended up in what locals describe as an institution in Coconut grove, called *"Green Street Café"*, we managed to get a table outside on their bustling patio area. We all ordered coffee along with iced fresh pink grapefruit juice and gorged on a variety of pancakes, my particular favourite being the blueberry granola ones. A great way to fuel up for the day. Nathan had to go into his office for the day in downtown Miami, but suggested he dropped us of at the famous South Beach area, where we could explore the shops and art deco hotels, cafes and bars. It was during breakfast that he informed us that he'd organised a birthday party event for the following evening at his home, with a group of his inner circle, they called themselves the "Mandingos", but this evening he was taking us as his guest to a club that he went to on occasion and said we'd enjoy.

We spent a great day just generally chilling out, shopping and taking in the amazing ambience of the area. We both bought a few slinky and kinky party dresses at a little boutique and some wild high shoes from the Steve Madden store. We found a wonderful bar with prime seating area, where we people watched over a pitcher of sangria for a few hours, both agreeing we'd never seen so many vain people posing in one place ever. It was staggering to see, all the men were strutting around like prize peacocks, a great source of amusement and well worth the $40 drinks charge.

Over dinner at a local seafood restaurant favoured by Nathan, he told us that the club he was taking us to was called *"Miami Velvet"* and it normally only opens on Wednesday, Friday and Saturdays for members only, but tonight (Thursday) it was open for a private party in honour of a local hotelier who Nathan had done some financial trades for in the past and who'd just sold his business to a well known chain and was throwing a party for his inner circle in celebration of the completion of the deal.

He told us the club had a dress code, or rather a motto, which was "dress to impress – less is more" in other words, sexy and revealing for the ladies and classy casual for the men. No cardigans, pipe and slippers here! At that time it was being referred to as upscale club wear.

According to their marketing *"Miami Velvet"* is the largest Swinger's Club in the United States, with over 20,000 square feet of pleasure. Featuring 2 Main Dance Areas, 2 Lounges, 4 Multi-Bed Group Playrooms, and nearly 20 private rooms, there is plenty of space for you to live out your wildest fantasies. In my opinion they have got it spot on in all their claims. The club does allow single men, but also there are areas within the club that are designated as couples only. Strangely though for a club of this size it operates along the same lines as Penny and David's, with a "bring your own bottle" policy. You simply pay one entrance price and nothing else. They like to have a variety of "themed" nights, which are extensively advertised at their website. There are always a variety of exciting events to choose from.

Arriving at the club you are immediately taken aback by the vast array of exotic cars side by side in the car park, Lamborghini, Ferrari, Bugatti, oh and Hummers seemed the norm. Upon entering the plush reception area, complete with its large illuminated tropical fish tank you are immediately made to feel welcome by the friendly staff. Then once you enter through the large red velvet drapes, a large plush world of erotic debauchery awaits. We arrived around eleven and the party was well underway with a diverse mix of people across a wide age range, all relaxed and ready to play.

With drink in hand we spent the first twenty minutes being zipped around by Nathan and getting introduced to everyone he knew and some he didn't. As it was a private party the club was only half full or half empty depending on your point of view. However, those that were there had most definitely come to play. Nathan explained that several of the players were high profile movers and shakers on the Miami scene and normally wouldn't be seen out at a club such as this, preferring to partake in the private and secure environs of like minded peoples large "mansionesque" homes in the area. I must admit the club itself was well planned out and had a solid erotic vibe radiating from every corner, but to me it totally lacked that certain elegance and finesse you get in the Parisian clubs. We settled back into one of the areas near the small stage with the obligatory pole and watched as several frisky ladies put on a little exhibitionistic routine. I was quite happy to sit quietly and indulge in my large J D on the rocks giving g Sarah and Nathan my blessing to go and have some quality playtime. As I was sitting there, quietly taking in all the great R & B music the DJ was playing whilst also enjoying a bit of people watching, a very attractive young man in his mid to late twenties joined me. He had that finely chiselled model type of face, deep tan and regulation well buffed up body. He had everything going for him; apart from he was in competition with himself to become the planets most boring, egotistical man. He actually used the worst pick up line I'd ever heard uttered. He had this cheesy grin and I promise you that he actually said "do you have a mirror in your panties as I can see myself in them later?" My response was instant. I manoeuvred myself slightly, briefly exposing my unclad pussy to him whilst saying, "Sorry but I don't have any on, but there's sure to be one in the bathroom". After several minutes of inane chat he sloped off to chance his arm elsewhere. I hugged my drink chuckling to myself and firmly decided to save myself for the following evenings big shindig in honour of Sarah and her milestone fiftieth birthday. Nathan ribbed me on the way back, calling me a wallflower, and a pure English lady, little did he know, but he was definitely going to find out. I'm sure Mike and Sarah had mentioned Paul and I, but anyway my pride was at stake. Roll on tomorrow night, pure English lady, I'll show you I thought to myself. I do love a challenge; it never fails to get my imagination running wild.

Chapter Twenty: Mandingo Overload

Awoke on the Friday morning to another glorious Miami day, we all decided to take breakfast again at *"Green Street Café"*. Nathan was teasing Sarah, urging her to fill up on the pancakes, as she'd need plenty of stamina for the evening's entertainment.

We relaxed in the warm Florida sun and lazed by the pool until lunchtime, when Nathan drove us to *"Coco Walk"*, as he wanted us out of the way whilst preparations were made for the evening's celebration. We had four hours to amuse ourselves, and amuse ourselves we most certainly did. Coco Walk is a truly magical shopping experience, with many famous luxury brands lining its walkways. Lots of small courtyards with restaurants, bars and coffee shops to chose from. We upped our calorie intake and sampled the delights of the *"Cheesecake Factory"* where we over indulged in a selection from the vast array on offer.

When we arrived back late afternoon the pool area had been completely transformed. Several large cane sofas complete with huge white cushions were scattered around, and a large closed white canopy tent had been erected near the palm trees, enclosed on all sides and its entrance zipped closed. This already had my mind racing, intriguing and conjured up all kinds of naughty thoughts. Two large tables were set to one side beside an outdoor bar. The selected guests, or as Nathan referred to them "his team" were due to arrive at ten o'clock, when the festivities would well and truly begin. So after a catch up with Paul I managed to have a quick ninety-minute power nap. Fully refreshed I ran a bath, laced it with some divine smelling bubbles and poured a glass of chilled wine, climbed in and had a good long relaxing soak and a little stroke.

Sarah and I were struggling to choose what to wear, but we both finally settled on the very revealing and clingy dresses we'd bought that day and we were going to compliment them with a pair of our new super high Steve Madden heels. Minimal make up, but a good coating of my new bright fuchsia pink lip gloss was my look for the evening, just showing off the tanned face to sultry effect. I could hear voices from the pool area so sauntered out, careful as not to get stuck in the new heels I kept well and truly on the stone pathway.

Nathan was chatting to the barman he'd hired for the evening, swiftly he instructed him to make me his version of the blood orange mojito as a starter. Simply delicious. Sarah appeared from the lounge area looking quite stunning, her dress accentuating her figure in all the right places. The material had its work cut out restraining her large, firm natural breasts. Nathan's eyes lit up with a pure lustful glint. Two young girls from the catering company began to bring out varying platters of food for the tables. There were very colourful exotic salads, chilled lobster tails, crab, and langoustine. There was enough food for an army. Shortly the guests began to arrive, Nathan made great fanfare with the introductions. Within twenty minutes everyone was present and accounted for, the front gates to the house were firmly and securely locked. I had a little check in my clutch, one iPhone set to camera function, one smuggled vial of poppers, one packet of St Moritz menthol, one gold Cartier lighter. All present and correct, lighting a cigarette I put on my party persona, determined to make the most of the occasion.

I did a swift head count and took a big breath when I realised that including Nathan there were eleven absolutely ripped, gym fit, handsome black men in attendance (the twelfth member was away in New York, so sadly couldn't attend). I could sense by Sarah's demeanour and general body language that she was in her element, like Santa had come early. The evening was balmy, in the mid-seventies and there was a constant soundtrack of chill out jazzy music discreetly playing.

The first hour or so was taken with general flirtatious conversation, mixing and getting acquainted with the entire "team". The drinks flowed, the barman was a magician and during all of this everyone helped themselves to the gorgeous food. Then the two young waitresses appeared to great fanfare carrying between them a large exotic pineapple based birthday cake, everyone sang a raucous rendition of happy birthday as Sarah blew out the one big candle, which was in the shape of a question mark. Most considerate.

Shortly Nathan disappeared escorting the two young girls back to their catering van and securely locking the gates as they drove off. This seemed to signal that the real festivities could begin. It brought on a very intense sexual tingle, knowing that it was just Sarah and myself at the mercy of these eleven huge black men. Nathan had explained to me earlier in the evening that it was by sheer coincidence that he'd formed this group, that he called "*Miami Mandingos*". He was at a party where the host had approached him late in the evening and asked him if he'd be interested in servicing his wife. He agreed and was surprised that he had thoroughly enjoyed the scenario. Basically pleasuring the mans wife whilst he discreetly watched. From that meeting the gent asked if he had a friend, as the wife wanted to take things a bit further and to have two black men pleasure her at. Things apparently escalated by word of mouth, and very soon he was being invited to many upscale house parties. Over a few months his group of guys grew to what it is today, and they are very much in demand all over Florida. Their reputation firmly precedes them, they are greeted warmly and revered by some on Florida's most needy wives. They are all charming and respectful and know what's expected of them. Any ground rules are strictly adhered to, ensuring things run smoothly and everyone is satisfied.

After the waitresses had left things moved on quite rapidly. Nathan asked Sarah and myself to follow him to the kitchen on the ruse of helping him carry a few bottles out to the barman. But once there he produced two elasticated blindfolds from his pocket and placed them securely over both our heads, immersing us in total darkness for what seemed like an eternity. Eventually leading us both back outside, where he instructed us to take a deep breath and discard our blindfolds. Upon removing my mask I was totally unprepared for what confronted me; standing to attention on the far side of the pool were ten completely naked black men, all proudly sporting large swaying black erections, and each toasting us with a glass of Champagne. Sarah audibly gasped and turned to me grinning said, "hope you're ready for this, it could be a long night", to which my reply was "just try stopping me, game on".

In short order I wriggled out of my dress and stood for a moment, hands provocatively on hips, naked and legs slightly splayed perusing the scene in front of me, whilst inwardly weighing up the enormity of the task at hand. These were some seriously big and powerful men in all departments. I noticed that the canopy was now open, and inside was a low double plinth covered in a massive white fake fur rug. My vagina was now positively throbbing and glistening with a mixture of my juices and the generous layer of Chanel body velvet I'd rubbed into it earlier. I grabbed my clutch and made my way around one side of the pool, whilst Sarah took the opposite side.

We were instantly enclosed in the middle of this group of ripped black sexual athletes, surrounded by shiny black meat, these men were so tall, even in my heels their erections were nudging my ribs, they were just enormous. Sarah began to whimper as many hands began to caress her body and fingers probed into her available and willing holes. I grinned as I noticed her eyes balls had rolled up into her head as she wrapped her hands around two colossal twitching black cocks. I left her to her own devices, as I had my own problems to deal with, albeit extremely pleasant ones.

My thighs parted automatically as a variety of fingers began to dance a sensuous tango over my swollen clitoris, gently teasing my labia and delicately stroking my anus. My breasts and rock solid nipples were also getting their fair share of attention, tweaked, pinched and sucked on by an assortment of men, I was in heaven. It was like a fantasy, a pure joy having this skilful team of black men giving every part of my willing body their undivided attention, it was a pure unadulterated dream like scenario. Wave after wave of bone wracking orgasms swept over me, my juices erupting in furious torrents over the many hands working on my vagina. I was physically lifted and carried over to one of the sofas, where a large pillow was placed on the ground. I took the hint and seductively looked each one of the men firmly in the eye as I sank to my knees, ready for them to feed my hungry mouth with their huge black meat. I wiggled my jawbone from side to side, working the muscles loose, in preparation for the onslaught. Taking a quick sip of a mojito, I then started to eagerly to lick the closest cocks to me, soon there were five, all patiently waiting for my tongue to work on them. I remember hearing Nathan jokingly exclaim, "Not so prim and pure now are you?" as his erection fought its way through the crowd to feed me. All I could see was a sea of hard, pulsating black meat in front of me, all waiting to use my eager, skilled mouth. I was being face fucked in true Mandingo style, my throat expanding to swallow each of them as they took turns, like a well-drilled team. I was salivating profusely and gagging noisily as I slurped on each of them. It was a true meat feast, one that from the sounds drifting my way Sarah was also enjoying. I devoured them one after another, using every last ounce of my experience to please these demanding men and their divine appendages.

After this endless entrée, I decided it was time for the main course, but no, these guys had other ideas. As if a silent instruction had passed between them my guys became Sarah's new feast and her guys became mine. Nathan or "Hammer" as I referred to him later, for obvious reasons, was acting like a ringmaster at the circus. He was strutting and posturing, drink in hand and flexing his mighty weapon as he issued very lewd and decadent instructions to both his squad and us. Every once in a while he would squat down behind me and slide a finger into my anus, whilst whispering in my ear a plethora of filthy, disgusting things he was personally going to do to me later. This in itself brought on an instant spine-shattering climax, soaking his wrist in my ejaculate. He loved the power he had to make both Sarah and myself squirt uncontrollably just by his touch alone. All the while I was trying to concentrate on the five brand new ebony poles plundering my mouth. It had now degenerated into pure unbridled lust, total animalistic sex. I took a very brief break for a drink and seized the opportunity to grab my clutch, retrieve the iPhone and take a multitude of photos, also my little bottle of poppers magically appeared in my hand. I quickly re joined the fray and was unceremoniously spread open on the sofa, enjoying the men staring at my gaping, wet pussy as they took turns in repaying the compliment and working on me with their tongues. I was climaxing in rapid succession and could feel a monumental orgasm building; I brought it to earthquake like proportions with a massive double hit of amyl, rapidly resulting in several formidable jets of my ejaculate squirting from me, drenching two of the men in close proximity. Cheers and applause reverberated around. It was mayhem, a total frenzy had set in and the poppers were passed to Sarah who almost immediately inundated her group of men with her own copious juices. Then all hell broke loose as they began fucking us, drilling their massive cocks into us, time after time, guy after guy. It was relentless, on top, from behind; they penetrated us from every conceivable angle. It was pleasure being heaped upon pleasure. My vaginal muscles clasping and milking automatically, working from its well experienced muscle memory.

 Sarah was by this stage on the fur plinth, being brutally pounded by the men in turn; grunting loudly her approval as they spit roasted her over and over again, she was like a rag doll in their powerful hands, a sight to behold. She was now getting very vocal and demanding, much to the delight of the men. This newly fifty year old would put ladies half her age to shame with this level of sexual performance. Thankfully Nathan had taken upon himself to record more damning evidence of her unbridled performance for Mike on my iPhone.

 As the debauchery continued several of the guys who were busy working me began reaching their own orgasms, two of them simultaneously flooding my mouth with profuse amounts of hot sticky sperm, several jets splashing off my cheekbones and running off my chin in great gooey torrents. This instantly sparked off a cum feeding frenzy, a sperm extravaganza, with load after load being ejaculated for our delectation. It was incredible; it was like being in the centre of a tsunami of semen, within minutes we were both saturated in it, our faces taking the most of their outpourings. It was a wonderful and truly empowering experience. After several minutes Sarah and I jumped under the poolside shower to cleanse off the aftermath, whilst the barman looked on nonchalantly as he fixed us a long, well deserved refreshing cocktail. We all lounged around chatting and drinking, and yes, much to the disgust of these health freak guys I enjoyed a St Moritz. Eventually many bade their farewells leaving two of Nathans closest buddies who were going to stay over until the morning. The barman whipped up a jug of some potent mix before leaving, happy with the very large tip from Nathan.

    We all nibbled on some late night snacks and talked some more until Sarah got her second wind and initiated a nice relaxed, less frenetic threesome with Nathans pals.

    Nathan and I left them to it and retired into the kitchen area, where he had a nice bottle of Jack Daniels with my name on it! No sooner than I'd had a sip he casually said, "It's now time to show you why they call me "the hammer". I just stood there and gulped as he became fully erect in seconds. It throbbed and flexed angrily, this penis definitely had a mind of it's own, and I sensed that it had me firmly in its sights. I was at this stage barefoot having discarded my heels by the shower; this had the effect of him being even taller than his six-feet plus height, he towered over me. He easily lifted me like a small doll and placed me with legs spread wide onto the square marble topped preparation surface. He grabbed a large can of squirty cream from the fridge and liberally spayed a splodge on both nipples before delicately decorating my gaping vagina with several cold squirts. The feeling of the chilled cream on my hot pussy was astonishing; instead of cooling me down it had the opposite effect. My pussy was on fire. He bent forward and lapped the cream from my nipples, he scooped up some of the excess and I lewdly sucked it of his fingers, tongue darting and twirling over them in a most provocative fashion. He worked his way down to eat the cream that was beginning to melt and drip from my labia onto the floor. His long tongue lapped away at me, gently chewing my engorged creamy lips and teasingly probing my anus. It was heaven; I could have stayed in that position until dawn and still wanted more. His tongue was methodically working on my ever eager pussy, totally licking every inch clean until there was no trace of cream left, just my smooth, wet expectant vagina, gaping wide for him, inviting him inside.

    Wanting to get more comfortable he pulled me down from the work surface and took me through to what he called his "den", where I immediately knelt in front of him, excitedly I began to worship his mighty cock, vocally praising it majestic appearance. He loved this, as by now this not so pure English lady was paying full respect to him, he groaned as I wrapped my hand around its girth and slapped my face with it, whilst my spare hand feverishly worked at my throbbing love bean. He looked surprised as I took him deep into my throat, gagging as I swallowed him inch by solid inch until his balls nestled on my chin. I kept him deep in my throat for a good thirty seconds as we locked eyes and just starred at one another. I nearly choked on him as a violent climax raged from me, causing me to thrash and jerk until it subsided. Eventually, he knelt me on his large leather office chair, I thrust my bottom in the air, inviting him into me. He reached into a draw and produced a tube of lube; I instantly took the hint and lewdly reached around and spread myself. He unleashed a large dollop onto one of my cheeks and slowly began scooping bits with his fingers and delicately working it in and around my anus. One finger then two gently easing me open, exploring deep into my rectum, the cool lube gave my insides a feeling that I simply can't describe. His strong black fingers worked their magic on my bud as my juices flowed in a continual torrent from my vagina, it simply poured from me in one long wet orgasm. I nearly fainted with sheer pleasure as he began to ease his solid ebony cock into me, my anus opened to its advances like an old friend, its muscle loosening to grip its large end, clamping it solidly and pulling him inside, bit by beautiful bit. It took several minutes for him to be fully inside me, such was its size. Holding the position perfectly still as my anus became fully accustomed to this most welcome intruder. Then slowly at first, he began to build up his rhythm until he was totally in full stride and living up to his moniker, I was being "Hammered" quite literally by "The Hammer". It was intense, pounding at me with a ferocity I'd not experienced in a while. It was sheer wanton fucking at its finest, both parties on the same plateau of sexual release. I gasped and gripped him as he began to buck and twitch behind me as he released a delicious stream of hot sperm deep into my rectum, filling me up, oozing out of me, with copious amounts dripping onto the floor. He didn't stop pumping into me for several ecstatic minutes, eventually leaving his meat inside me until his hardness had fully subsided.

The last thing I can recall from that epic evening was Nathan throwing me over his shoulder and carrying me to the bungalow. I awoke at eleven in the morning feeling a little battle weary. I ached in places that I never knew could ache, but it was all in a very nice way. I staggered to the pool, where Sarah was sitting with a coffee, looking very much how I felt. Needless to say we spent the day very quietly recuperating by the pool, making the most of our last day in Florida, as we were flying back on the early evening flight which arrived at Heathrow at Seven a.m. on the Sunday morning.

Before Nathan drove us to the airport we had a farewell mojito, where he cheekily presented us both with a Tee shirt, which had written on it "Visited Miami, Got Hammered". Hilarious and most apt. I still have it to this day. Yes we did sleep for pretty much the entire return flight.

On a humorous note we did teach him a little English slang when we explained to him what Sarah meant when she remarked that the guys had given us both some serious "Welly!" during the previous evening. He has now put the expression into his vernacular.

Chapter Twenty-One: London Awakens 2

Back on schedule; it was a month away from Valentines Day, and as promised David and Penny dropped by one Sunday lunchtime with photographs of their completed party venue. On time, but quite a bit over budget, the large viewing panels in the upper room were £550 each and there were five of them. Also as an extra attraction they'd spent a small fortune on a large covered outdoor cooking area complete with a top of the range Napoleon Oasis 400 Built In BBQ. Plus any array of outdoor tables and loungers to finish it off.

By this time word of mouth had escalated the numbers of interested couples, the only fly in the ointment being the car parking, which at a stretch would just take fifty five cars (later extended to seventy five by laying an adjoining small plot to gravel), during the invitation process we asked that where possible couples, that either knew each other, or lived nearby doubled up in one car so we could satisfy the demand to attend. I handled all the invitations myself, and between David and Mike the nitty gritty logistics were implemented.

On a very sad note, two weeks prior to the party, I received a phone call from Marc in Paris informing me that Yves had quietly passed away in his sleep. Paul and I were devastated, not only had he been a guiding light and had mentored me fully, opening me up to a whole new sexual side of my existence in the early nineties and beyond, but he'd also been a good and loyal friend to Paul. Due to the nature of our friendship we did not attend the funeral, which was held near the Palace of Versailles. We did however make a donation to his favoured charity, which looked after families of French soldiers who'd lost their lives in service of their country. It was very dear to his very large, ebullient French heart. Marc said that I'd be required to come to Paris at some stage to meet with Yves's lawyers, as there were several possessions that he'd bequeathed to me. There is not a day that goes by that I don't think about him, and remember him fondly. So many good memories, they always make me smile and if I'm somewhere decadent participating in some outrageous act I often glance up thinking "I know you're up there watching with that devilish glint in your eye". Paul and I feel proud and blessed to have known him. May his spirit party on for all eternity.

During this period we were also kept busy by the children, who were both now at university, fortunately they'd both passed their driving tests, and using some of the money my aunt had left in trust for them and a little extra from Paul and I, they had both gotten a car each, which made them truly independent. However, we both found we worried more about them until they text or called, especially if they were making a long trip. Pauls Mum and Dad were also toying with the idea of selling up in South West France and returning to Surrey to buy something smaller and more manageable, as they were both now into their seventies. So I was forever popping in to various estate agents in and around Kew and Guildford, collating details of anything that might be suitable for them.

Paul was also very busy on finding and securing music for a new U.S T.V series that had just been given the green light. However, the novelty of being in New York almost on a weekly basis was wearing thin and he kept threatening to severely cut back his workload and spend more time in the U.K.

Finally, Valentines weekend was upon us and we had the guest list finalised, sixty five couples in total, all of whom had confirmed by email on the Thursday of their attendance. Full location details and other pertinent information were only then released (still wary of the NOTW). David and Penny had been to a large local wholesaler and loaded their 4x4 with a vast selection of mixers, soft drinks and snacks. Obviously, being February the outdoor BBQ wouldn't be making its debut, instead they'd organised a local catering firm to deliver a full buffet for the relevant number of guests.

Paul and I arrived lunchtime on the Saturday to help with the final preparations. It was a hive of activity, everyone rushing around ensuring that everything was where it should be, and a quick check that all the various electrical bits and pieces all worked together and didn't cause any trips when fully powered. Thankfully it all worked, it would have been dreadful to have encountered any last minute technical issues that would have put a damper on this special night, a night that had been long in the planning. Everyone had everything firmly crossed, but thankfully everything went to plan on the evening.

Come eight o'clock the buffet area was getting stocked in preparation for the nine thirty start. Also a nice touch was David had done a deal with a local vintner and had thirty bottles of Champagne being chilled so that every guest would get a welcome drink on arrival.

They'd also employed three security guards from a local company that catered to this type of private event. They were worth their weight in gold, really ensuring that the parking was taken care of smoothly and in order. They generally kept a very watchful eye over the nights proceedings. One of them manned the main gate, and on strict instructions only admitted people who presented him with their confirmation emails. Then the other two guards guided people to the laid out parking bays. From the parking area the guests simply followed the cute illuminated cupids arrows leading them along the path to the venue. It ran like clockwork, in no small part to this trio of security experts.

Thankfully, as requested all guests had arrived by ten thirty and the main gates were securely locked, we'd made it a firm instruction that there was to be no admittance after this time.

Everybody had made a massive effort, with all the ladies glamming it up, all dressed in a diverse array of sexy revealing club attire, possibly something to do with a few prizes that were handed out for various categories, including "most erotic outfit", incidentally won by lady in a custom made leather harness that struggled to contain her modesty, but was certainly a hit amongst the gents and also many of the ladies present. She was letting her hair down to celebrate her twentieth wedding anniversary; her husband was one proud man and just adored showing her off.

Antonia had brought along as her significant other a very attractive much younger man, who during the early part of the party had a very bewildered look on his face, but was to be found later on in a very fun looking six way romp up in the group play room. Paul and I spent the majority of the evening playing co-hosts with David and Penny, keeping all areas running smoothly. David and Paul were very busy doing the bar duties, whilst Penny and I were generally keeping tables cleared and making sure things were okay in the pool and Jacuzzi zone.

Every room was being well used, and all the guests were really enjoying the facilities, throughout the evening people would wander up to both Penny and myself full of compliments. Everyone felt comfortable and secure in this well controlled environment, being able to party hard with like-minded people was absolutely the key to its success. Everyone was there for pure decadent fun, and that is what they all got by the bucket load.

We did an "after party" email questionnaire which gained a lot of valuable feedback with positive suggestions for future events. All in all this first party proved to be a huge success. It demonstrated to me that London was ready for much more of the same. Elegant, sophisticated people occasionally unleashing their inbuilt British inhibitions and getting decadent and debauched in a secure upmarket venue.

The parties went from strength to strength, incorporating many and varied themed spectaculars. In particular "greedy ladies" parties, where three guys were invited for everyone lady attending. As Penny and I thought, these proved a huge success, with a record Friday afternoon that saw thirty ladies and around ninety selected gentlemen getting down and dirty with one another. Another most popular event turned out to be, weather permitting, the Sunday afternoon "fun in the sun" BBQ. Word travelled quickly along the swinger's grapevine and soon we had to decline more people than we could accommodate.

On several occasions' members of various press organisations, most notably "The News of The World" tried to infiltrate the guest list. Some of the ludicrous lengths they went to did give everyone a good laugh. There was one incident where a couple turned up saying they'd mislaid their invitation, and during the conversation the female got a call on her mobile, inadvertently she let it slip to whoever was on the other end of the line "that she was out working and would be back in the office later", needless to say they were unceremoniously turned away (after taking a picture of them). The strict rules and vetting procedures that had been put in place definitely served their purpose on more than one occasion over the years. Eventually, it was run along the lines of a membership only venue and admittance was only granted upon production of the laminated photo I.D that was issued to the individual member. Also guests had to be vouched for at the discretion of the member, and where necessary a temporary membership issued upon production of a drivers license, passport or similar.

Along with success also came the numerous imitators and within six months many other people tried to emulate our success, with several similar styles of house party events springing up in various parts. Mainly London and the Home counties, a few had limited success, but the vast majority sunk without trace. Purely run by people who had limited or no experience of the lifestyle, or the calibre of people in it. However, David and Penny's events prospered and their reputation as hosts flourished over time. Things really started to take off in London and the U.K. in general from early 2011, a most significant date as I'll explain later in the book.

Chapter Twenty-Two: Marbella Madness

During one of David and Penny's soirees we met a couple that Paul and I immediately hit it off with, James and Amanda, he was late fifties and an ex racing driver and she was his much younger trophy wife. They were in the final stages of completing building works on their new property in Southern Spain.

Over the coming months we became good friends, amazed that we'd never bumped into them previously, as they'd regularly visited many of the clubs in Paris that were our favourite haunts. In particular they'd been to *"ChrisetManu2"* on numerous occasions over the years.

James was, and still is a serious player and loves nothing better than orchestrating a little afternoon delight for a willing wife. Amanda fully accepts and frequently participates in his hobby.

One occasion that springs to mind, is when a Welsh couple had contacted him; the husband was a recently retired international rugby player. He wanted to fulfil a fantasy that both he and his wife had and they had chosen James to organise the event. James in turn roped in Paul to help with the planning and recruiting of willing participants.

The plan was for the husband to put his pretty thirty-year-old blonde wife on a train from Cardiff to Paddington, where she'd be collected by Paul and driven to the Grosvenor House Hotel, where awaiting her in a suite would be eight gentlemen for her pleasure. The whole event was to be filmed and plenty of photographs taken for her voyeur husband. After being well used for several hours, she'd be put back on the five o'clock train to Cardiff, complete with several memory sticks full of photo's and video clips as a memento for them both. The event went as planned, much to the Welsh couples delight. I only include this snippet, as I recently stumbled upon a folder on one of my external hard drives that was a record of the afternoon in question. The young wife did look like she was well and truly put through her paces by the final picture. Paul and James over the years have organised a number of such events. I can only surmise that they are from the same gene pool, as their quest to impart pleasure to the female race is limitless. Well it keeps them off the streets I suppose.

James and Paul became really firm friends and through James, Paul was able to attend many F1 races, both at Silverstone and abroad. Meeting many of the famous drivers and celebrities that hang around these events. He always arrived home buzzing with a multitude of stories.

Anyway, once their house was completed and they'd fully moved in they decided to christen their new home with a party. They'd already made big strides into the Marbella swinging circle, already having been to several house parties, garnering many good contacts along Spain's southern coast.

The party was arranged for early summer and David, Penny, Mike, Sarah, Paul and I decided to make a long weekend of it, flying into Malaga on the Thursday and returning on the Monday. James had arranged the use of a large villa for us, at the nearby Puerto Sotogrande, we got mates rates which made it even better.

We arrived to a typical Andalusian June day, with clear skies and temperatures in the low eighties. As pre booked there was a people carrier waiting for us as we exited arrivals that whisked us down the A 7 motorway to our destination in under an hour.

Later that first evening we all met up with James and Amanda for dinner, at a fantastic Argentinian restaurant called *"La Quinta"*, as you'd expect the speciality was meat, meat and more meat. Everyone had the large Solomillo (fillet steak), cooked traditionally over an open wood burning fire. It was so tender you could cut it with a spoon as they say. Over the course of the evening they told us the back story of several of the other couples that would be attending the soiree the following evening, also they had a special surprise in store, but no matter how much we badgered them, their lips were sealed, but Amanda said it would be a big hit. She winked at us three ladies in that knowing way us women have when we have a little secrets.

The following day was spent lounging in the sun around the pool area chatting and drinking. Just generally relaxing until it was time to get ready for the evenings fun and frolics.

The dress code for the evening was casual; shorts and polo shirts for the men and skimpy-barely there dresses for the ladies. By the allotted time everyone was ready and the taxis arrived to ferry us the short distance to the house, well more like mansion. It was set on a large plot overlooking one of the greens at La Reserva Golf Club, one of the most exclusive members only clubs in Europe. The house it self was very imposing, with a large marble central hall that swept through to a massive lounge, then on to an enormous infinity pool, complete with stunning views of the Mediterranean and Gibraltar in the distance. It was breath taking. James greeted us and led us through to the large patio-lounge-eating area by the pool and introduced us to the other guests, as Amanda thrust a glass of Champagne in our hands. We were the final guests, making it a fairly intimate affair, with ten couples of varying nationalities. A veritable United Nations Swingers gathering. The pool really was the centrepiece, looking majestic, with it's under water lighting making it glow a stunning azure blue under the dark Mediterranean night sky. There was food and drink in plentiful supply and very subtle mood music playing, creating a wonderful atmosphere. Everybody was mixing, chatting and openly flirting with one another. It wasn't long until the French couple stripped off and slid enticingly into the pool, this tempted a few others to follow in rapid succession.

    Whilst chatting to the husband of a Dutch couple and discussing our experiences in Amsterdam I noticed Amanda discreetly slip away into the house. I thought no more about it until ten minutes later she reappeared and beckoned me over. I followed her into the kitchen, where she excitedly informed me that the entertainment had arrived, explaining that she'd been accepted into the inner circle of a group of golfers wives and that they'd been meeting up for lunch weekly, and unbeknownst to their husbands they'd all used the services of four South African masseurs, who catered for "needy golf widows" as they were referred to. To cut a long story short, she'd told James all about it, and he simply loved the scenario. He had Amanda arrange for them visit the house and give her their special service a few weeks previously, and she was now hooked. One of the two ground level bedroom suites had been converted into a sensual tantric massage area, complete with massage table and large sofa. For the party the second bedroom suite had also been appropriately rearranged, there would two masseurs in each waiting to treat any ladies that desired sampling their special touch. She was most excited by the little surprise they'd organised and told me to tell Penny and Sarah situation. She also told me that James had installed discreet cameras in the first bedroom suite and loved to watch her with the masseurs from his study upstairs on his large screen iMac. I knew immediately that Paul had definitely had some input in this novel and most voyeuristic scenario. She did promise that the cameras had been deactivated for the party, and that nobody would be taking a sneaky peak of what anyone was up to.

I quickly told Paul before telling Sarah and Penny, he just told me to go and play to my hearts content, as always the ever-thoughtful understanding husband. Sarah was excited by the idea, but David and Penny were already in the pool otherwise engaged enjoying the intimate company of the French couple.

I indulged in another glass of bubbly, enjoying the sensation as my over excitable urges began to send their usual signals to my brain and back to my loins in a split second. Once this occurs I'm pretty much an unstoppable force. These urges have seemed to get progressively stronger as I get older, many friends have shared my observations, saying that since they hit their forties the greater their needs and desires became. It's no wonder that today's cougars are much in demand by their many young admirers. I'm certainly not ageist when it comes to sexual encounters, and can definitely appreciate what a man in his twenties can bring to the bedroom, or anywhere else the opportunity arises.

Finishing my drink I quickly told Amanda I was going AWOL for a while, with a wicked grin and a raised eyebrow she shooed me off in the direction of the masseurs. I had a choice of room; I was instinctively drawn toward the right hand side bedroom suite. My heels echoed on the marble flooring as I made my way down the corridor to the room, my insides churning with lust as to what may be in store on the other side of the door. I stood trembling with pleasure for a few moments before taking the "Do Not Disturb" sign off the small table and hanging it on the door handle. I knocked gently as I opened the door, quivering even more as my imagination ran amok in those initial brief seconds of stepping into the unknown. It's a combination of all my emotions, fear, anticipation, lust, expectation and desire all bundled up into one large butterfly flapping its wings furiously in the pit of my stomach, it's a wonderful feeling.

As soon as I closed the door I was startled by how good looking these two white South African men were, rugged, chiselled and suntanned type of guys. The room was gently illuminated by a variety of scented candles that gave off a lovely Mediterranean aroma. They immediately took charge, putting me at my ease firmly instructing me to remove my dress. As I was slipping it over my head I felt an authoritative strong pair of hands deftly peel my panties down, instinctively I stepped out of them, leaving me just in my heels, completely at their mercy, I adore this feeling of vulnerability. At this point I began to get very turned on, their accents alone made wet and shiver with unbridled lust. They helped me up on to the quilted massage couch; face down at first, positioning my head in the padded area and slotting my toes into the footholds. I quickly relaxed as they began to drench my body with sandalwood infused oil, the smell was quite exquisite. Four powerful hands began to massage my body, one pair starting on my shoulders, whilst the other set worked on my calves, firmly working the muscles. Slowly and methodically they both worked their way towards my bottom. The feeling of anticipation in those few minutes is the thing that orgasms are made from. Eventually their hands met and both of them began sensually kneading and manipulating my cheeks. More oil was applied, flowing in a warm tingling trickle down the crease and over my anus, and settling in a warm pool on my clitoris. My legs were gently eased apart as they massaged the tops of my inner thighs, fleetingly brushing my labia and clitty with their long skilful fingers. They could tell when they hit the right spots as I let my pleasure be known with audible whimpers and squeals. As they flipped me over onto my back my legs automatically opened by pure lustful reflex, they both took a fleeting moment to admire my vagina whose lips were engorged and open, shimmering with my juices in the candle light. They stood either side of me massaging my nipples, and that most sensitive area around my pussy lips, skilled fingers soon released my throbbing clitoris. Their fingers worked on me with complete dexterity, slipping into both my vagina and anus with equal vigour. They brought me higher and higher, until with a muffled scream I let rip a rapturous bone shaking orgasm, great torrents of fluid ejaculated from me, hot powerful jets squirting in huge arcs everywhere. They let me come down gently, stroking me and bathing my vagina with a chilled flannel, gently massaging my temples and forehead, transporting me onto a divine level of peaceful calm. I felt all my muscles release as a strange sensation of tension flowed out from my toes away from my body; it was just one the most delicate post orgasm feelings ever.

    I re-joined the party and grabbed a much-needed drink; things were well underway at this stage. Paul was reclined on a lounger with the French lady firmly impaled upon him, he did look most contented. Penny joined me for a few moments before disappearing to put herself in the very capable hands of the masseurs. Everyone was getting well into the spirit of things, with lots of squeals and groans coming from all areas, all enhanced by the warm evening breeze wafting across the Mediterranean from North Africa.

Call me greedy, but I was still excited from my experience with the two South African masseurs, and decided that the only thing for it was wander off to the second bedroom and see if the other two masseurs were available. As luck would have it they were. I brazenly knocked and entered, I was pleased at their reaction as their eyes scanned me naked body up and down. Both were just in a towel, and my entrance immediately produced the effect every woman looks for, movement! There was certainly a large degree of movement as they welcomed me inside the room, one of them swiftly locking the door behind me. It quickly turned into one of those situations where few words were spoken and the fun just flowed naturally. They were both late twenties, but between them seemed to have a hundred years of experience in pleasuring a woman. With just a look from me they removed their towels releasing two fine hard cocks for my admiration and appraisal. I swiftly knelt down open mouthed, inviting them to feed me, which they did, both jostling for prime position in my mouth, they both gasped as I took each one in turn deep into my throat. Once they realised that they had a pure slut on their hands they took full control of me, each taking his turn to stand behind me holding my head in a vice like grip as the other brutally fucked my mouth. I was gagging, yet loving every filthy minute of this oral abuse. After the initial boisterous onslaught things settled down, and we all got more comfortable on the large bed, where as they requested I took turns in riding their erections, nimbly alternating between the two of them. It developed progressively into a very natural rhythm, what started in a lust fuelled frenzy between the three of us was now a slow sensual moment in time, where each of us was in tune with one another. I swapped between them multiple times, on each occasion milking their cocks with no movement, just squatting over each erection, inserting just the tip of the cock and letting my powerful vaginal muscles grip and flex, edging them ever closer to climax. I was now controlling their pleasure, and revelling in the feeling of pure sexual release. For what seemed like an hour, but in reality was only about twenty minutes we all three fucked each other in a variety of positions, each one urging the other on to orgasm. Eventually, I climbed back on top of an erection, taking it inside me to the hilt and then arching my bottom, inviting the other to use my anus, it was mind numbing as I felt him gently entering me. We held perfectly still for a moment, as both my vagina and anus accepted these two muscular men. Then like a pair of steam train pistons they began to pump me, building up the pace little by little until for the final few minutes I was being unceremoniously pounded, my vicious wet climax spurred them on to even harder and faster thrusts, culminating with both of them flooding me with powerful spurts of their searing hot sperm, it was a gratifying feeling of fullness, having both orifices full and overflowing with their cum. After a swift cleansing shower I pecked them on the cheek, thanking them for making me one very satisfied lady. Before leaving the room I did accept their business cards for future reference.

As I entered the large kitchen Sarah was freshening her drink, she looked up at me smiling and simply said, "you're pure filth", takes one to know one did cross my mind as we toasted each other with a smirk. Incidentally, Sarah had just returned from a similar encounter with the initial pair of masseurs and women being women we did compare notes.

The house warming was a great success, with much inter couple playing going on until the early hours of Saturday morning, eventually taxis were called, and exhausted guests bade their farewells and went in search of some much need sleep.

Some of the men had arranged to play a lunch time round of golf on the Saturday, whilst several of us ladies met up at a fantastic nearby beach "chiringuito" for a lazy Spanish lunch in the warm sun. It was during this lunch that two of the ladies who lived there all year round filled us in on the local gossip; we were all ears as it centred around a minor English celebrity, who the press had nick named "The Cad". He'd recently opened, to much fanfare, a restaurant on the "golden mile" in Marbella. It had quickly gained notoriety for more than just its food. Rumour had it that the owner had turned his office above the restaurant into a bit of a boudoir, and treated many of the golf widows to his rather large endowment (which I have since found out from someone who was privy to a dabble, does live up to its reputation). One of the ladies told us that the queue of wives wanting to experience the pleasure was huge, and quite often the husbands would be taking a complimentary drink at the bar whilst their wives or partners were having a different kind of "cocktail" up in the boudoir office, occasionally catering to two at a time. The local joke was that he would be soon catering to coach parties. Sadly, and with much weeping and wailing from "The Real Housewives of Marbella" it shut its doors in 2013, and this lounge lizard returned to the U.K.

James and Amanda still host the occasional party at their home, but still prefer to travel to the clubs of Paris for the odd weekend of debauchery. They are very much like Paul and I in this respect, even after all these years the anonymity of the Paris scene is still a major turn on.

Chapter Twenty-Three: Moulded In His Image

Ever since our visit to Paris Penny has never forgotten the Parisian Fire-fighters, especially the bull with the gargantuan, harnessed penis. In fact he became a topic of conversation during the house parties, which incidentally were still hugely popular and always had a long membership pending list. One of the aforementioned venues that had opened a few years previously, just after the inception of David and Penny's house party concept, and was designed and run along very similar lines was gathering rave reviews and going from strength to strength was the *"Radlett House Parties"*. I have met a number of people who've attended recently who all give it a massive thumbs up. In fact Mike and Sarah attended a recent event and only have glowing reports regarding the venue, quality of party guests and according to them the hosts Richard and Janet are a delight. High praise indeed! I suggest you check out the website as I have, and I'm definitely going to be attending one of their events when time permits, definitely before the coming summer. I look forward to meeting the infamous Tyson Brown!

Anyway, Penny was fast approaching her big four zero and I had a plan to give her a surprise present, which involved me going to Paris to source and have manufactured whilst there.

I had planned the visit to coincide with the over due meeting with Yves lawyers, in their quest to close the book on his estate. After several calls and emails to various individuals all was set for a Wednesday to Saturday solo visit in early September. This also was convenient as Paul and the children were going to be at Pauls parents in South West France, helping them pack personal items for their impending move back to Surrey. They'd recently fallen in love with a cosy cottage in a small village between Guildford and Woking called Mayford. They'd made an offer that was accepted and were due to move in during early November, so they needed all the help we could muster. I promised to also go early October in the 4x4 with Paul and bring back any valuable or fragile items for them and store things at ours until everything was ready.

I caught the mid morning Eurostar to Paris, and as promised Marc was at the Gare du Nord to collect me, he was now driving for an elderly former colleague of Yves, so there was no problem. Also, at this stage the apartment was still mine to use as and when I needed.

We pulled in to a small side street and had a coffee and brandy, and had a good catch up on all things Paris and many things Yves. It brought back many fond memories and to be honest unburdened my conscience, as I didn't no quite how I'd feel knowing that my mentor had gone, and I'd not see his cheeky grin again.

First thing on the agenda for the afternoon was to get a few essentials from the local Franprix convenience store. Stopping off at my local bar for a mid afternoon snack I also got all the local news and gossip from the ever present staff, who by now were like an extended family, and it was always a major struggle to get them to take any money off me in payment. I always took them a bag full of English goodies such as chocolate, cheddar cheese and bizarrely Colemans English mustard, oh and Branston pickle, which they found most odd but loved it all the same.

I'd explained my idea regarding my present for Penny to an old colleague called Anton from the website days who was going to be taking care of the finer details of my scheme. He popped by early that evening with what was required for my part in the process, which all sounded simple enough, if not a tad messy. When he arrived we reminisced over a glass of wine as he showed me what I needed to do step by step and that he'd stop by the following morning on his way to his office to collect the result and return the finished article to me Friday evening on his way home.

Now all that was required was my pre arranged nine o'clock meeting with Monsieur Gargantuan Cock himself (tracked down after numerous phone calls, I'm nothing if not determined). His name is actually Rémi and he's thirty-eight but his dark swarthy looks make him appear older. He remembered Penny and myself most vividly and he thought my idea was both fun, and a compliment to him. Yes, you guessed correctly, I was going to take a plaster cast mould of his full-blown erection and Anton was going to fabricate it into a unique true to life personal dildo for Penny. It was going to be identical in every way, even down to the skin tone, as Anton had instructed me to take a photo of said member and email it to him so he could adjust the tone of the silicon moulding material.

Rémi arrived promptly at nine looking exactly as I remembered and smelling gorgeous. In a distinct effort to put him at his ease after I'd had a quick soak in the tub earlier I just slipped on an old large white shirt that I'd used in Kew when decorating. It had old paint stains on it and was the perfect garment for the occasion. We had a good chat, reminiscing about our visit to the Fire Station; apparently I had become legendary amongst the fire fighting fraternity. Whilst enjoying a couple of glasses of chilled Sancerre and much to my surprise he joined me in a St Moritz. He gave me a good update on the new clubs that had sprung up around Paris since my last visit. One in particular called *"Moon City"* piqued my interest and I made a mental note to check it out on the Internet later.

    I showed him to the second bedroom where I'd placed a robe on the bed for him to wear once he'd undressed. The whole procedure was very time sensitive (and messy). He had to be solidly erect for it to work properly, so I put an erotic DVD on to aid the process. I needn't have worried as when he opened the robe his penis was already well on the way to its epic proportion. He relaxed with his wine; gently stroking himself whilst I rushed to the kitchen to prepare the moulding substance, it had to be exactly the right consistency, not to runny and definitely not to dense. It set very quickly, so timing was everything. It was a most awkward procedure; as once the Perspex container was filled and ready he had to lay at a slight angle, his legs and feet inclined upwards. Thankfully he remained solidly erect as I quickly manoeuvred the container over his penis, immersing it fully until his sac was resting on the top of the mix. It was fiddly but I managed it. Holding the container in place for the few minutes as instructed allowing it to solidify slightly. Once that stage was reached I had to ease the Perspex contain off, then with my hands I had to firmly squeeze and mould the substance to him, ensuring every ridge and veined contour had been encompassed. Leaving it again for precisely three minutes until the cast was almost set it was now time to gently remove the mould from his penis and putting it safely in the fridge to fully set ready for Anton to collect the following morning. Rémi's groin and stomach was a sight for sore eyes, still erect but with solidifying bits of excess dotted everywhere, we laughed at all the palaver it had been as I showed him to the shower. I myself went to the kitchen to wash the remnants off my hands and opened a fresh bottle of wine. I then remembered that I needed to take a few pictures on my iPhone for matching his skin tone for the finished article.

    He returned from the shower in the robe and grinned when I told him I needed to take a few pictures. I told him not to worry, as he needn't be erect as it was simply for colour match. He stood there and opened the robe laughing as his colossal cock leapt free, as I grabbed the camera he reached into his jacket pocket and produced a brand new chrome and leather cock harness. I let out a gasp as he fitted it on his mighty erection and heavy balls. I took several photos as I anticipated a few would be blurred as my hands were trembling so much. As a little added extra I flipped it to video mode and made him say in his sexy French accent "all for you Penny, enjoy me at your leisure", my immediate reply captured on the video was "but it's all mine at the moment" as I got down on my knees in front of him. The effect his harness had was astounding; it just made him appear even larger if that was possible. It accentuated his immense girth and it was so engorged it pulsated aggressively in front of me. I took a final sip of my wine, and then we locked eyes as he watched me go through my mouth and jaw ritual, something I always do when confronted by a penis of such gigantic proportions. Also, it is a point in time when my sexual energy releases itself in the form of a hot tingling wave pulsating from head to toe. It's an indescribable feeling of pure unrestrained desire. I gripped on to his muscled thighs and began to work my tongue on him, spending time on his balls, tasting them individually and getting an extra frisson of excitement as I felt the stainless steel and leather on my tongue. Not losing eye contact for even a brief moment I clasped my hands together behind my back, inviting him to feed and fuck my eager mouth. He placed its enormous end on my outstretched tongue and probed and eased himself gently to the back of my throat. My cheeks were bulging and I was gagging on its sheer size, whilst at the same time jerking and shuddering with my own mini climaxes. The decadent feeling of my juices flowing out of me and soaking my thighs was phenomenal. He firmly gripped my head as he sensually used my mouth and throat for his pleasure. Eventually he relented and lay back on the sofa, his erection flexing angrily. I crawled seductively forward with my tongue eager to lap his balls again, I couldn't get enough of this man, wave after wave of lust cursed through me. I began to run my tongue up and down his thighs, down to his feet, sucking his toes and working my way slowly back up to my prize. He groaned with pleasure when I parted his thighs further and with lizard like flicks my tongue danced over his freshly showered rectum. He was trembling with decadent pleasure as my tongue gently probed his anus, tasting him fully, encircling his beautiful sphincter muscle. He begged me not to stop; this spurred me on to even more lewd tongue work, my saliva was soaking both my face and his bottom, it was a crazy and frenzied ten-minute interlude of pure anal worship, which I adored. We needed a quick wine break at which stage I removed my shirt, leaving me fully naked, and without any heels on he seemed even larger (height wise), in fact when stood face to face his erection would nudge the top of my rib cage. We commenced where we left off, him laying back on the sofa with his mammoth cock beckoning, daring me to climb on. I eagerly clambered on the sofa kneeling either side of his large thighs, as I lowered myself onto him I could feel my labia part in preparation, ready to welcome his huge engorged helmet. I loosened instinctively as my walls were firmly stretched, my wetness helping ease its passage inside me. The sheer effort in accommodating his vast manhood left me breathless for a few moments; it really was the ultimate in pleasurable pain. Once my vagina was sufficiently in tune with its guest intruder I began a series of slow and gentle hip rotations, coupled with a relaxed riding motion. All the while his large fingers were tweaking, and pinching at my extended nipples. I slowly but surely increased the speed until I was pounding up and down on him, whimpering as the climaxes continually washed over me. I would ease up slowly, almost releasing him then hold for several moments before slamming down hard on him. At one stage I thought I was passing out through lack of oxygen, as during a particular vicious climax he grabbed my hair, pulling my face to his and thrusting his tongue down my throat. It was so lust driven, pure animalistic sex in its rawest form. We fucked each other hard over the next half hour, both taking our pleasure from each other's bodies, I lost count of my orgasms and just rode wave after wave of pleasure, savouring every moment. He got close several times but was determined to ensure maximum satisfaction for me as a priority. However, when he did eventually orgasm it was incredible. He made me kneel before him with my mouth open, and with just two strokes on his cock he put his hands on his hips and his cock began to shudder violently, releasing torrent after torrent of his cream into my mouth, over my face, it was squirting everywhere in a vast outpouring. It was phenomenal to watch, it was never ending. I was drenched, covered in his warm cum. When it eventually subsided I cleaned him up with my tongue, draining every last drop from him. It was a session of immense proportions in every way. We were both drained, exhausted from our exertions, but we finished the evening off at my bar opposite with a lovely large brandy whilst he waited for his taxi. After he left with a flourish of kisses I suddenly realised I was famished, and the ever attentive waiter had a stunning T-bone steak and salad cooked for me. I'd been fed so much meat that evening I collapsed into bed one very full and contented lady.

    Anton arrived as promised and took a quick coffee with me as he collect the mould, confirming he'd deliver the finished article Friday evening around six-thirty. Once he left I got ready for my scheduled eleven o'clock meeting with Yves's estate lawyers at their offices located on the close by Rue du Faubourg Saint Honore.

It was very informal, and they read the relevant parts of his last will & testament in both French and English. The bulk of the estate had already been executed and the few final items pertinent to me were presented on the firm's embossed legal paper that simply required stamping and my signature along with both lawyers. He'd left me the full use of the apartment until 2017, when its ownership would be transferred to his goddaughter upon her twenty-first birthday, several pieces of jewellery and "the fur coat". That brought both a smile to my face and a tear to my eye. Finally they handed me a large sealed padded envelope with the explicit instruction "to opened and read alone in the apartment". Typical mischievous Yves, bless him, secretive and intriguing from beyond the grave. The two lawyers duly signed along with myself; it was job done, the end of an era, but as it would transpire not quite full closure.

Walking back to the apartment I stopped off at a small bar in a little side street and enjoyed a café and cognac whilst letting my mind explore the possibilities of what was awaiting me inside the envelope. A million and one things flew around inside my brain, but impatience got the better of me and I was back at the apartment within ten minutes, positively excited but apprehensive about the contents. I grabbed a cold Page24 beer from the fridge, lit a cigarette and anxiously stared at the package for a few minutes until my curiosity overcame me. I carefully broke the seal and peeled open the envelope, inside were two envelopes, one addressed to Paul and a larger one to myself. I kept Paul's sealed, but subsequently when we opened it together we were flabbergasted by both his generosity and thoughtfulness, as inside were two one thousand pound Ralph Lauren gift certificates to be spent at any store across Europe, Paul was most touched by the gesture and took a moment to reflect on the man and his ebullient character. Opening mine alone in the apartment was a sombre moment, but instantly uplifting by the very nature of its contents. There was a lovely long letter, which is far too personal to go into here, but included was twenty five hundred euro notes attached to another small note explaining his wish was that I used the money to celebrate life on the first five anniversaries of his passing in Paris, indulging in fine food and even finer sex. That made me chuckle; only Yves could come up with something like this in his final days. I do miss him, but his memory lives on in true decadent style, especially when I'm in Paris. Even today when I'm at the apartment I can sense him there somewhere looking down smiling in appreciation of my "joie de vivre" and cavalier attitude to enjoying all things Paris has to offer a liberated woman. I quietly toasted him saying "bon voyage" as I sat alone for a few moments contemplation before returning to the land of the living.

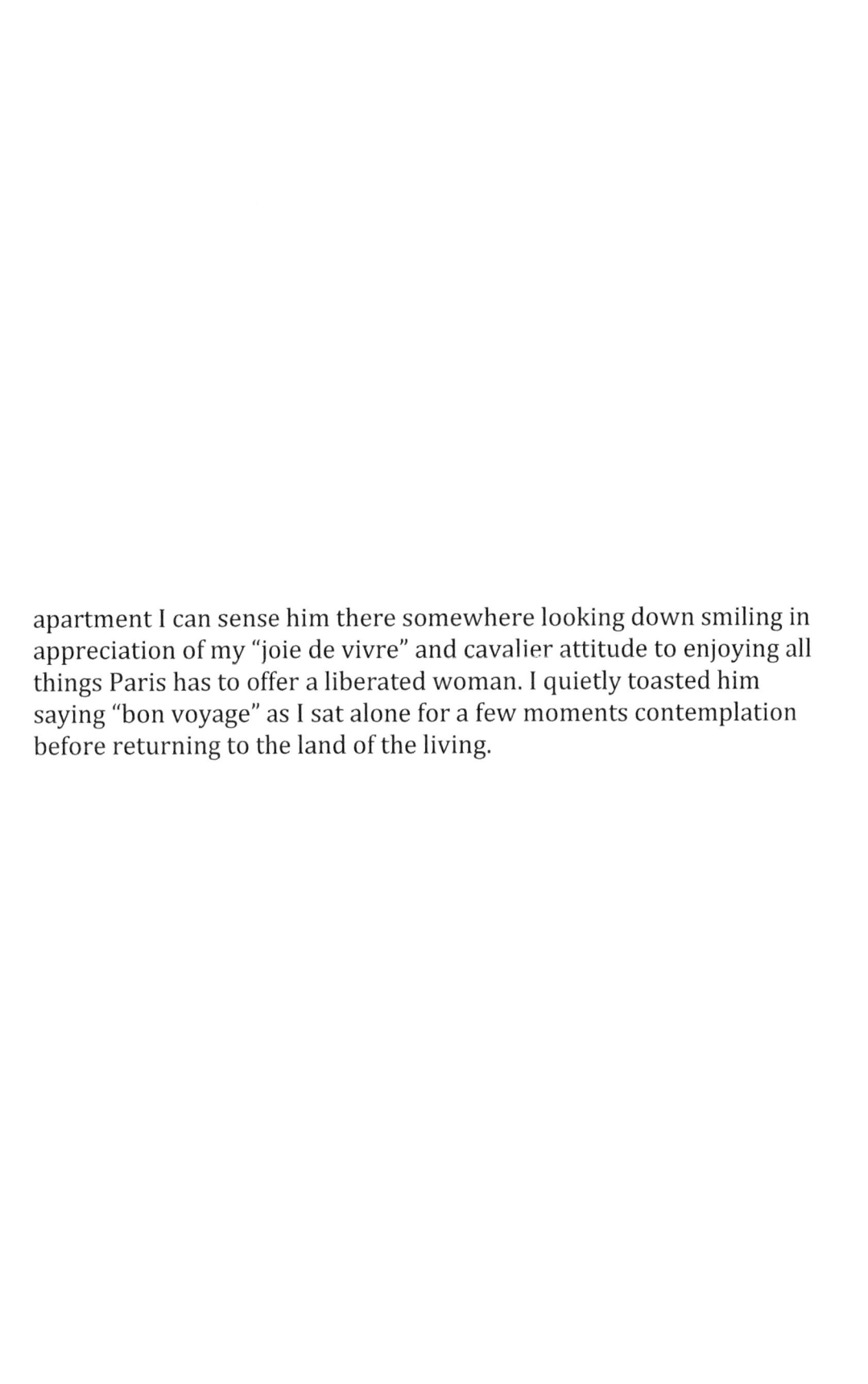

Chapter Twenty-Four: Moon City

After a quiet evening in the apartment catching up with both Paul and the children on Skype I awoke refreshed and ready to enjoy my Friday in Paris with some playtime. I decided to go and check out this new club Rémi had talked about. I looked at their website and liked the concept, and they were also open during the afternoon, which was exactly what I was hoping for. I decided to treat myself to a nice lunch to get in the mood before visiting.

The club is situated on Boulevard de Clichy, in the Pigalle district, very close to the world famous *"Moulin Rouge"*. The area is a mecca for tourists, and has many sex shops and kinky clothing boutiques on every street.

I decided to have lunch at a restaurant close to the club, one that I'd been recommended a few years previously by Charli, but had never had the opportunity to sample its delights. It's called *"Buvette"* and is on Rue Henry Monnier in the South Pigalle area. In French, the word "buvette" describes a laid-back place to eat or drink no matter the time of day, and it certainly delivers on that front. The restaurant is owner Jody Williams's second establishment, the first being in Manhattan's West Village, New York. What a find, great décor mixing Parisian art deco with a smidgeon of Manhattan chic. I kept it light and simple with a very tasty "Croque Madame" and two thirst quenching mugs of local artisan cider. Well worth the visit and very inexpensive for Paris. My total bill was under twenty euros.

Upon arrival at the club I was instantly impressed by the very ornate and welcoming façade, complete with two imposing traditional ancient oriental warriors on plinths either side of the entrance, both holding a spear, as if guarding the establishment and its guests. It is really a most impressive first impression. A very pleasant young girl on reception explained that as a single female I was welcome to use the facilities free of charge, as it was Friday and they allowed single males, also my first two drinks were complimentary. She explained that it was usual for the single ladies to be offered drinks by the single gents after that. My ears certainly pricked up, I wondered where the catch was, but I needn't have worried as everything was exactly as described and so much more. I was shown to the very plush oriental themed changing area where I was given a key to a large locker. Upon opening the locker I was impressed by its contents, two large fluffy white towels and a very pretty floral sarong. I excitedly undressed and wrapped it around my waist casually and popped a towel over my shoulder. Slipping the elasticated key band around wrist I followed my nose along to the most enchanting main area, with its Asian décor and wonderful seating areas. I casually headed to the bar. I admit I felt a bit self conscious at first as dotted around on various comfy sofas and easy chairs were a number of men drinking cocktails, a few were chatting to a couple that seemed to be regulars. Everyone was most courteous and just raised their glasses in a discreet welcoming fashion. I ordered a Jack Daniels on the rocks to get my senses flowing; it was served in a beautiful cut crystal tumbler. I settled on a very comfortable bar stool to get my bearings and generally get a feel for the place. Everyone seemed relaxed and respectful; there was a great no pressure ambience to the place, with several men introducing themselves and making general chitchat. I was totally taken by the overriding atmosphere so far, and had a good feeling creeping through me, always a good sign. I was also getting a good overview of the facilities from the barman. I finished my drink, which had certainly taken the edge off and as usual gave me a high level of confidence and bravado. I wandered off in search of the steam room, hanging my towel and sarong on a peg outside, I took a big breath and went in. The interior was wonderfully hot and steamy, the ultra violet and red lighting made it very hypnotizing. I took little steps, finding my way to the tiled seating levels, I settled on the middle level, letting the hot steam coat my body in a film of condensation; I breathed a large lung full of the eucalyptus infused air. That really opened the tubes and was a marvellous sensation. It soon became apparent that there were several other people enjoying the heat. I got chatting to an older French man who introduced himself and was a wealth of information regarding the current swinging scene in the area, he was most intrigued by my extensive knowledge and experience of Paris and it clubs. He was very easy to talk to, all in French I might add, as his grasp of English was basic to say the least. After a while he suggested we continue our conversation at the bar, which suited me, as I was now getting uncomfortably hot. The barman poured me a fresh Jack Daniels and I discreetly noted it was added to this gents tab. It turned out over the years we'd been to many of the same clubs; he was currently enjoying life as a single man after divorcing the previous year. At his suggestion we headed of to the Jacuzzi, leaving our drinks at the bar I followed him to what can only be described as a large whirlpool set into a grotto, glowing red lights illuminated the statues and rock formation. It was fantastically relaxing, it wasn't long until he really turned on the charm, complimenting me on my body in a way only the French and the occasional Italian can get away with without getting a sharp dig in the ribs. He wanted to show me his favourite room in the club, and as he put it pay homage to my "yoni", which in this very eastern and oriental themed club was the perfect word to use. He was tempting me by explaining in detail how he'd worship at my "yoni". I did play hard to get, insisting that I wanted to relax at the bar for a while and take in the atmosphere. By now it was mid afternoon and the club was quite busy, and there appeared to be a steady flow of men and couples wandering off to play in the maze of rooms. I had a little mosey around the corridors stopping to watch a very enthusiastic young lady being treated to a plethora of Friday afternoon cock by her vocally encouraging partner. It was empowering to wander fully naked around the corridors, having the men look at me and often fleetingly touch my body along the way. I adore watching the effect my body has on a man, or even better a group of men when I'm in these kinds of situations. Today was no different, hard cocks were presenting themselves at every turn, making me wet and horny. I was in need of an orgasm, but one where I could relax into it with just myself to please. I scooted back to the bar area to find my new friend the "yoni" master. He didn't need asking twice, he quickly took my hand and escorted me to the room in question. It was at the furthest end of the maze of themed rooms, small and private. It consisted of just large well-cushioned bamboo and wicker seat with leg supports and a padded kneeling stool, similar to what you'd see in a church pew strategically placed in front. I'd noticed he'd brought a small toiletries bag along with him, I was curious as to what was inside.

 As I got myself positioned in the seat he closed the door and slid the bolt across for privacy. The chair was very well designed, with the front edge slightly raised so when you placed your legs into the supports everything was open and fully accessible. He swiftly knelt on the stool whilst admiring my openness and very obvious aroused state. I watched as he produced a small tube of oil from his case, which he explained had been infused with a few rare chilli seeds, I was apprehensive at first but he assured me it was absolutely fine. He then took each of my labia in turn coating them in the concoction before peeling the hood and exposing my engorged clitoris and liberally coating it also. He very briefly massaged it in before drying off his hands with a small towel. My vagina began to tingle and my mind began to race as he produced a large thumb sized lump of fresh ginger root. Then astonishingly from his bag he produced a small vegetable peeler, like you'd find in any kitchen and delicately stripped the stem of its outer skin, just leaving the creamy white flesh. I was massively intrigued and captivated by the moment as he tenderly inserted the root into my anus until it was completely secure and gripped by my sphincter muscle. This was a definite first for me, quite bizarre but intensely erotic. He told me to close my eyes and let the feelings take over me. It was simply a whole new sensation for me, my vagina was now palpitating and my anus was spreading a hot tingling sensation up through my abdomen, it was what can only be described as the most pleasurable sensation, hot, all-consuming pleasure, throbbing intensely in places I'd never felt before. In seconds my entire body started to shudder as an irrepressible surge of orgasm raced through me, instantly triggering an enormous, powerful ejaculation, squirt after squirt of my juices came spewing from me. I'd not felt this kind of sensation before, the ginger root had most definitely triggered this response. I heard him gasp, and as I opened my eyes I saw him knelt on his haunches dripping from head to toe in my female ejaculate, he was totally and utterly drenched, saturated, transfixed watching my vagina and anus spasm unaided by human hand. I closed my eyes as my body relaxed into its post orgasm state and felt him gently remove the ginger root, instantly replacing it with his tongue. I looked down at him, he just instructed me to allow him to perform his own special style of masterful tongue work. His adulation of both my pussy and anus was overwhelming, bringing me to several more vicious climaxes. His worshipful feasting on me was insatiable, he'd have been happy to continue all night. Once I got my body back under control we returned to the bar where he thanked me profusely over a very welcome glass of Champagne.

I noticed that the club was now very busy with lots of comings and goings to the various play areas; it seemed a very popular Friday afternoon haunt for Parisians starting the weekend early and with a bang. I decided to stay for another hour or so, as it turned out I was glad I did.

Sipping on my refreshed glass of bubbly I got talking to a very attractive young man who'd recently arrived with a friend who he worked with, and the friends secretary, who was married but playing as her husband was working until eight, giving her the perfect opportunity to have some illicit playtime. They'd gone off to relax in the steam room together. He introduced himself as Dominic, he was twenty-two and was from Lille, but had been living and working in Paris for the last year as a graphics designer for a popular French magazine. He was nice to talk to, but even better to look at, I instantly made up my mind that I was going to let him fuck me, in fact I took the initiative and suggested much to his pleasure that we continued our little chat in the Jacuzzi. As we made our way to the grotto my "Yoni" devotee gave me a cheeky little wink and a look that said "be gentle with him, he's only young".

    There were a few other people relaxing in the warm bubbling water, and a general feeling of "le weekend" was very apparent, with everyone chatting and enjoying the atmosphere. We sat in the far corner and joined in the general conversation, several of the men complimented me on my ability to switch between French and English without a moments hesitation. Dominic, hesitantly at first brushed my thigh with his fingertips, discreetly, under the water and out of sight, when he realised I hadn't pulled away he let his hand rest on the top of my thigh. I smiled at him out of the corner of my eye encouraging him, as only I knew how, I reached across and in turn placed my hand on his thigh giving it a friendly squeeze. I edged a little closer, and whilst speaking to several of the men I moved my hand across and wrapped my fingers around his submerged erection. It was such a turn on, nobody suspecting a thing; I carried on talking whilst gently and seductively stroking my fingers up and down his powerful young aroused cock, he repaid me in kind and slipped his hand between my open thighs and gave my clitoris a nice under water massage, exploring me with relish and enthusiasm. The whole situation had made me want his young cock inside me as a matter of urgency. It caused a lot of raucous laughter from the other people when I loudly announced in French that I needed "a good fucking, and I needed it now" and proceeded to drag a slightly embarrassed young French guy from the water by his erection, to a few shouts of encouragement we made our way to the first vacant room to continue our fun. This happened to be a small room for two, but with a window where people could look through and enjoy the show, and boy did we put on show! We used our mouths and tongues on each other in a ferocious display of depraved lust, he was massively turned on as a young girl was watching us as things evolved, I must admit I was also putting my all into it, showing that the older ladies still have all the moves and more. The young girl who would have been around Dominic's age vocally expressed her appreciation with a vast variety of encouraging and often explicit remarks. I rode him, he rode me, we enjoyed each other in a melange of positions over the next twenty or so minutes, with the young girl squealing every time he brought me to climax. On occasion various men would appear behind her, but she waved them away, she was purely and simply getting off on watching a young Frenchman servicing an older English lady, who was certainly old enough to be his mother. Eventually the decadent scenario reached its crescendo as he powerfully thrust into me from behind, groaning loudly as he pumped his hot seed deep inside me. We took a few moments before enjoying a relaxing warm shower together. As we headed back to the bar things were really rocking in these play areas, with much giggling and moaning coming from all the rooms. All in all it was a special afternoon in a most wonderful setting, the staff and their enthusiastic hospitality are a joy. I had a coffee at the bar before saying my goodbyes to my new "yoni" master and young Dominic. One very contented and happy lady had a well-deserved cigarette before climbing in a taxi and heading back to the apartment.

My timing was exceptional, as I hadn't been back more than five minutes when I got a text from Anton telling me he'd be delivering Penny's gift shortly. I popped the coffee machine on, as I knew he'd be craving a cup or two before he headed off home. When he arrived and presented me with the finished product, I was to say the least astounded by its detail and accuracy in replicating the real thing. It was exact in every way and the texture of the silicon was breath taking. It would be difficult to tell it from the real thing. I knew Penny would adore it and hopefully she'd get as much pleasure from it as I'd experienced designing and researching it. It was a masterpiece and came beautifully encased in its own embossed padded velvet case, a delightful finishing touch.

I was due to catch the Eurostar the following lunchtime, but had one last thing on my agenda for this evening, a quick visit to see Amanda and Costas, as they'd be upset if they ever found out I'd been in Paris and not dropped by to say hello. After Anton departed happy and clutching a hundred euro note I had a quick ninety-minute power nap, strolled across the road and enjoyed a simple yet tasty steak and chips and a bowl of fresh raspberries and cream. As always delicious and hit all the right taste buds.

I had a hot shower, slathered on some Chanel velvet body cream and wriggled into an body contoured LBD and a suitable pair of heels and called for a taxi. To this day I always get a tingle of magic in my bones as the taxi drives over the "Pont Marie" on its way to deliver me to the door of *"L'Escapade"* (now Le Taken). I often, as I did on this occasion wander the twenty or so metres and lean over the wall having a quick St Moritz whilst enjoying the view over the Seine and the close by Notre Dame Cathedral, it never fails to impress. It is always a postcard perfect scene every single time, watching Paris coming alive at around eleven o'clock in the evening is an awe inspiring sight.

Amanda was her usual bubbly self, however on this occasion more than usual. She had big news, they were going to sell the club and retire. I was shocked, but happy for them. She explained that they'd been approached by a couple called Isa and Alain who'd been running a strictly couples only club called *"No Comment"* near the Champs Elysées and had made them a serious offer, which they had all but accepted, it was now just a matter of ironing out a few minor details. I was pleased for them both as they'd worked non-stop running the club for peoples pleasure for a great many years and they did deserve to step back and enjoy an easier pace life. She assured me that the new owners were a most "Sympatico" couple and would only try to improve on what in my opinion was perfection. Over a glass of Jack on ice I wished them all the best for whatever the future held for them.

Being a Friday night the club was busy with a wide assortment of people letting their down and partying. I on the other hand was absolutely knackered from my afternoon exertions and was quite happy to chat at the bar and soak up some male attention with absolutely no pressure to participate. I chuckled to myself thinking that I must be getting old, reminiscing that when we'd first discovered the club on that fateful night way back in about 1992 I'd have partied until dawn. But hey occasionally it's all about quality not quantity. After a farewell nightcap I climbed into the taxi looking forward to a good long sleep before catching the lunchtime Eurostar back to London.

Chapter Twenty-Five: A Monumental Event

2011 saw an incident that changed the "Swinging" landscape in London and across Britain forever. This event was the scandal involving "The News Of The World" and its unceremonious closure on the 4th of July this year. Below is a quote from Wikipedia.

"The newspaper concentrated on celebrity-based scoops and populist news. Its fondness for sex scandals gained it the nicknames News of the Screws and Screws of the World. It had a reputation for exposing national or local celebrities' drug use, sexual peccadilloes, or criminal acts, setting up insiders and journalists in disguise to provide either video or photographic evidence and phone hacking in on going police investigations".

Prior to this event any activities connected with swinging was always operated under ground and in private, but always with the shadow hanging over them that they'd suddenly find themselves exposed and labelled with all sorts of unsavoury titles. Hence prior to this date there was always an air of paranoia and any kind of "on premise" establishment ran the risk of being hung out to dry by this publication and suffer the wide ranging back lash resulting from such unwarranted press attention. They certainly had a knack in ruining many peoples lives and their personal standing in the community and workplace were destroyed. The underhand and in many cases (as the phone hacking scandal went on to illustrate) illegal practises knew no bounds, they really did sink to new lows in their standard of journalism. They really did pander to the "Angry of Mayfair, Disgusted of Tunbridge wells" brigade. It was both laughable and annoying that they could weald such influence over the lives of the general public. It simply wouldn't have been tolerated in any other European country. I always like to use the following example; if a British government Minister was exposed as attending a swingers club or party he would be hounded out of office in disgrace, whereas his equivalent in France would be applauded and his popularity would rise significantly. That was the difference back pre 2011, attitudes in the U.K are changing, albeit slowly.

Out of the ashes of NOTW came a fresh new acceptance of swinging and all things erotic. It seemed like a big weight had been lifted and resulted in an explosion of clubs across the length and breadth of Britain. Venues and events catering to many fetishes from the vanilla through to the harder BDSM lifestyle flourished over the coming years. Many of which I've sampled and will detail a few of the finer ones shortly. Thankfully private house parties are slightly more relaxed now regarding the security and guest lists. The worry of exposure is now mainly a thing of the past.

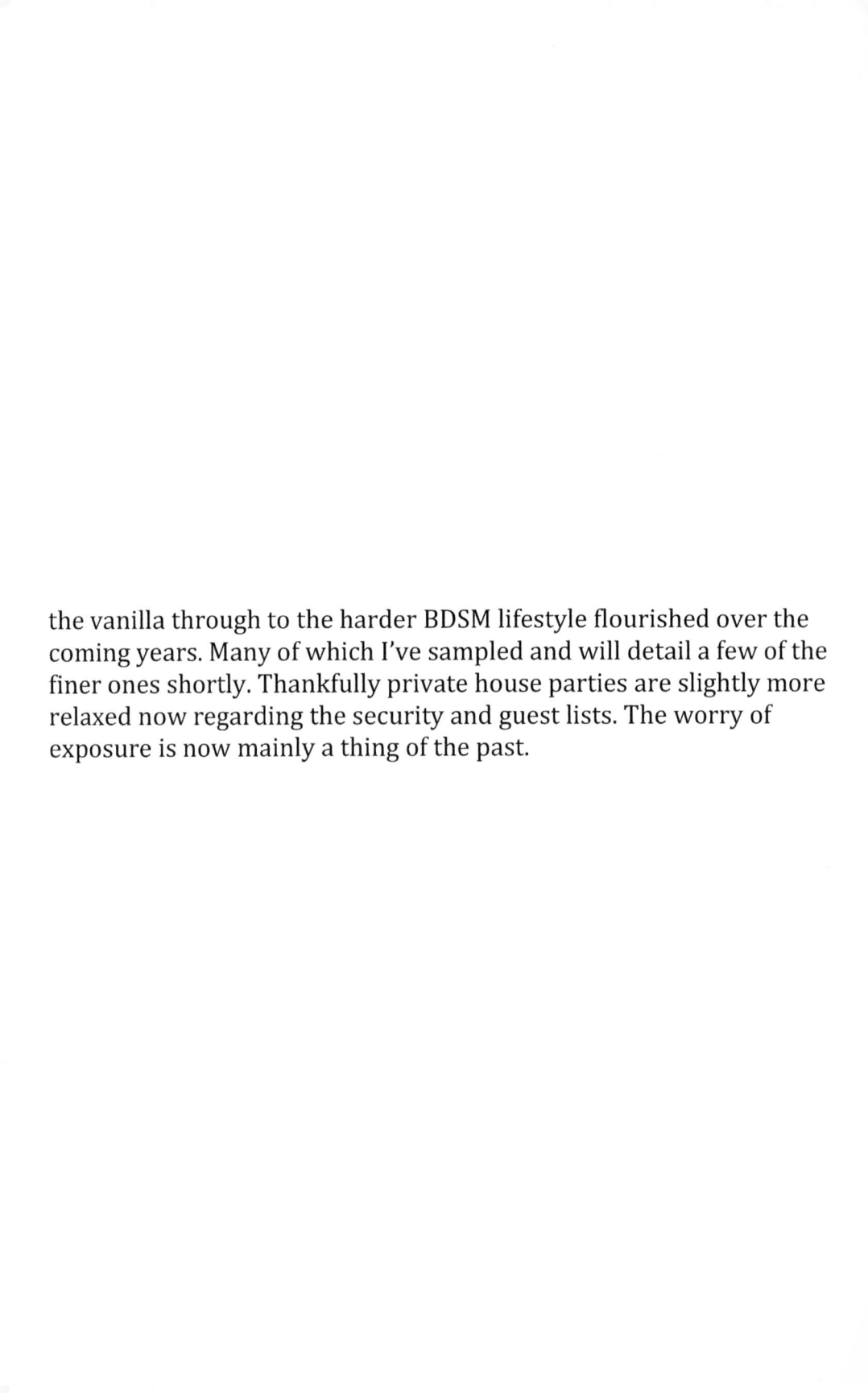

Chapter Twenty-Six: Showboating!

Since Penny's birthday, which was celebrated in fine style with a themed party where she shared the spotlight with her special present, "silicon Rèmi", which all the female guests were intrigued by Many ladies expressed a desire to have one of their own, but when I explained the story behind its inception they looked on open mouthed, and I could sense that many a husband and partner would be getting badgered to arrange a weekend break to Paris. If I'd had a supply of this object of desire I think I could have probably sold a few dozen that night. She'd been on at me to take her back to Paris for another round with France's finest, as she couldn't get the experience out of her head. Even with her new toy, which had been put to good use over the months I understood her need to sample the real thing again. Part of the thrill for her was being abroad; free to play whilst David was at home taking care of business. I completely understood her thought process and agreed to organise some more fun and games for us both. She left the details for me to arrange.

Since the first trip, I'd been back to Amsterdam frequently to play at the *"Paradise Club"* both solo and with Paul. However, the opportunity had never arisen to visit the *"Showboat"*, so this was the perfect opportunity to satisfy Penny's desires and my long standing wish to visit and experience this well established venue.

I had scheduled us a Wednesday morning flight from Heathrow, getting us into Schiphol at lunchtime. No expense spared I booked us in at the "Grand Hotel Krasnapolsky" on Dam Square. I'd got us a good deal on a two bedroomed suite for three nights. The hotel is wonderfully situated for shopping and doing general tourist activities.

All the way there on the plane Penny was over excited, and reminded me of myself in the early days of my solo excursions abroad. Its always amazed me how ones mind can be such a great stimulant, mine always tends to run riot, plotting and scheming in silence.

That first afternoon was manic, shopping, drinking and generally behaving like two wives set loose to enjoy themselves in anonymous surroundings; free to do as they please in their own time frame, no pressure, just pure fun. During the evening we went to one of my favourite Indian restaurants anywhere "Koh-i-Noor", where the food never lets me down. Afterwards, we went to a very bizarre but fun place called *"Sameplace".* It's a very odd concept, it's an erotic bar/café where anything and everything goes. As soon as you enter you can feel the sexual tension in the air, immediately in front of you there is a large U shaped bar, where you can sit, drink and chat with the other customers, just like a normal bar. However, that's where normal ends, as beside the bar there is a dance floor that has two fully functional BDSM bondage poles, complete with full restraints for all conceivable body parts. The stage area, which is curtained off, is fully equipped with slings, chains and all manner of bondage toys. For the braver, more adventurous people there is a downstairs cellar where you will find a glory hole and a darkroom designed for those anonymous moments. There is also a SM area with a full harness sling and a chill out zone with comfortable sofas. We both had a very enjoyable if not slightly unusual couple of hours, watching a very wide range of people, from a girl who arrived for a beer dressed as Charlie Chaplin to an elderly gent who thought it quite normal to be in full leather body harness with all his gentleman parts on show, all topped off with a bowler hat and eye patch. You just couldn't make it up.

Thursday afternoon had become legendary recently at *"Showboat"* judging by recent reviews on an Amsterdam xxx web forum, which was a good site to read recommendations and impartial reviews. So that was my big plan for us for the day. The theme was called "Slutty Girl" which left nothing to the imagination. I'd rang the club a few months before and had a long chat with the manager who explained the best idea would be to turn up in normal day clothes and bring what ever we wanted to wear at the event in a holdall, as there were large showers and changing rooms at the venue. So this is exactly what we did, doing it this way gave us carte blanche to be as daring and outrageous as possible. That's like a red rag to a bull as far as I'm concerned; luckily Penny was cut from similar cloth.

We jumped in a cab outside the hotel and handed the driver the address, he seemed to know it as he smirked handing it back telling us he knew the place well and it was about a twenty minute ride.

As you pull up to the mooring the first thing that struck me was the size of the boat and its beautiful pristine condition. We were shown aboard and immediately made to feel welcome. The manager led us through to the changing area and told us to have fun and give him a shout if we needed anything.

We both stripped off and had a shower in the large wet area, this certainly got the attention of the guys already in there, but they were most polite and respectful. As we sat at the large vanity area putting on some lippy and sorting our hair I couldn't help but notice how busy it was becoming, with several couples excitedly making their way to the showers. A very attractive German lady who spoke good English came and joined us and gave us a quick low down of what the general etiquette was at this event, she'd been attending regularly for over a year and said she'd always had a wonderful few hours fun and met some great people. The afternoon we were there was apparently pretty much the norm, with a diverse cross section of people, lawyers, and doctors mixed easily with builders and truck drivers. It was definitely a case in point where sex is a great leveller.

We didn't bother putting our dresses on, as the German lady said just pop your heels on and wrap the towel around you otherwise you'll feel very over dressed. I must warn you this venue is not for the feint hearted or people of a shy disposition. It is completely "hard core" in every respect. This afternoon caters purely for the ladies that enjoy being at the centre of a large group of rampant men. The women here are treated as queens and their every need catered for in a manner that she dictates. We got acclimatised to the scenario with a few drinks at the bar and had a few nibbles from the very plentiful buffet. It was a very relaxed yet sensual ambience, many men making pleasant conversation with no hidden agendas, purely open and friendly. One very pleasant Dutch guy gave is a whistle stop tour of the various play rooms, which were all getting busy by this stage. The rooms are varied, from large orgy areas to glory holes and grope boxes that Penny fully enjoyed. Also, they have a wonderfully equipped SM fetish play room, with cage, slings, swings, leather restraint benches, its pretty much a fetishist's paradise. Penny was game for trying everything so I shadowed her for a while, but once she found her feet and locked herself in the grope box I knew she'd be fine. I wandered back to the bar to the squeals of delight as several men began to fondle her through the many holes around the box.

I was in my element; there were men in various states of arousal everywhere, and ladies being pleasured in every nook and cranny of this floating palace of debauchery. I got myself a drink and went and sat in one of the large sumptuous corner sofa chairs, almost instantly a man who I'd chatted to earlier knelt in front of me begging me to allow him the pleasure of servicing me with his tongue whilst I enjoyed my drink. I more than gladly accepted his kind offer and opened myself up for him, he swiftly got to work on me, and was very skilled, paying attention to all the right areas, as he was enjoying himself two gents came and sat either side of me, both naked and both already fully erect. The elder of the two offered me a cigarette, which I gratefully accepted, it was a most decadent but empowering feeling having a conversation with two men whilst a third ate my pussy. Whilst I relaxed into the flow I became very aroused as the younger guy began issuing instructions to my tongue specialist, urging him to probe me deeper in both anus and vagina, he was getting very animated. I became increasingly more turned on the more he licked and sucked on me. The two guys urging me on and on until I began to boil over and delivered an almighty stream of ejaculate into this anonymous mans grateful mouth, he made a great spectacle of swallowing all my juices. He didn't falter, and continued to devour my pussy, urging me to give him more to drink, I was absolutely into the moment, watching the guys either side stroking their erections in appreciation of the spectacle and my gushing prowess. I played my part by repeatedly squirting into his mouth and at one stage the younger guy crouched forward slightly and unleashed a stream of own cum into the mans mouth, he was almost drowning in my juice and this guys semen. It was a fantastic sight, by this stage there were several other men gathered around to witness the unfolding decadence. I was totally absorbed by the situation; all I could see was a sea of hard cock, all varying shapes and sizes, all fighting to be noticed. After a few minutes the elder gent suggested we take the action to a more suitable room, I nodded my agreement and he led me to an Egyptian themed room with a large central bed, we were obviously followed by the large group of expectant men, once in the room he took total control, instructing the pussy mechanic to lay on the bed and for me to sit on his face. His tongue instantly found its way into my anus, causing me to squirt over his chin, many of the men were stood around me on the bed feeding me their erections, which at this stage I was devouring with relish, often two at a time. It had turned into a complete sperm extravaganza, with cock after cock ejaculating over my face, breasts and chest of the gent, who was still busily gorging himself on my rectum. There was semen flying everywhere, as soon as they came their places were rapidly taken by more throbbing erections. It was a frenzied twenty minutes with my pussy seemingly having a mind of its own and in an almost permanent state of ejaculation. I was overwhelmed by a greedy lust and accepted all that was thrown at me, eventually the feverish activity subsided leaving me and the most grateful tongue man drenched from head to toe in a potent mixture of sticky cum and my sweet juices. As we made our way to the large wet room to shower I caught Penny wandering back to the bar with three men in tow, she looked aghast and said "what the fuck happened to you!", I said "you really had to be there", she chuckled and I went and showered myself into a more presentable state. It was one of those innocent moments that suddenly turned into an unforgettable scene, one that will always be etched on my mind. Filthy but so much fun. Needless to say there were quite a few drinks waiting at the bar upon my return from various grateful and impressed gentlemen.

We stayed until around seven when most of the afternoon crowd started to leave and be replaced by the after office crowd, who in turn would be replaced by the night time party crowd. The manager rang for a taxi and we were deposited back at the hotel in double quick time.

We decided to throw on some casual clothes and go in search of a quiet restaurant where we could unwind and indulge in some girlie chat, and compare notes from our afternoon of smut. We didn't want anywhere stuffy or fine dining, simply tasty food in a pleasant laid back atmosphere. If in doubt just ask the doorman is always my best tip, it worked a treat, he'd pointed us in the direction of an Argentinian steak house called "L'Estancia", about a ten minute stroll from the square. We both ordered a large sirloin steak and side salad accompanied by a bottle of house red wine. Absolutely delicious and certainly refuelled us. Over the meal Penny said she'd had a great afternoon and really had enjoyed some decadent fun, but it really hadn't come near the highs of our trip to Paris years earlier, admittedly I'd initiated her pretty near the top of the erotic tree as far as clubs and elegance goes. She wanted more than just play, she wanted to be used, fucked hard like her time with *"Les Pompiers"* of good old Paris. The following day, Friday was our last evening and with her requirements in mind there was no other place to take her, *"Club Paradise"*. Friday nights are "Night of the Bull", where gentlemen who are hung like the proverbial are welcomed warmly by single ladies and wives who are size aficionados. Once fed and back at the hotel cocktail bar that overlooks the hustle and bustle of the square with a large Jack on ice in our hands I told her my plan for the final evening. That set her off, tomorrow daytime we had to shop for party shoes, from past experience this was all that was required (at this juncture I'd revisited the club on several occasions).

After a most welcomed lazy morning we had a bite to eat at a small café over looking a canal before eventually finding our destination. *"Webers"* is a unique sexy avant-garde fashion shop situated centrally at Kloveniersburgwal 26, it's a must visit if you are looking for something different and sexy. All their products are locally made in Amsterdam in limited editions and single pieces. They stock a very eclectic collection sexy platform stiletto high heels boots and shoes at very reasonable prices, perfect for a club like *"Paradise"* where you may end up in the shower or steam room still wearing your shoes for effect. We both bought a pair of Perspex "Adore" slip on platform heels; Penny opted for the clear effect whilst I chose the black stardust effect ones. It is well worth a visit, you'll always find a much classier range of sexy club wear than in the run of the mill sex shops.

We had dinner in a very good Chinese restaurant close to the hotel called "Mandarijn", again it was by recommendation by the hotel doorman who told us that it had a great reputation and is known for its Szechuan and Cantonese cuisine. We stuffed ourselves on Peking duck, pancakes, spring rolls accompanied by a variety of side dishes and dips. I highly recommend it.

Back at the hotel we showered and got our faces on for the evening of licentious fun ahead. We dressed in our normal clothes, just popping our new shoes in a bag to take with us. All very easy, but I did miss the fun of deciding what dress to wear and all the preparation that goes into a night in Paris; for me personally that is an event in itself.

By complete coincidence we jumped in to the first taxi outside the hotel to be confronted by our driver from the previous day. We had a good laugh, but what he must have thought of us, two complete nymphomaniacs on the loose in Amsterdam whilst their husbands were having a pie and a pint in the U.K.

As always a warm welcome awaited us at the club, we arrived around ten-thirty and looked forward to partying, the club closes at three in the morning on these Friday night extravaganzas, so plenty of opportunity to play. I led Penny to the large communal changing area where we secured out clothes and wrapped our towels around ourselves before climbing into our new heels and adding many inches to our legs. Whilst getting ready there were several very well endowed men also dressing down for the evening, as we left heading towards the main bar area Penny said "this is more like it, much more like it!" both grinning we ordered a glass of Champagne to begin our festivities. The atmosphere was already at a very intense level and the place was busy, but not oppressively so, at a rough guestimate there were fifteen couples, five or so single ladies and around eighty men. One of the single ladies made a beeline for us and struck up conversation, she was an American divorcee who was visiting Europe for six weeks, travelling around with no firm agenda. She'd read about this club on one of the forums and unbeknown to me recently the club had begun to put on a bit of entertainment for the ladies in the form of a group of six erotic male dancers. The look on Penny's face was one of "I've just won the lottery". She was called Catherine, but preferred Kate and was forty-seven and had just come out of a loveless marriage and was making up for lost time. She was riveted by our personal back-stories, and made me promise to email her with details of Paris, as she'd be going to visit there at some stage during her trip. She howled with laughter when I told her to be "careful what you wish for". She looked after our seats and drinks whilst I took Penny on a quick guided tour of the club and its extensive facilities, dodging many striking looking men along the way. She was most impressed and now felt confident that she could firmly relieve me of my chaperoning duties, which was a big relief to me as I was definitely in one of my own serious filthy play moods.

    As we got back to the bar two gents who were chatting to our new American friend Kate gave us our seats back and introduced themselves. No sooner had we sat than the DJ put on a very up tempo dance track and six bronzed men appeared on the stage, all resplendent in Navy Uniforms, a bit predictable but very effective as they launched into their routine. The ladies present were transfixed as they teasingly removed their outfits in a most provocative manner (think Chippendales with a massive amount of xxx). It was raucous and really got the captive audience whipped into a frenzy, one or two of the wives were enthusiastically squirting baby oil over the dancers chests, but the vast majority was aimed directly over their large endowments, encouraged vocally by their husbands, soon there was a mass of female hands stroking and teasing the oiled cocks to full erection. It was a sight to behold when one woman couldn't contain herself and forcibly dragged one away by his erection, immediately impaling herself on it whilst her partner held her drink and looked on mesmerised. The atmosphere was electric; this was a great addition to the evening. Penny was like a greyhound in a trap, she was itching to get amongst the action. These dancers raised the level of sexual anticipation in the air to a crescendo. I was pleased to see that after their routine they showered and came to the bar in towels ready to party. I thought they would probably be whisked away for another booking, so we were most delighted to know they were here for the long haul. The three of us sat at the bar presenting an easy target for them and we were soon engaged in some flirtatious banter with a few of them, along with several other gents who were already here to play. Penny was soon led astray by a few men and quickly disappeared to one of the playrooms.

    I ordered a Jack on ice, a glass of bubbly for Kate and continued overtly flirting with all the various men that were stood around us. I provocatively let my towel fall exposing my breasts, gaining many complimentary comments as my nipples visibly hardened, after a bit of playful goading Kate followed suit. I told her I was going to the steam room as I felt sure I'd be followed, she asked if she could join me as she said she'd feel more comfortable, I assumed it was all a bit new to her and a safety in numbers scenario would allow her to express herself fully with no anxiety.

    I had another sip of JD whilst she gulped a large mouthful of bubbly, then taking her by the hand we flirtatiously excused ourselves saying we were going to the steam room. I have always loved the feeling of being desired by a group of men and this was accentuated on this occasion, as there were two of us the number of men trailing us increased substantially. We hung our towels on the pegs outside and gingerly wandered in, and to my amazement it was empty, we found our way to the marble seating at the far end, and I whispered to her "watch this", literally for the next few minutes the door of the room resembled a barn door in a gale as man after man entered. I sensed her shiver slightly and utter a little squeak of delight. As our eyes adjusted to the steam enhanced dim lighting we could make out numerous men homing in on us, erections fully at the ready. Things began to happen in double quick time as hands began to touch our bodies and we both made a few encouraging noises to encourage the men. I knew from prior experience and warned Kate that we'd only last in here for ten or fifteen minutes until the heat overtook you and a cool shower was needed. We both willingly spread our legs allowing many anonymous hands to tweak, probe and play with us whilst we stroked each and every erection that came within our reach. It was a brief but enjoyable anonymous fumble fest, with both Kate and myself enjoying several orgasms along the way before succumbing to the heat.

    We showered and applied some lippy and returned to the bar for a debrief, I sensed that Kate was following my lead, but I just wanted to know that she was fully at ease with the situation. I needn't have worried as she told me she wanted and needed to be fucked, before I even had the chance to ask. I hatched a little plan and ran it by her and she was in total agreement. Over the next few minutes we selected our prey, and once we'd whittled it down a bit we invited eight of the horniest looking guys to join us upstairs in the orgy room. Towels draped over our shoulders we had the old pied piper experience as eight perfectly formed and impressively hung specimens followed along behind us. On the way up I told her initially to do what I did and that she'd soon be overtaken by the moment and it would all then follow on instinctively. Once everyone was in place I lay back on the huge bed legs apart inviting the men to come and eat my pussy and gave them a strict minute each. Kate followed suit and was totally overwhelmed as the first tongue touched her vagina, she emitted a soft scream of pleasure and came instantly. The men all waited their turns stroking themselves, lots of goading words of encouragement from all concerned. I pulled her up from the bed and told her to kneel with me back to back and indulge in a period of anonymous cock worship. She was now fully acting on instinct as we both took cock after cock in our mouths, seductively sucking them fevrishly; I was doubly aroused as Kate really was slurping vociferously on every erection presented to her. Out of the corner of my eye I noticed two of the male dancers intently watching me and talking intently to each other. I caught the eye of one of them who winked at me and gave me the most alluring smile. A few moments later another couple arrived with a single lady in tow and quickly joined the fun. Just as Kate was being lifted on to the bed and being prepared for fucking one of the dancers approached me and whispered in my ear to meet him and his friend by the changing room area as soon as I could get away from this scrum. I was tempted, in fact there was no way I was going to let this opportunity go wanting and checked if Kate was going to be fine if I left. She was very busy but said she'd meet up back at the bar at some stage and to go and destroy the guys, music to my ears.

    I grabbed my towel and made my way excitedly down stairs to the changing area. Standing there chatting casually was my prize for the next part of the evening. I had a feeling this was going to be something special as they took me by the hand and led me through the changing area to a secluded private room that I never knew existed. No sooner were we inside than these two guys set about me in a most dominating fashion, they took control from the outset in a most erotic and intriguing manner. The only piece of furniture in the room was a large red velvet sofa situated along the far wall, however central to the room hanging from the ceiling was a beautiful leather sex swing, complete with a set of leather stirrups, a large leather pillow, and the customary D-rings. My pussy really started to tingle and throb with anticipation. I could feel my entire body quivering with delight as they lifted me on to the swing, once comfortably positioned they cuffed my wrists to the top chains and put my legs through the raised stirrups. Once restrained and completely helpless they walked around me talking to one another as if I wasn't there, deciding what they were going to do to me, it was intense watching them as they continually moved around me, erections visibly throbbing and glistening in the dimly glowing violet light. Every so often one would tweak and twist my nipples as the other stretched and extended my swollen labia with his strong fingers; my juices were dripping from me soaking my anus and dripping from my thighs. This continued for several minutes, the more they teased the wetter I got, until one went to a small chest in the corner and produced a variety of toys. They discussed amongst themselves as to which they would use on me, my insides were on fire, and my whole body shook with pre orgasm delight. They looked on in awe as purely with mind and body control I unleashed an immense vaginal squirt accompanied by a guttural scream of pleasure. It was then that they inserted (I later found out what it was called and have since bought several from the company "Lelo") a remote controlled vibrating bullet into my receptive anus. They went and sat on the sofa, both stroking their cocks whilst watching me squirm with intense pleasure as they remotely increased and decreased its vibrations. It was mind blowing; the only way it could get better was if I had a hit of amyl. I mentioned it and to my surprise there was a wide selection in the pleasure chest, I left the choice to them, just thrilled to have another of my favoured items join the fun. The bullet was throbbing on a nice slow intensity deep in my rectum as they held the vial under each nostril in turn for me to sniff. Seconds later a tidal flood of ejaculate erupted from me, large arcing streams pulsed everywhere, as I began to scream, I was quickly silenced as two large cocks were forced into my mouth, I was in amyl heaven, right on the crest of an orgasmic plateau. They had me restrained, in all sorts of trouble and begging for more. We all took great pleasure as they cock slapped my face in between gagging me on their hard pulsating meat. I'm sure my eyeballs rolled up into my skull as the more vocal of the two men began to slap my clitoris for a while before his accomplice spread my labia, holding me open for his friend to fuck. All three of us were in the zone, they let me have a constant supply of amyl as they took turns in pounding my soaking vagina, and pound they did, relentless hard fucking, drilling into me ferociously. Using me as their very own personal fuck toy, I wasn't complaining, I was positively encouraging them in the sluttiest tone possible. The feeling of the bullet in my anus, together with the large erection embedded deep in my pussy and a large cock to slurp on was definitely a divine feeling. We built to a crescendo, all three of us with one goal in mind and it was rapidly approaching, eventually the heady atmosphere overtook us as we succumbed to that awesome moment, that exquisite point of no return. It got very wet and messy rapidly; I came powerfully as I watched these two cocks as they began to twitch and jerk in unison, spraying torrential streams of hot thick sperm over me, totally drenching me, glowing on my torso in brilliant white streams under the ultra violet lighting. I came down slowly letting the last of my fluids flow freely from me, allowing my body to reenergise slightly before they freed me from the various leather restraints and gently lifted me down onto my shaky legs. These two had certainly put me through my paces, showing me no mercy whatsoever, relentless power fucking at its finest. Thankfully, a large well-earned Jack Daniels was waiting for me at the bar as I returned from the shower. Penny was sat smiling like the cat that had got her cream, which after what she later told me she'd gotten up to she most certainly had. Kate staggered back a while later looking equally pleased with herself. Three very happy and well-used ladies exchanged snippets of their shenanigans as they relaxed over a drink.

Chapter Twenty-Seven: The Rise & Rise Of Social Media

The relentless rise of the Internet was one of the key factors in the unyielding growth of Swinging across Great Britain. As with everything, once the British came on board they did so with huge enthusiasm and relish.

As often with the French they are pioneers when it comes to all things erotic. Even back before the Internet our cousins across the channel were leading the way. When Paul and I first ventured to Paris back in the early nineties they had their own telecom system in place, which was called "Minitel", a large proportion of people had it in their homes, especially Parisians, it was like an advanced "Ceefax". It was linked up to the telephone system and you rented the equipment from France Telecom; it consisted of a small monitor and keyboard. It had many individual sections, I can only describe it as an interactive "Yellow Pages", and yes you've guessed it, that by far and away biggest subscribed section was the "Adult xxx", which was broken down into many individual sub-sections, such as "women seeking men – Couples seeking couples" etcetera. This enabled like-minded individuals to instantly connect with others, it was a huge success, and in fact in the early days Paul and I met many couples who themselves had hooked up via this system. It was like a very primitive version of on line dating sites such as "Grindr – Tinder – Plenty of Fish etc", nowadays the list and niches that these sites cater to are endless.

Back in the early days of our personal foray into swinging all we had to guide us was a little handbook that was published once a year by the legendary Tuppy Owens called "The Sex Maniacs Diary". It was that little diary, coupled with word of mouth and a huge chunk of good fortune that enabled us to indulge in the delights. Today everything is accessible to all at just the touch of a button. The big problem now is that its very tempting to over indulge. Probably no such thing when you're in your twenties and thirties, but as you get older you do need to be more selective, and pace yourself somewhat.

One of the first things I did after publishing "First Tango In Paris" was to set up a "Twitter" account to promote the book, and the interaction I've had with readers and other self-published authors is hugely satisfying. I find it a great way to keep abreast of current trends and obviously it opens so many other mesmerising doors to the swinging lifestyle, whether it be people wishing to meet others or clubs promoting events its all freely searchable. In many ways I'm envious of todays Swingers, but I also think that the pioneering spirit we had back then added to the whole sensuality and mystique of such occasions. There is something to be said for "Seek and ye shall find" as todays "Search and ye shall find" is sometimes a bit too clinical and can take the edge off the all important anticipation aspect of things.

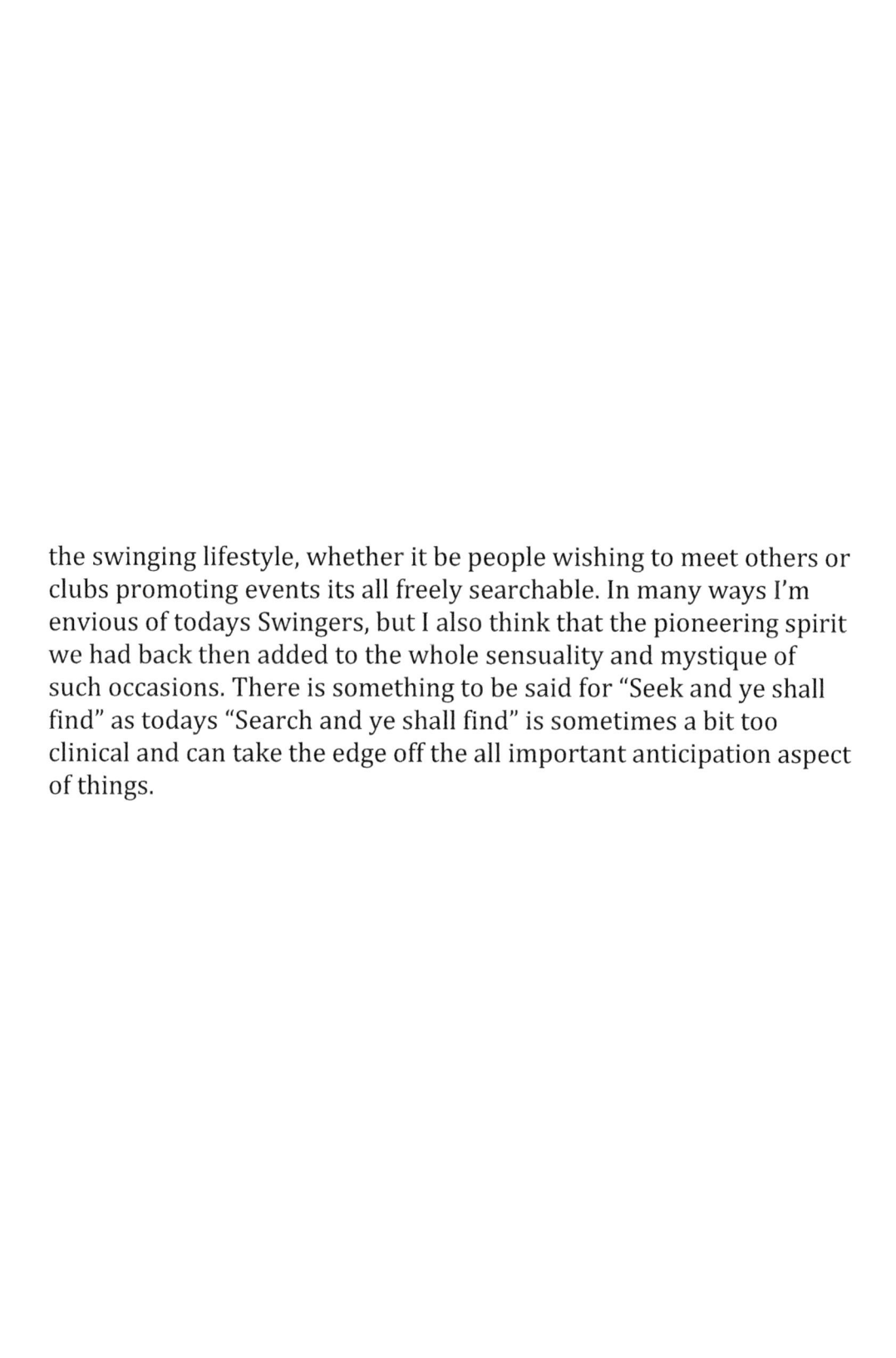

Chapter Twenty-Eight: Post NOTW

Things really opened up with the demise of "The News of The World", there was a definite shift in peoples perceptions of recreational sex, in particular swinging. The stigma that the NOTW portrayed that all Swingers were perverts and wore raincoats was finally beginning to be dispelled. Various groups and individuals grasped the opportunity to host parties on an elegant, sophisticated yet debauched level and openly advertised them; quietly confident they wouldn't be splashed across the tabloids in lurid detail.

One such group is *"Fever Parties"* who began hosting house parties similar to David and Penny around 2009, but have since gone on to host very successful and upmarket club nights at select venues across London, sometimes further afield. They cater most definitely for the under forties crowd and they do have a very competitive and strict vetting process. I did attend several parties, which were very well represented by a wide cross section of London's "beautiful" people. They have a most informative web site that will certainly steer you in the right direction.

Another group worth mentioning is *"Killing Kittens"*, since their inception in 2005 they have grown from a small, intimate group to an international online community of almost 40,000 members, including a high percentage of single females. My namesake Emma Sayles, whose battle cry is "Girls, we make the rules and we can break the rules", founded it and it has remained on top of its game throughout the years. Again they have a most informative web site.

They also host parties for the more mature group of swingers, which has really exploded recently due in part to the increased acceptance to this kind of entertainment, plus the availability of Viagra! They label the events *"Silver Kittens"* where you'll meet a cross section of society aged 45 and above, all letting themselves enjoy their new found freedom. I appreciate it does sound a bit ageist but it seems to work, judging by the attendance of these events.

Over recent years many "On Premise" clubs have sprung up to such a degree that every major town and city has at least one purpose built club to cater to the ever-increasing demand. I will list some of the ones that in my opinion are the best at the end of the book. However, I must make particular mention of one that is dear to my heart, and local to me in this section of the book. *"Kestrel Hydro"* is a haven for naturists and swingers alike. Located near to Heathrow airport, it is a very relaxed, fun adult spa. It's a wonderful no pressure environment where you can either simply chill out and get the full benefits and pleasures of the sauna, heated swimming pool, and both the indoor and an outdoor Jacuzzis or take things further. When weather permits there's a great sunbathing area, wonderful for showing and teasing. There are several playrooms and a really fun outdoor log cabin where you can play as a couple or group. It's mixed so there's always a selection of single men to play with if that's what you're looking for, all the men were most respectful towards the single ladies the times I've attended, both accompanied and as a single female.

The first time I went was several years ago, and it was on the spur of the moment. It sticks in the memory because of the circumstances and the visit itself. It was a Friday morning and I'd just arrived back from Southern Spain a few days previously, Paul was in Germany until the Saturday afternoon. I was in one of the video chat rooms at the previously mentioned FAB Swingers website, just generally flitting around and chatting to various people I'd met on line when a private message popped up from a guy called Nick, who told me he'd just seen my profile, told me that he was local to me and would I care to chat for a while. I quickly looked at his profile and he looked most appealing in his photos, also he had several glowing verifications from other members, many of whom he'd met up with. All in all he seemed a decent kind of person, so we chatted for a while and as these things go the conversation got raunchier (well it is a swinging site), after a while once we'd both switched our web cams on to confirm we both were actually who we said we were, we exchanged Skype details and decided to talk one to one. Having explained that I'd just returned from the sun and my skin needed some serious moisturising he suggested a massage was in order, and why as we were both only fifteen minutes from each other and ten minutes from *"Kestrel Hydro"* didn't we meet for a drink and go and try out the facilities. I think he was a bit surprised when I readily agreed, and we soon decided that we'd meet at one o'clock at the "Swan Inn" in Stanwell, which was only a short drive from the spa.

As arranged Nick was waiting inside this typical old English pub with my chosen tipple ready and waiting. We connected instantly and the conversation flowed freely and thankfully with no awkward silences whatsoever. At thirty he was considerably younger than me, which thankfully turned us both on as we flirted over our drinks. Eventually we dragged ourselves away from the pub, and I followed his Range Rover to the large parking area behind the spa. It was a pleasant sunny day and the pool and sun deck area was already busy with people enjoying an early start to the weekend. The pleasant staff gave us a quick tour and left us at the changing room ready to get better acquainted in what was a really chilled out atmosphere.

    We both undressed, snatching little glances at each other, laughing when we caught each other doing so. We immediately showered and went outside to the pool area, where we swiftly climbed in the hot tub where we chatted with two other guys who were regulars and they explained things in more detail. After a while and before turning into a prune I went and got two sun loungers. Nick went back to the lockers to get the massage oil he'd brought with him especially for our meet. I lay on my front as requested and told him to drench me in the oil, as my skin was so dehydrated from the strong Spanish sun, I knew it would be absorbed rapidly. His hands were firm and authoritative as they oiled from the soles of my feet to the nape of my neck, blissful and erotic, it wasn't long until my juices began to flow. His fingers worked all the right areas with finesse and super sensuality, often running an oiled finger from the top of my inner thigh slowly lingering on my labia and the occasional fleeting feather like strokes over my anus. It was heavenly, sun on my back whilst being lubricated by a most skilled and attentive young man. I could see out of the corner of my eye a few other men and a couple discreetly watching proceedings from their sunbeds, which just enhanced the intensity of the situation. The couple thankfully soon started getting frisky, relieving me from being the sole focus of attention. As he flipped me over to work on my front I couldn't help but notice he was attached to a rather impressive looking erection, this reaction never fails to please me and raise my core temperature up a notch or two in readiness for some impending physical pleasure. Decadently I took the opportunity to light a St Moritz whilst his nimble fingers stroked, tweaked, and generally manipulated my body, which I'd pretty much surrendered fully to him from his initial touch. Every now and then he vocally expressed his desire and how much he was going to enjoy pleasuring me in any way I craved. His occasional murmurings got more and more explicit with every little twitch of my body. He'd brought me to such a high state of arousal that I knew just the tiniest bit of encouragement from my over active imagination would quickly bring on a series of my mini orgasms.

After prolonging the body oiling and pampering to a point where we both needed to take it up a notch or two, I reached towards him and firmly wrapped my fingers around his solid young erection, and suggested we go and get more comfortable in the nearest log cabin. Leading him around the pool toward the wooden dolls house like outdoor cabin by his erection was a hoot, causing a few shouts of encouragement from a couple of nearby guys. His cock was dancing in my hand with excitement as we entered; I immediately pushed him down on to the soft beanbag and began to use my tongue on him. His sac was large and heavy, it tasted so good as I gently sucked and nibbled on each of his testes in turn. Delicately raking my nails up and down his entire length. After a while I sensed the two guys from the sun beds watching avidly through the window, this turned me on even more, and I played up to them by pushing my bottom up and spreading my thighs, ensuring my vagina gaped wide for them to admire. I turned slightly toward them so they could also enjoy an uninterrupted view of me with my drool covered mouth stuffed full of young hard cock. To make things even lewder I reached under and slid two fingers up into myself, promptly bringing on the first of many gushes I attained over the next hour or two. There really is a distinct decadent feeling when you are being watched, whether it be openly or discreetly. I was sorely tempted to invite them inside to join the fun, but was too into the moment with young Nick. I gave him an impish grin as I mounted him, my well trained pussy lips wrapping themselves snuggly around the tip of his cock, taking only an inch or two inside me at a time, ensuring the voyeurs had a good view of me being penetrated by this solid piece of meat. I tensed my thigh muscles as I began the sensual cock milking that I have trained my vagina to achieve over the years. Shortly the exhibitionist in him came to the fore as he flipped me over onto all fours and began to drive his cock into me with ever creasing formidable thrusts, powerful and dominating my willing pussy. The men at the window were transfixed, and I played up to them by keeping full eye contact with them both. It definitely was turning into an afternoon of unexpected pleasure; I went into full wet mode when he withdrew from me leaving my gaping vagina on full show as he came around and gathered up my hair, twisting it around his hand until he held my head firmly to one side, he told me to beg for it as he slapped my face with his hard cock; once satisfied he had me under his full control he began to use my mouth solely for his pleasure, making me keep him deep in my throat as he counted up to thirty before pulling out, he repeatedly made me gag on him, saliva and spittle dripping from both his cock and my chin, much to the delight of the watchers. I loved every moment, all the while urging him, and begging him to keep feeding me his rock like cock. Time after time he brought himself to the edge of his own climax, then holding perfectly still as his glistening penis danced just millimetres from my lips. After many rounds of this self pleasure he began the tell tale thigh muscle tensing, slightly bending at the knee he plunged himself back into my enthusiastic mouth, as he did so I quickly reached under and worked my forefinger deep into his tight anus. This prompted an almost instantaneous effect, as I felt him begin to throb with a much increased intensity, the end of his cock seemed to double in size as he started to violently flood my throat and mouth with his hot sweet cum, my cheeks bulged as I tried in vain to swallow it all, it just kept pumping from him in big thick jets. I must have looked a sight as his milk ran from the sides of my mouth, my eyes were watering intensely, it seemed like forever but it did eventually subside, he was dripping in sweat and I leant back on my haunches with my face contorted in the sheer ecstasy of the moment, cum running of my happy face. We both collapsed into the beanbag for a while, both spent and totally exhausted, trying to regain some energy and a little bit of decorum. The two gents at the window silently applauded their appreciation of the exhibition, all very decadent, but also most civilised behaviour in my humble and smutty opinion. By the time we headed off to the large shower area I noticed several more people had turned up and there was a lot of playing occurring in the hot tub and on the various sun loungers. It really is a top place to while away a few hours in the company of like- minded people. You can simply turn up, and there is no pressure to participate, you can just do your own thing. On the occasions I've attended the people have always been extremely friendly and courteous, which in my opinion goes a long way in making a club successful. I've met a wide variety of people here and played with many, on one visit a really memorable time was had with a lovely blonde lady who had fabulous nipple and pussy piercings, she was a fellow devotee of the squirting pussy and we had a great wet session as her elder husband looked on with several other males. One of the naughtiest ladies around, if you're reading this you know who you are!! See you in the local Ascot/Sunningdale Waitrose sometime.

    This kind of venue seems to be very popular now and several similar types of facility have opened across the U.K, some have been running for may years under the guise of a naturist club; such as Eureka's in Kent, which now welcomes Swingers with open arms, and in fact host a wide variety of themed events, such as "Cougars and Cubs" nights, which is where the more mature lady is encouraged to hunt for a younger male or two for her evenings pleasure or bring one along to share, also their regular hosting of the Black Mans Fan Club events, which is pretty self explanatory. In fact our good friends Mike and Sarah have attended several of these evenings, where Sarah indulges her desire for all things "big and black". The club has certainly embraced the thriving swinging lifestyle that has swept across the U.K in recent years and shows no signs of abatting. Plus by all accounts their facilities are first class and spotlessly clean. I most definitely will pay a visit once this book is finished and I get a few moments to myself. I certainly like the thought of relaxing naked for an afternoon in early June, indulging in a bit of exhibitionistic play, anyone want to join me? Below is a bit of blurb from their website.

"Eureka is a private members club for naturists and is open from 10am, 364 days of the year, with 23 acres of grounds, onsite parking for 75 cars, onsite accommodation, large dance floor, seating for 180 people, 60ft x30ft outdoor heated swimming pool (during the summer), and also a wet area in use at all times that features two 8 person Jacuzzis, sauna and steam room. All this in addition to the rest areas, huge sunbathing fields and walkways through the wooded area.

Located in Kent, the 'Garden Of England', Eureka certainly lives up to this reputation with its 23 acres of beautiful landscaped lawns, fields and woodlands where you can relax and laze around the tranquil grounds. Or take a stroll through the peaceful woodlands,you'll never know who you may bump into".

So, to sum up this chapter, the demise of "The News Of The World" has seen a general loosening of attitudes in regard to anything sexual and erotic, allowing the general British public to enjoy themselves (and each other) in a more relaxed and liberal society. In my opinion this can only be a good thing. I always think that if you work hard you should be allowed to play hard without fear of any repercussions!

Chapter Twenty-Nine: The Accidental Exhibitionist

As you are well aware, especially if you read "First Tango 1" I love exhibitionistic behaviour, and do indulge as frequently as the situation allows. This next chapter is one that I regret not featuring in the first book; however, I think you'll agree its one worth including here. It happened quite a number of years ago when the children were small, it was around the time Paul and I were first discovering Paris and its delights.

It occurred in Portugal, Paul was employed at the time by the U.K arm of a major American record company and as part of that years incentive scheme was a week of luxury at the "Four Seasons Fairways" at Quinta do Lago in the heart of the Algarve. I would have been in my late twenties at the time and we'd reserved a week late May when Pauls parents were able to have the children, something they always loved doing.

We flew in on a Friday to Faro airport where a taxi was waiting to take us the short distance to the resort. I remember it well as it was so plush and exclusive you had to be checked in at a security gate where someone would come in a golf buggy to vet you and take you to the reception area.

The grounds were beautifully landscaped and sub tropical plants were in abundance, giving it a very private secluded ambience. We were showed to a stunning spacious luxury three bedroomed villa/apartment, complete with its own small swimming pool, perfect if you wanted to relax away from the main clubhouse and busy pool area. They were built in private blocks of four, one set back above and two adjacent. All surrounded with exotic plants and bushes, giving you the feeling of total seclusion.

We didn't venture from the resort for the first few days, just relaxing by the pool and playing a bit of tennis. During the second day Paul got chatting to a couple of other Brits who were there on a golfing break, and they invited him to join them the following day for a knock around. Paul wasn't a keen golfer but agreed and soon sorted out the club hire and shoes. He met them at the clubhouse at midday as arranged, leaving me to sunbathe at the villa. Being pretty secluded I plonked myself down with a nice glass of wine on one of our pool loungers, naked as I don't like to have any tan lines. I recall I had a clunky Sony Discman back then and was listening to the Lighthouse Family on a loop. I lay out chilling and occasionally applying sun cream over the next few hours until Paul returned. He had enjoyed the afternoon and asked if I minded if he joined them again the next day. I didn't have a problem with it as I'd enjoyed the solitude and the warm May sun on my body.

We showered and went for dinner at the gorgous poolside restaurant, and after a meal of local seafood we retired to the bar for a few nightcaps. His two golfing partners were sitting over in the far corner and he sauntered over to arrange the following days tee time. As he did a very distinguished looking guy who was in his mid to late fifties, elegantly attired in pristine white polo and navy blazer appeared at the bar to order drinks for his table. I was completely taken aback when he casually enquired if I'd enjoyed my afternoon sunbathing; he winked at me and told me he was staying in the upper apartment adjacent to ours. He told me not to worry as my secret nakedness was safe with him, and anyway he said he'd very much enjoyed what he saw. The whole encounter lasted no more than a minute, but it left me incredibly turned on, so much so I literally ripped Pauls clothes off before we even got through the villa door.

My mind raced overnight, the very thought that this elder gentleman had been watching me sunbathing naked as I remained totally unaware made me incredibly wet and horny. I woke up excited, went for breakfast excited, well excited really doesn't cover it, I was buzzing internally. I couldn't wait until Paul went for his game of golf and I could indulge myself a little.

Eventually he left, dragging his clubs behind him. I went to the pool and made a bit of a noise moving the sun loungers around, hoping to attract attention of any elegant neighbour who may be around. I dashed in showered, put a hint of make up and a good smattering of lipstick on and stepped into a pair of wedge sandals. I stood in the kitchen and sprayed a light coating of sun oil on my naked body, which made my skin glisten. My hands trembled uncontrollably as I poured myself a large glass of wine to take to the pool area. I actually was so turned on and shaking I had to lean on the kitchen counter and have a cigarette to calm me down. This was a completely new sensation for me.

I had positioned my lounger in full view of the corner of the upper terrace, the area where I'd quickly deduced I had been seen from, I thought I saw a fleeting movement out of the corner of my eye whilst I was arranging my wine and cigarettes on the small table, this made me feel all the more wet and aroused. At that time it really was a new and massively exciting feeling. I lay down a tad deflated that I hadn't caught sight of him yet, but the not knowing was making me even hotter, causing my tummy to churn. My mind was in overdrive with very explicit thoughts. At that precise moment I felt like the naughtiest girl on the planet, just wanting to expose myself to this much older man, a relatively total stranger. He kept me in suspense for what seemed like hours but in reality was only about twenty minutes until he appeared, gin and tonic in hand; he'd obviously seen Paul leave because as he raised his glass to me he said "good morning my dear, you're looking perky today" as his eyes lingered on my exposed breasts. I told him Paul was at golf and I was just going to stay here by the pool enjoying the sun. He explained to me that he was staying here for six weeks, and that he'd already been here a week and his son and his family would be joining him the following week, then he cheekily told me he was just "taking in the sights and enjoying some most unexpected and stimulating views". I giggled like a teenager as he said, "just shout if you need any help with the sun cream", I nearly came on the spot. I noticed that he had pulled his sun lounger closer, so as he could keep me discreetly in his sights, I realised that this was my first real full on exhibitionistic opportunity, and I instantly decided to take full advantage of the situation. After deliberately showing off my body front and rear as I made a faff of going to top up my wine and get organised, I lit a cigarette and lay back on lounger this time with legs slightly parted, allowing him a glimpse of my exposed pussy lips. He pushed his sunglasses up and said "do carry on my lovely, you know you want to". My aroused state quickly overtook my shyness and I opened wider for him to see, my labia parted automatically showing off my wetness. I finished my cigarette and grabbed my sun cream spraying it liberally over my breasts, rubbing it in as seductively and provocatively as I could, working my nipples into a state where I thought they'd explode. It was pre my squirting days, but a definite river of juices ran from me, making my vagina shimmer and open even wider without even touching it. It was absolute heaven. Decadent, filthy, unadulterated and so totally depraved. Every so often our eyes met and he raised his glass in full appreciation and admiration. I played with my pussy continually over the next few hours for him, making myself cum on numerous occasions. We both enjoyed this depraved interlude. Paul played golf on two more instances during our stay, and on both occasions I played enthusiastically for my older, appreciative voyeur, getting more and more daring each time, until on the final time I just couldn't resist any longer and beckoned him down. I was shaking with total lust as I rushed naked and wet to answer the door to him. He quickly slipped in, and as I closed the door and leant back against it opening my legs I said "five minutes only", he nodded his understanding and immediately began to use his deliciously long fingers on my pussy, bringing me expertly to orgasm in the allotted time frame. He then kissed me on each cheek and slipped out door smiling. It was quick, it was naughty and it was highly enjoyable.

Soon after I went and crashed out on the bed and enjoyed a long lazy nap until Paul returned from his golf. I know which game was the more enjoyable, and it didn't involve any clubs or trudging about in loud patterned culottes.

Dinner that evening was a major turn on, as I hadn't told Paul what I'd been up to during the afternoon, and my watcher was giving me the occasional knowing smile across the room as he ate his salad, discreetly raising his glass in salute. It was this few days in the Algarve that really unleashed my exhibitionistic side and my desire to show myself at any given opportunity remains as high as ever. I particularly enjoy showing at secluded nudist beaches, as you'll be aware if you read *"Distracted"*, which was set on a beach in Southern Spain during the period I was going through my diaries in preparation for writing this book. The feeling lying naked under a hot Spanish sun and being admired by the odd voyeur or three never fails to raise my temperature, and my inner devil raises its often-naughty side. On a side note, a quite amazing place to put on a little exhibition is a spa I visited recently in Brighton called *"Bristol Gardens"*, well worth a visit. However, exhibitionism is all about the daring and unexpected, hence the places and situations that this can occur are of an incredibly wide ranging variety. I recently read an article where one lady caught a train to Birmingham once a month, with the sole intention of exhibiting her panty less state to fellow male passengers. She bought a return ticket and she never actually got off the train, just there and back enjoying a good few hours of her own personal fetish. Each to their own; the opportunities for us females to explore the exhibitionist side of ourselves are truly endless and the variety of appreciative voyeurs across all ages is most diverse. Everyone enjoys being watched and admired; to what degree is entirely up to the individual. Try it; you never know you may just like it!

Chapter Thirty: Beach Life

After selling our villa in Southern Spain in 2012, both Paul and I soon realised we'd made a huge mistake. We both missed being able to just jump on a cheap flight for a long weekend in the sun whenever time permitted, we both enjoyed the slower pace of life that Southern Spain and Andalucia in particular offered. This was further amplified when I had to rent a place whilst I was preparing to write this book; however nice the house was it just wasn't home. So after completing the most unexpected novella "Distracted", having had so much fun doing so I decided that we should find ourselves another property to call our own on this wonderful part of the costa. Thankfully Paul agreed wholeheartedly with my feelings. We settled on the Almayate area, as during my stay there I'd made a few friends amongst the locals, and had fallen head over heels in love with the area in general. We scoured the Internet and eventually found a few places that matched our criteria. We arranged viewings and booked a flight over for a long weekend. Sadly, none of the properties were quite right once seen in the flesh as it were, however, talking to the locals in the bar in Almayate (they remembered me well, this strange English lady who had stayed for a while in the house a few doors up the road), as so often happens so and so knew so and so who possibly had a place that we'd love. Well it turned out that we did and put in an offer there and then, which on a handshake was accepted immediately. It was perfect; it was an old fisherman's cottage, virtually on the beach, detached with a small piece of land either side. It had been reformed five years earlier and just needed a few finishing touches to finish it off. Then it would be down to individual touches here and there to make it our own. In fact, it's where I'm writing this particular section of the book, hammering away at the keyboard whilst glancing across the beach to the shimmering Mediterranean.

Paul flew over six weeks later to complete the paperwork and go to the notary with the lawyer to finalise the purchase. It was my job to equip the interior and put our own personal stamp on it.

I'd booked to go early October, and the first thing on my list of things to do was buy a car which would be left in the detached garage cum workshop that came along with the property. My old Dutch friend Rubens who still lived nearby was a great help during this phase, and we ended up in the Land Rover concession in Malaga, where after sending Paul several texts and pictures I purchased a nearly new Range Rover Evoque that the garage had been using as a demonstrator. It only had 6k Kilometres on the clock and was in pristine condition, but more importantly it was a great price. Forty-eight hours later with all the relevant Spanish paperwork completed it was ours. The dealer presented the keys to me along with a bottle of Champagne and a huge bouquet of flowers. A nice touch I thought. Now being mobile my tasks became much easier and I got swept up in the fun and excitement of buying furniture, bedding and everything that's needed to furnish a new home. I had an absolute blast. I wanted all the interior rooms to be repainted in the local Andalusian brilliant white emulsion before the furniture was delivered, so I arranged with a local builders merchant to send in a team of painters to do the work as a matter of urgency. I remember the first few nights vividly as I was sleeping on a sun lounger with just a sheet, thankfully the weather was kind and waking up to glorious sunshine was as always a treat, a positive start to the day.

    One quite erotic interlude occurred when I became a nuisance and was getting in the way of the painters, slowing them down, and generally getting in the way. I grabbed my rucksack threw in a towel and left them to it. I crossed the narrow road onto the sandy beach (if you go to Google Maps or Earth and look for Almayate Playa and look for Chiringuito "*Vargas*" you'll see where I mean and get a feel for the beach and its opportunity to chill out or play!), being October the beach was very sparsely populated, just a few souls dotted at intervals taking in the still very warm sun. I walked towards the Almanat naturist site and after a few minutes found a nice secluded spot at the back of the beach, sheltered each side by vegetation with three agricultural fields behind growing an assortment of crops. I placed my towel and inflated my newly purchased pillow and stripped off ready for an afternoon of complete unhindered relaxation. I poured a glass of wine and sprayed a liberal amount of sun oil over my body, getting a little aroused as I rubbed it in, it was a blissful scene, a moment to saviour. The feeling walking down to the waters edge totally naked, skin glistening with oil is always exquisitely erotic, the chance of being seen always heightens my sexual awareness to exhibitionistic levels, hoping someone may just wander along, it's just such a heady feeling of freedom mixed with total decadence.

    Whilst walking back to my towel I noticed that there were a couple of farmer's busy working in the fields, both wearing the traditional blue work trousers and straw sun hats. They both glanced my way and nodded a greeting to me. This got my pulse racing a bit as I layback on the towel giving myself another liberal spray of oil. It wasn't long before I sensed that I was being watched (its strange but you always seem to get a sixth sense in these kind of situations), this sensation spurred me on to really massage the oil in more enthusiastically than normal. After several long minutes of provocative rubbing and stroking I glanced behind to see the two elderly farmers watching discreetly, I adore that brief moment and always enjoy a quick orgasm. Encouraged by their smiles I swivelled around on the towel and slowly spread my legs for them, working the muscles in my abdomen and groin to stimulate my already wet vagina to open up for them. My nipples were rock solid from the oily tweaking; I was firmly in the mood to play for them. Glancing along the beach to confirm that no one was walking my way I ran a finger slowly over my clitoris and in between my already butterflied labia, my juices were already flowing from me, coating my fingers, which I occasionally licked and sucked in a filthy fashion for my watching workers. They looked on approvingly as I worked feverishly on my pussy; this triggered my stomach muscles to heave violently as I began to accelerate rapidly to my point of no return, the point where a gushing orgasm was imminent. I took the bull by the horns and beckoned them to come closer, which they both did, kneeling in front of my spread legs, enjoying watching me pleasure myself. The look on their faces was priceless as I took them by surprise unleashing several monstrous arcing streams of my juice for them. My thighs jerked uncontrollably and my legs turned to jelly such were the ferocity of my climaxes. They were two impeccably well behaved "up close and personal" voyeurs, or rather in this case "admirers", and it was such fun playing for them. Something that I've done several times since, and on each occasion I get rewarded with several bags of fresh produce from their crops. A fair exchange and a most enjoyable scenario.

 Later that afternoon the local telecom company arrived and much to my surprise, as everyone told me it could never happen that quickly our broadband was hooked up and good to go. Surprising both Paul and I with decent speeds, enabling us to Skype and allow Paul to see the progress so far on video.

 The next few days were filled with more of the same, including a trip into Malaga city to buy the T.V Paul had seen online at Wortens the big electrical outlet on the coast and various other bits and pieces that were needed.

I kept the Thursday free for a fun trip in the new car, as Friday was already taken up with deliveries from a variety of sources, most importantly the beds and general furniture. I was so looking forward to a good nights sleep in a new bed, as the sun lounger was taking its toll on the body.

After reading many good reports online I'd decided to drive down the coast to Cabopino beach for a spot of lunch and whatever else might titillate me and sneak onto my very open agenda.

That evening I strolled a few hundred metres along the small road and stumbled upon a wonderful small family run beach bar, where I was served sardines fresh off the open wood fired barbeque with a scrumptious tropical salad all washed down with a few glasses of chilled white wine. I had a good feeling we were going to have many happy short breaks on this most unspoilt little stretch of the coast. It just felt comfortable and very tranquil, a million miles away from the hustle and bustle of London and Paris.

Chapter Thirty-One: Cabopino Playa

Thursday morning arrived with another clear warm day along with the painters who were almost on the final straight, just the utility room and a few recoats here and there and it would be ready for the furniture to be delivered.

Packing a few essentials into my new large beach bag and popping them into the boot of the new Range Rover I had the entire day ahead of me to do as I pleased. No need to programme the satnav as it was motorway all the way to my destination of Cabopino, and in particular the "Dunas de Artola o Cabopino" and its vast beach.

I initially headed for the very pretty and busy port area with its cafes and bars, and perused the multitude of smaller yachts and motorboats bobbing on their moorings. I found a nice table outside a great restaurant called "Alberts" and people watched for an hour or so with a glass of chilled white and a most devine bowl of steamed clams with fresh crusty bread, the sun was warm giving the whole area a definite "St Tropez" feel without the "St Tropez" prices.

I eventually dragged myself away and drove the few minutes to the beginning of the beach with its large sand dunes and sporadic wooded areas. There were cars and motorhomes dotted around, I drove along the track at the back of the dunes for a few hundred metres and found a good spot to park up and get my bearings before deciding on where to make my pitch. From my vantage point I could see a good span of the area in front of me and I could definitely sense there was fun to be had, as there were a dozen or so beach umbrellas in view and a steady volume of people openly wandering around naked, intentionally flaunting themselves. There was an abundance of wooded areas that seemed to be the focus of many of the people who were meandering around singularly and in pairs. My interest was definitely piqued. I noticed several cars parking up and the occupants disrobing and grabbing their beach bags before disappearing off in many directions along the well-worn paths to the dunes and beach. I could imagine that during the high summer months this area would be packed and possibly a bit oppressive, I enjoy it when its quieter, as it seems to bring the classier person out to play and enjoy the freedom that beaches like this encourage and allow.

I undressed and threw a sarong around myself, grabbed my bag and headed off to find a quiet spot in the dunes but a little closer to the beach. I passed several men, all of who were most well mannered and imparted the customary greeting, the simple, universal nod and smile used when you're unsure as to the nationality of the person. I eventually found what turned out to be a perfect spot, a small sandy nook in front of a cluster of trees and pitched my towel and inflated my pillow. As usual as soon as I got naked I gave myself a liberal spray of sun oil and relaxed back in the sun and watched the various comings and goings in my immediate vicinity. Occasionally a gent or two would stop for a chat, it was all very relaxed and civilised but with a very strong undercurrent of sexual shenanigans. A large area about a hundred metres away appeared to be where the action was, as people were wandering in to the dense trees along various worn foot paths, this always gives my stomach a nice sensation from the little butterflies fluttering their wings, never fails to get me aroused to a level where I lose all self control and the sexual devil in me appears. The turning point or rather the catalyst to my afternoons fun was when I watched a very tanned couple stroll in to the undergrowth with several men following at a discreet distance, all in various states of arousal. I love that feeling of being followed and the apprehension coupled with anticipation of what may follow, but equally enjoy watching another female being followed, knowing what she's feeling inside. I viewed the steady procession of men, and after several minutes decided to go and see what if anything exciting was occuring. I grabbed my little beach security bag and slipped on my wedge sandals and ambled along the nearest path into the densely treed area where instinct and awareness from my many dalliances at Almayate beach took over, giving me an immediate feeling of confidence and sensual abandon. This feeling is hard to describe, but for me it's a combination of mental as well as physical factors that make it so erotic and decadent.

I stopped for a moment letting my eyes adjust to the shade. I immediately sensed this was going to be fun, as ahead of me I heard the tell tale murmuring of different voices and in particular a female obviously already in a state of orgasmic elation. Very shortly I saw a throng of people who were intently watching the couple and several men also playing with one another, the lady was wholeheartedly enjoying all the attention she was getting, and her husband was very vocal in his encouragement. Several of the men were both surprised and obviously pleased to see me by their reactions, a single female coming into the unfolding scenario definitely raised the "naughty" factor by a quite few degrees. The many approving and leering looks made me quiver a little in pure shameless pleasure. As I stood appreciating the view several discreet hands began to stroke and caress my body, tentatively at first, but when I parted my legs slightly it signalled an instant frenzy, an onslaught of hands and fingers tweaking and probing me. Just like the other female I was outnumbered by a large factor, but eager and fully willing for some group fun and games. Everywhere I looked there were erections of all shapes and sizes on offer, the two men behind me were rapidly bringing me to orgasm with their accomplished fingers, working both my pussy and anus with equal measure. Juices were streaming down my thighs, soaking all the attentive hands; I got busy stroking cock after cock, in what was turning into a naked free for all, no limits, just how I like it. I had a small yet powerful squirting orgasm as I nodded my approval to a guy who was unfurling a condom onto his thick manhood, and then as if by telepathy the guys beside me lifted me up by the legs, giving him a welcome gaping target to penetrate, and boy did he hit the right spot, straight in hard and deep, no messing around, he made it clear he just wanted to pound me. He was thrusting mercilessly into me, and the two men holding me were rocking me back and forth meeting his thrusts with a powerful collision of flesh on flesh. The other female was getting very similar treatment, and there was a sea of men masturbating everywhere I looked, a blur of hands pumping hard glistening cock. As soon as my guy came, a powerful older gent who just by his demeanour gave an aura of dominating experience replaced him, swiftly driving his thick weapon forcefully into me, making me whimper with glee when his thumb reached under and plugged my anus, the men sensed I was in heaven and reacted accordingly, every part of me tingled and was on fire as they took turns in using me. I was being firmly controlled by this group of men, fully dominated, but all in a very respectful way. It was just perfect, we all seamed to be in tune with each other, one simple goal in mind, which was to extract the maximum pleasure from the moment. I was being given climax upon climax physically, and the mental stimulation of seeing more inexperienced men being overwhelmed by the spectacle and ejaculating on the spot was a sight to behold. The bull fucking me just kept pumping into me like an automated machine, never missing a beat, causing wave after wave of internal pleasure to encompass me. My body was racked with a continual spasmodic pulsating feeling; my vagina was gripping on to this powerhouse of pleasure, matching his demon like thrusts with a powerful steady milking action, urging him on towards his own climax. His piercing eyes locked onto mine as if we were in battle, both urging each other on to higher plateaus of gratification. I felt sorry for the ladies husband, as he was torn between watching his wife and was mesmerised by what was happening to me only a few feet away, he had a grin that stretched from ear to ear, he was taking his pleasure from his partners total uninhibited sexual indulgence. This decadent scene went on and on, eventually the bull withdrew and stood transfixed, staring at my gaping vagina, slapping my labia and clit with his meat, he just seemed to know what I required and his timing was impeccable, this induced several more violent liquid orgasms. After a while he spoke to me in broken English and led me away from the melee, leaving the lady and her husband at the mercy of group of guys that were left. She didn't look like she'd be complaining anytime soon. He gripped my hand firmly as we exited the under growth into the warm sunshine. I eagerly followed him until we reach his private spot, which was sheltered by a strategically placed windbreaker. He lay back on his towel holding his vastly thick erection upright inviting me to get on top, I'd not had chance before due to the intensity of the action in the woods, so reaching into my small beach purse I retrieved a small bottle of amyl, taking a massive hit in either nostril. As the effect began to rage through my body I clamped my labia around his bulbous tip and allowed my vagina to work him inside me bit by bit until I could feel him throbbing deep within my abdomen. His powerful hands locked on to my hips and he began to rhythmically bounce me up and down, some times delicately and every now and then violently, which felt like a small rabbit punch to my womb, exquisite and the moment was enhanced as my juices squirted uncontrollably in all directions, in a wild arcing spray. He fucked me in a variety of positions over the next hour, never giving me time to draw breathe, he was relentless, just persistently working me again and again. I was in a consistent state of extreme orgasm, until eventually he flipped me on to my stomach and knelt in front of me and began to feed me his cock, his balls were swollen and heavy in my hands, I relaxed my jaw as he placed a hand under my chin and one solidly on the top of my head and began for ferociously fuck my mouth until I was drooling copious amounts of saliva over him in between sharp bouts of gagging. I had my work cut out as he drove his meat into my mouth with an unnerving force. Much to my pleasure and relief I won the contest, the battle of wills as it had become by this stage by sliding two fingers into his anus and feverishly manipulated his prostate, this instantly caused him to buck and jerk like a bronco bull, and he began filling my mouth and throat with abundant amounts of his hot sweet semen, which I enthusiastically swallowed, lewdly scooping any excess that dribbled onto my chin with my fingers and eating it with porn star like gusto. It was an extraordinary afternoon of sheer filth, and total slut like behaviour.

 Time was racing by, but he insisted I follow him so he could buy me a drink as a token of thanks, and we could swap contact details. We drove literally three minutes to a small beach bar called "Andys", where sadly as I was driving I could only indulge in an ice cold coke, but it was delicious, one of those rare moments where it lives up to the adverts, most "refreshing". He belatedly introduced himself as Jorge, he was thirty six and single, originally from Portugal, but living and running his own business in sports management in Malaga. We did swap details and I have subsequently met him again on several occasions, both with Paul and solo. In fact he and Paul have become good friends and they have partied together with a lady Jorge knows in Seville, much to Pauls enjoyment. With a sore neck and aching jaw I drove back to Almayate just in time to catch the painters before they left and pay them for a job well done.

 The majority of the items I'd purchased were delivered the following day, and over the next few days I got the "cottage" by the beach well and truly transformed and fully liveable. It was wonderful that first night in the new bed listening to the sound of the sea whilst resting my weary bones. Needless to say my vegetable supply grew over the coming days! Also importantly I established a friendship with the locals, who always keep an eye on the place when neither of us is there.

Chapter Thirty-Two: A Staring Role

During the following month I arranged one of my regular solo excursions to Paris, this one in particular was dedicated to the memory of Yves. It was one of the more unusual and quite frankly most depraved and debauched afternoons that I'd so far celebrated in his honour, one of which I'm sure he'd have applauded wildly, and thoroughly approved of.

As per normal I hopped the Eurostar to Gare du Nord, where Marc was waiting to drive me to the apartment. I'd called him the previous week just to let him know I'd be in town for a couple of days. We had our customary catch up over a drink, and being ever thoughtful he told me he'd been to the apartment and had gotten a few essentials in for me. He would never take any payment, each time simply telling me that "it had been taken care off", I can only assume Yves had made some arrangement with him, it is something that is never discussed. However, he did accept my goody bag of gifts that I'd brought for him, he was particularly fond of a mature Cheddar cheese and Jacobs cream crackers, complimented by some Branston pickle, most strange for a Parisian. They will often like such things, but heaven forbid them ever admitting to it, in this respect they are "les tossers" (written with a big grin).

I'd often wondered what had become of the magnificent home in the South of France that Yves had owned and entertained Paul and I at all those years ago. Marc informed me that he'd bequeathed it to his beloved "Military" and as was his wish it was being used as a place for servicemen recuperating from life changing injuries sustained during active duty. This was typical of the man we knew, always thinking of others less fortunate than him, and so very patriotic.

My tribute to Yves began the following morning after breakfast with a trip to the lingerie department of Les Galeries Lafayette where I indulged myself in a stunning pair of Wolford – Silk crystal Hold-ups, always such fun and a great precursor to some naughtiness is a little shopping trip to this amazing store.

After a small light lunch I returned to the apartment where I booked a taxi before luxuriating in the bath for a while with a glass of wine, getting slowly turned on as I allowed my mind to wander, imagining every scenario that could happen in the execution of my "tribute". I liberally coated my body with my favourite Chanel Body Velvet and encased my legs in my new hold-ups, accentuating the look further with a pair of high black patent platform heels. Feeling a warm glow of anticipation I went to the wardrobe and retrieved the "fur coat" from its protective cover and slipped into it with an overwhelmingly decadent feeling engulfing me. I had just enough time to demolish a nice large Jack Daniels before the taxi arrived.

I gave the taxi driver the address of my destination, which was located about fifteen minutes away in the second arrondissement. I'd read about it over the years and heard many people discuss it with great enthusiasm. It was a cinema, not just any cinema, but Paris's oldest and only surviving adult porn cinema. It has a great reputation of being very welcoming and safe, with its huge exposed-brick wall and expansive red-leather-style seats, it ranks alongside the very best small cinemas in Paris in terms of both comfort and retro chic style. I'd rang the previous evening and spoke to the owner Maurice Laroche, a pleasant smiling young seventy something who'd been running it for well over thirty years. I explained my request and he told me that it would be no problem whatsoever, and that he'd meet me in the reception at three o'clock, which he explained would be the best time for a good cross section of clientele that would work perfectly for what I was looking to experience. True to his word a smiling Maurice was waiting to greet me and whisked me quickly into his projection room, where he poured me a nerve calming large glass of white wine and lit us both a cigarette. He was so charming and put my mind at rest and any last minute reservations were well and truly replaced by an overwhelming aura of daring. Once ready he showed me to the entrance of the small narrow theatre with its legendary brick wall and its twelve rows of seating, he told me he'd reserved three seats on the back row just for me, and to go and enjoy the experience. The rows of seats had around seven or eight per row, so I had an unobstructed few steps to my seats. Discreetly, as I was getting seated many heads turned to look at the new arrival (having certainly been primed by Maurice). Once accustomed to the dark atmosphere I quickly saw that the place was about half full, with most customers in the rows nearing the rear. The film was a high quality stylish French affair, which added to the elegant yet "sleazy" ambience, which was exactly what I was looking for. I felt very secure, safe in the knowledge that Maurice would be keeping an eye on things from his projection booth; this feeling of security was reassuring and relaxed me very quickly into the moment. Over the next ten or so minutes I slowly undid the three coat buttons and untied the belt so that the heavy fur draped loosely over me, just exposing the tops of my hold-ups and a glimpse of cleavage, several men by this stage had moved to the row directly in front of me and were busy alternating between watching the film and checking out what I was up to behind them. Two men came and sat at either end of my row with just a couple of seats between them and me, I was instantly on fire, and felt my wetness begin to flow as I reached between my legs to prepare my vagina for public display, butterflying my labia and unleashing my engorged clitoris, which was dying to be touched by a few strange anonymous hands. Eventually all eyes were peering back my way, the film had become just a background enhancement, the audio giving this seedy scenario another kinky dimension. I could sense as well as see that many of the men were openly masturbating at the unfolding situation. It was at this point I snatched a huge hit of my poppers just before I let my coat fall totally open, fully exposing my naked body. I opened my legs as wide as possible, placing my heels on the tops of the seats in front of me, giving full easy access to my expectant pussy. This was like lighting a very short fuse, as in seconds numerous hands were coming at me from all directions, stroking and probing me, many vocally commenting on my wetness. It was sleazy in the extreme, with numerous men queuing to take turns in kneeling in between my legs and use their tongues lapping at my anus and vagina in equal measure, pure vagina worship which I love. Many skilled fingers and thumbs masturbated my protruding clitoris into their willing mouths, my ejaculations began to come thick and fast, each one more violent than the last, until I was being kept on the crest of one powerful gushing tsunami of female ejaculate after another. Men were gently jostling for position to drink from me, while many were happy just to watch and pleasure themselves. At one stage there was a gent tonguing my anus as another nibbled on my clit, I was squirting like an uncontrollable burst pipe. It just wasn't subsiding and it felt like there was an unending fluid producing machine deep inside me. I think it was the pure seediness of the situation and the novelty of the location that was making everything feel more intense and depraved. It was like my inner slut had escaped and was showing the audience how a true "salope" should behave in such sleazy company. It was everything filthy wanton sex should be, and I adored every cum filled minute. It was two hours of pure debauched filth, and one that lives on in my memory, and hopefully Yves had looked down on me approvingly!

      Enjoying a wind down vino and cigarette with Maurice I thanked him profusely and we chatted away until my taxi came to take me back to reality. Just as a side note he holds couples only evenings on Thursday and Saturday, well worth a visit, I'm definitely dragging Paul along soon, as I know he'd relish the decadence of it all. Just go and have a look at the web site for any relevant information. This establishment definitely caters to the more outrageous amongst us.

Chapter Thirty-Three: First Tango - The Upshot

After self publishing "First Tango In Paris pt1" during the summer of 2013 on Amazon I was amazed by the reaction it had, and still has on people. I was quite frankly astounded by the success it achieved and reaching the top 15 in the mainstream book chart and number one for many weeks in the Erotic chart was beyond my wildest expectations. What started as a dinner party dare had become a best selling monster that created a wide variety of responses from its readers. Both good and bad reviews litter the Amazon sales page, as you'd expect from this kind of warts and all memoir. Over the following months my inbox was deluged with emails from PR companies who wanted a bit of the action, wanting to get me on all kinds of daytime television shows, I resisted all offers, as basically when it came down to it the whole purpose of writing the book was simply to see if I could, and in no way was it a mega money making venture.

Also I received vast amounts of emails from readers and I'm pleased to say not one from "Outraged of Tunbridge Wells". I took the time to reply to each and everyone; even it was just a simple "thank you for the kind words" reply. Many emails were from couples who said the book inspired them to dip their toes in the water and use my book as a guide, in fact the level of British people visiting the clubs mentioned in the book increased dramatically. "Chris et Manu" even presented me with a very tongue in cheek bottle of vintage Champagne for services to the Parisian tourist industry. It was interesting to note that the book appealed to both sexes, and most definitely inspired many "masked" parties across the U.K, from small intimate events in peoples houses to full blown events in larger club venues. I just wish I had a pound for every Venetian style mask sold over the last few years!

Out of the many emails several caught my eye and deserved a more in depth response that just a curt "thank you", and this one in particular is more than worth a chapter here, it is extremely recent so the details are very fresh in my mind.

Chapter Thirty-Four: Mentoring Karen

Karen's email piqued my interest solely on the grounds of its one word subject line, which was "HELP". She went on to explain that she'd read both my books and desperately wanted to indulge but lacked the self-assurance to take the next step. Her husband had sadly died a few years previously, her two children had grown up and were pretty much leading their own lives and she felt that she both needed and deserved a bit of sexual adventure in her life. After several emails and chats on the phone we decided it would be nice to meet for a coffee and discuss her desires face to face.

We met in a nice quiet café in Kensington Hight St, where we instantly struck up an easy rapport, it was a most strange initial few minutes as our paths had never crossed previously, but it seemed we'd known each other for years. Obviously she knew a great deal about me from the books, so the majority of our conversation was about her and what had brought her to this moment in time. It became evident very quickly that we did indeed have much in common and only circumstance had deprived her of living out her dreams and fantasies. However, she'd now reached a point where she wanted to take the plunge. She was in her late forties, looked younger, was a natural blonde and figure wise looked in great shape, but she just lacked a bit of confidence. Easily remedied when you're working with the right ingredients.

She explained the reason she kept getting drawn back to "Distracted" was that she vaguely knew the area of Spain where I had written it, and where many of the sexual adventures took place. She knew this part of the coast due to the fact that her Father who had recently passed away had lived for the last fifteen years of his life in a town called Nerja, twenty minutes along the coast from Almayate, and she'd visited on numerous occasions. She was currently in the process of clearing his apartment with the view of selling it.

The upshot of our conversation was that we'd arranged to meet up in Spain the following month, as I had a few days planned at the new cottage and she was there cataloguing her late fathers extensive collection of jazz records, which she was going to sell on E-Bay over time, simply because the cost of shipping them back to the U.K was prohibitive due to the weight. But was hopeful that once catalogued she would get a collector to buy them as a job lot.

It was early summer, and I arrived on a Sunday morning to a sultry 26 degrees and clear blue Andalusian skies. The first thing I did was make myself a coffee, pour a small brandy and sit on the large rock on the beach twenty feet from the front door and breath in the wonderful Mediterranean sea air and feel the warm sun on me. Being May the beach was quiet with just a few people dotted around, no tourists to speak of in sight. The afternoon was spent lazing naked in my spot of choice topping up the tan. Sadly no farmers around to play up to earn my fresh vegetables, but tomorrow was another day. To be honest the days all roll into one here as the pace of life is so tranquil and unhurried.

I met Karen at midday on the Monday at a café outside the town hall in nearby Velez Malaga where she'd had to go and sort out some paperwork. As we'd agreed back in London this was going to be a journey of discovery for her and she was placing herself, as she put it in "my very capable hands" over the next few days. She gave me carte blanche, promising that she'd left all her inhibitions back in London.

She arrived as planned at the cottage late morning the following day, where over a little vino blanco I outlined the day ahead, to which she thoroughly approved and by the sparkle in her eyes I sensed that she couldn't wait to get started.

We both popped our things in the boot of the Range Rover and headed to the area of Almayate beach heavily featured in "Distracted", the one Karen had been dreaming about, but had never had the courage to visit alone. It is in fact only a twenty-minute walk along the beach from the cottage, however for ease and convenience the car was the best option, also there were two comfy beach loungers stowed in the boot. As we turned onto the track that would take us down to the "fun" area of the beach Karen got visibly and vocally more and more excitable the closer we got, possibly aided by her recollections of the book and my running commentary of the things that awaited just minutes away. My excitement grew simultaneously with hers, as it always did, as fleeting memories of the filthy times I'd had there on many previous occasions came to mind. Being a Tuesday I was confident that it would be the perfect day to expose Karen to the delights of the great outdoors, in other words not too crowded, but enough people to ease her gently into the scene. Dependant on how today went and her reactions I had several other plans in the pipeline for the rest of the week. This first day was a trial run, testing the water as it were. I wanted to ensure that her realisation of her fantasies went smoothly with no untoward hiccups.

Parking as normal on the scorched earth behind the beach we quickly grabbed our things and headed towards what I now refer to as my lucky spot. Looking around I briefly noted with much elation nothing had really changed since my last visit. I could see the well trodden pathways into the palm tree area was still well worn, in fact there appeared to be a couple more little tracks. First thing we did was lay our beach mats down and unfold the lightweight beach loungers, and then at my suggestion I poured us both a large white wine from the chilled litre screw top bottle I'd packed to bring with us. I enjoyed a cigarette whilst pointing out various things of interest to her that she instantly recognised from the book, the whole time I was explaining things to her she acted like a meerkat, head swivelling and bobbing uncontrollably taking everything in, not wanting to miss a thing. A bit reminiscent of my first days here many moons ago with Rubens.

As we stripped off several men casually wandered by nodding the customary welcome greeting, much to Karen's delight, squealing like a teenager as she noticed one was proudly flexing a semi erect manhood as he walked, pointedly slowing his stride for us to appraise it. A good start, and hopefully much more of the same to come. We liberally coated ourselves with sun oil, which always manages to produce a warm tingling glow deep inside me, and I sensed it had a similar effect on my protégée.

We both lay there naked and glistening in the sun, enjoying a drink and discreetly teasing any beach walkers that came close by, always good fun to see the effect a glimpse of oiled, slightly open pussy has on a man, its interesting to see the various reactions from the bold to the timid, the talkers and the gawkers as I humorously refer to them. Soon Karen was firmly into the swing of things and was thoroughly enjoying her newfound freedom. She was getting a huge thrill subtly playing with herself for the passing men. She was becoming more and more daring as the time went on, and after another glass of wine she really opened up, quite literally, giving herself several climaxes as a small group of men stopped to watch approvingly, uttering many words of encouragement and two or three of them ejaculating into the sand before moving on. This really was turning her on, and for once I was enjoying not being the centre of attention and simply watching and encouraging her to let herself get immersed into the moment. During a break in her exhibition she expressed her desire to go into the wooded area and experience for real what I'd encountered on my visits. I agreed that we'd venture in together, but before we did I offered her a small sniff of my poppers, which she tentatively accepted at first, but was soon asking for more. It certainly gave her another dimension to her new found sexual awareness. She was taking to the whole exhibitionistic game like the proverbial duck to water. I kept my eye on the pathways and the general level of sexual adventurers entering the palms and when it felt right I quickly popped our valuables into the car and grabbed her by the hand and headed off to the woods. I could feel her entire body trembling with anticipation as we approached along one of the well-trodden paths. I told her to relax and enjoy the sensation, and that I'd be there to keep a semblance of order if things got to overwhelming for her. I needn't have wasted my breath, as soon as we were well inside and our eyes had become accustomed to the shade we encountered several men waiting to greet us, provocatively stroking their erections. Karen groaned with delight as a hand reached out and tweaked her erect nipples, I signalled to the men that I was overseeing events and that Karen should be the object of their attention. They nodded their understanding, and slowly went to work on her body, fingers and tongues licking and probing her every orifice simultaneously. Her orgasm erupted furiously from her within seconds of me giving her a sniff of my amyl, she was whimpering loudly as her secondary orgasm hit, brought on by the sight of a guy ejaculating heavily just inches from her, this had a domino effect, causing several other men to unload their semen for her watch and enjoy, from the mewling sounds coming from her mouth she was fully appreciating the spectacle these erupting cocks delivered.

Our brief but intense playtime left Karen on a sexual high, and once back on our loungers in the sun she continued to flirt with anyone who passed anywhere remotely close to us. I felt she'd really embraced the situation and had most definitely put a large tick on one of her to do fantasies, definitely earned her stripes. Her ability to overcome any reservations that she may have had even surprised her, and she expressed a firm desire to take things up a notch. With this and everything else that had so far been accepted by her I was confident that what I had planned next for her would open her floodgates even further, and there'd be no looking back in regard to her wish to visit and discover "my" Paris (which she has since done and ticked many more boxes on her ever expanding list).

That evening, after sending a very happy and satisfied lady back to Nerja I met up with Rubens for a spot of supper at a family run beach "chiringuito" a short stroll from the cottage, where over a chilled bottle of fruity Spanish white and a large dish of assorted fried fish I told him about the day and how Karen had let herself be swept up in the moment and wanted to experience much more, and that she had a lot of catching up to do. As we'd tentatively arranged a few days earlier, both Rubens and I agreed that we should give the lady an night to remember. Rubens eyes lit up and we agreed that we'd have an evening of good food and debauched decadence around the pool in his courtyard. We arranged to meet up the following lunchtime and go shopping for the evenings feast.

Rubens picked me up at the agreed time, and we headed straight to the large Eroski supermarket at the local mall and stocked up on wines, bread and a range of cheeses and salad stuffs, before heading in land to a local butcher he gotten to know over his time in the area. After the introductions and a small glass of fino he prepared for us three kilos of his finest "solomillo" (filet steak), along with some very finely carved and outrageously expensive "Jamón Joselito Gran Reserva Bellota". He gave us a few slivers to sample, and it was delicious, melted on the tongue and the flavour was like no other Spanish ham I'd ever tasted. Rubens dropped me off around four, which meant I had three hours to kill until Karen arrived to get ready with me for the evenings soiree. As it was such a glorious day I wandered along the beach and entertained the two field workers for an hour, my excuse was that I was simply topping up my tan, nothing exhibitionistic in that! It does however simplify vegetable shopping to a large degree.

Karen turned up promptly at seven excitedly clutching her overnight bag, still unaware as to where we were going or what was in store fore her. I felt the unknown element would add to her overall enjoyment of the occasion. We both showered and moisturised before slipping into our full-length clingy summer t-shirt dresses and heels. Just a minimal amount of make up and we both wore our hair up to add a touch of elegance and we were ready to party. She did look a tad confused when I grabbed my small overnight bag as we headed off, suggesting she did the same. She grinned when I said "be prepared it may be a long night".

Arriving at Rubens I noticed two other cars already there, one a beautiful Arctic white Porsche Cayenne Turbo with French registration plates with the 75 department number on them, denoting it was from the Paris region. This immediately gave me a very hot flush in anticipation of who may be the owner of such a stunning beast.

Rubens came to greet us at the entrance, took our bags and dumped them by the coat rack in the hallway before enthusiastically embracing us both and producing a welcoming glass of bubbly from nowhere, a most impressive trick.

Leading us with a flourish through to the courtyard, informing us everyone had already arrived, I felt Karen tremble slightly and squeeze my arm, I responded with a wink and a grin.

Rubens introduced us to the other guests, or as I prefer to refer to them "our evenings playthings". There were five deeply tanned handsome men smiling at us, all elegantly attired in casual polo style shirts and cargo shorts or jeans and loafers. It was a bit like a scene from a "Dolce and Gabbana" photo shoot. As you may be aware Rubens is a photographer, and these were good friends of his, not just random rent a gent people, they'd all worked together on various projects over the years. It transpired that the Porsche driver was in fact from Paris, where he'd recently sold a fashion based magazine that he'd built up from nothing to a half million plus pan European distribution figure. A big corporation had made him a good offer and he'd snapped their hand off and was currently to be found enjoying the proceeds on the southern coast of Spain. He was, as were all the other gents most charming and exuded an air of decadent sophistication. The drinks were refreshed as everyone flirted and got to know one another, whilst some soothing Strawberry Jazz played in the background. Rubens had laid out the large wooden dining table and I left Karen in the clutches of the men whilst I helped him bring out the salads and the beautiful warm crusty bread. Everyone was summonsed to the table as the platter of "Jamon" was presented reverently, as its cost demanded. Everyone helped themselves and savoured its delightful texture and flavour, unsurpassed quality in my opinion. I did my part in clearing away the empty plates whilst Rubens fired up his extravagant gas BBQ, uncovering the mound of steaks that he'd brought out earlier to reach their ambient cooking temperature. I brought the two large dishes of poor mans potato that he'd prepared that afternoon from the oven, the smell was most rustic. I took everyone's individual steak preference, and handed the tongs to Rubens who began to griddle up a storm. One of the guys poured everyone a glass of a beautiful French red from one of the three bottles that had been opened and were breathing on the old farmhouse dresser along the back wall of the courtyard. As always things were silent as the first mouthfuls of the steak were appreciated. Melt in the mouth and cooked to perfection was the general consensus. As I cleared the plates I could sense a most definite sense of anticipation building and that frisson of sexual expectation began to fill the air.

Rubens brought in a tray with six large warmed brandy balloons, which signalled one of the French contingent to produce a rather spectacular bottle of "Chateau de Laubade Vintage 1978 Armagnac", a gorgeous smooth, creamy brandy with a distinct caramel flavour, possibly one of the finest brandies I've had the good fortune to drink. A larger than expected measure was poured into the balloons and Rubens made a toast in a pretty bizarre mix of Dutch and French words with a few English phrases thrown in for good measure. This seemed to be the signal for International hostilities to commence, Karen and myself pitted against the might and skill of three French men, two Dutch and one Spaniard. I will dispense with individual names, as they did blur into one as soon as the brandy worked its magic, I will simply refer to them by nationality. Rubens had primed his friends that the main purpose of the evening was the initiation of Karen; therefore their initial focus was to be primarily all on her. She let out a small trembling sigh as four men began to remove her dress, eventually leaving her quivering with pleasure in her heels and thong, which was seductively removed by an enthusiastic Dutchman who knelt and dragged it stylishly down with his teeth. My Porsche driving Parisian, who I do recall was called Pascal stood beside me watching whilst his hand gently stroked the crease of my bottom through my dress. I quickly grabbed my trusty clutch bag and retrieved my bottle of amyl and my pack of St Moritz. I gave Karen a double hit to get her juices really flowing before lighting myself a cigarette to accompany the little brandy I had left. It was a sight to behold as the four guys stroked, licked and probed Karen, two sucking her erect nipples, as the others fingered her front and rear, she was on tip toe as two strong orgasms swept over her. The men were unrelenting in their ministrations, as soon as one climax subsided they worked her up to another, her thighs and their hands were shimmering in the courtyard lighting with her juices. Rubens had quickly cleared the table and she was placed on it with her legs held wide open for the men to take turns in eating her heavy lipped vagina, which caused her to utter a stream of mewling, guttural sounds from deep inside her. After a while a cushion was positioned for her to kneel on as the men began to enthusiastically feed her eager drooling mouth with their throbbing erections, she looked up at me and said "you wait two years for one to turn up, then four come along at once", which made us both giggle. She then really set about her task with vigour, slurping and sucking their cocks in turn, gagging and drooling large amounts of saliva upon them. My Parisian took it upon himself to undress me whilst Rubens sat back admiring the scene with brandy and cigar to hand. I decided Karen was well engrossed in all the attention she was getting and relaxed onto Pascal's adept fingers, simultaneously taking a hit of poppers. He wasted no time in getting naked and manoeuvring me onto my back in one of the large cushioned recliners. I murmured my approval as he knelt in between my out stretched thighs and began a very pleasurable session of vagina worship, his darting tongue explored every nook and crevice, also taking long lingering moments on my anus, which he seemed most keen on pleasing. I soon reached forward and began to tease my erect, protruding clitoris, which rapidly caused a deep bone-shaking climax along with several powerful streams of my ejaculate drenching his startled but grateful face. His surprise at my wetness soon had him begging me for more, so for that next segment of our liaison I took control, riding his face in many different positions and flooding his mouth on many occasions with my copious juices, he couldn't get enough. Karen was being ridden hard by the men, but did take a small time out to watch me attempt to drown this avid French pussy connoisseur. In fact they did give me a brief animated round of applause as they watched, as Pascal struggled to breathe such was the volume of fluid flowing from me in torrents. Eventually my legs gave out and I had to call a short intermission, a drink and cigarette break was in order to allow some energy to return to my muscles. Karen was grateful of the small break, but was back into the fray in double quick time ensuring each and every hard cock was given her undivided attention, whilst she was in full attack mode, and fucking and being fucked at a frenzied pace I lay back and enjoyed Pascal's slower pace, his slow but deeply powerful thrusts were both relaxing but at the same time keeping me on the brink of orgasm, every now and then tipping me over the edge and producing a languid hot wetness that engulfed both of us. Pascal's tranquil approach continued with a sensual hypnotic rhythm, bringing me to new levels of pleasure with each deep penetrative thrust, until with an unexpectedly powerful movement of his hips he began to empty himself inside me, flooding me with his hot cum, it felt exquisite and my vagina milked him of every last drop, clamping him firmly inside me until his erection fully subsided.

The other men were working Karen hard, and Rubens had now joined the merriment and was engrossed in watching how Karen was skilfully surrendering herself to this onslaught of hard cock. She'd well and truly found her inner slut, and was actively issuing instructions as to what she wanted next. It wasn't long before every one of her orifices was plugged and she gurgled happily as the intense pounding continued. She had certainly found her feet quicker than I'd anticipated, and the look of pure lust on her face as the guys eventually lined up to feed her their cum was a joy to witness. She'd had a baptism of fire, and had emerged triumphant, if not a little messy by the end of it.

Everyone showered before exuberantly jumping into the pool to cool off before indulging in some cheese and a tot more brandy. The last thing I remember before sneaking off for some much needed sleep was Karen gearing up with several of the guys for another round of debauchery.

The scene that greeted me in the courtyard the following morning was one of total devastation, with several sleeping bodies awkwardly positioned in various sun loungers, Karen was curled up on a large bean bag partially covered by a duvet, totally out for the count. Once coffee was made and people surfaced bleary eyed the task of clearing up was slowly undertaken. Rubens appeared fresh faced and bushy tailed a few hours later, just as the last of the empties was binned, his timing was spot on as usual. It was late morning when Karen and I said our thanks and farewells, and we jumped in the car and drove to my bar in Almayate Alto for a debrief.

Karen was most animated as she recalled her evening and her own personal input to the proceedings. She said that it was the small details that boosted her confidence to the degree where she felt totally at ease in the situation and her ability to express her sexual needs fully. Simple things like a flirtatious look or a subtle touch were the things that worked for her. The only thing she felt that she was lacking in her toolbox so to speak, was the ability to fully achieve a squirting orgasm like the ones she'd witnessed of mine and read about in my books. I promised her that I'd arrange for her to meet Mike "Le Digit" for some of his much sought after guidance in all things regarding the turning on of the female tap. A promise I lived up to and a most successful outcome apparently transpired a few weeks after her return to London. We met up again for coffee a while later and I welcomed her to "the club".

I was due to fly back on Saturday evening, so the next couple of days were all mine to potter around doing things in the cottage, and chilling at my new agricultural spot on the beach, rewarded with a bag or two of avocado and mangoes! However, I had one date to attend on the Friday evening, as Jorge my Portuguese bull had invited me to dinner as he had someone he'd like me to meet. He wouldn't expand further, except to give me directions to his apartment in Malaga and a time to arrive. I was intrigued and excited as he told me just to bring a pair of heels as he had picked an outfit for me to wear. Friday night couldn't come quick enough.

Chapter Thirty-Five: A Soiree With A Difference

Excited, and slightly pensive at what the evening had in store I spent a wistful hour lazing in our newly purchased free standing hammock, glass of wine in hand and let my imagination run away with me. I knew that it would be demanding, if our first encounter at Cabopino was anything to go by. But even by my standards the evening turned out to be a very definite "first" for me, an experience to remember, hopefully to be repeated at some stage. It certainly opened my eyes and left me momentarily speechless.

I showered and packed a pair of high heels and make up bag as instructed and set of for Malaga. I took the old and very scenic coast road that skirts the Mediterranean all the way to the "Playa de la Malagueta", which fronted his rather impressive apartment building. Its setting is very eye catching, with a large busy promenade popular with the so called "beautiful people", all posing and parading at all times of the day and night. It's a most vibrant area with an absolute abundance of bars and restaurants. I eventually negotiated my way through the busy traffic and found the apartment buildings private underground parking and keyed in the code he'd given me. I drove down a few levels and pulled into the vacant bay next to his car. The lift took me swiftly to the top level where Jorge's impressively large apartment was located. So far I was most impressed, however, when he opened the door to greet me I was completely flabbergasted and overwhelmed by the sweeping views out to the terrace and the sparkling Mediterranean beyond.

Jorge poured me a glass of chilled white wine and gave me a whirlwind tour of his vast penthouse apartment, leaving the master bedroom suite till last, where upon he produced my evenings out fit. There wasn't much of it, just a very small clingy black cocktail dress, which only just managed to cover my modesty, both top and bottom. Once I managed to squeeze into it I felt like I was still naked, and had simply been poured into a small piece of material, it was ultra clingy, ultra tight and most importantly made me feel ultra sensual. The high black patent shoes elongated my tanned legs; I even impressed myself, which takes some doing.

I joined Jorge on the large terrace and admired the amazing view, both over the sea and over the newly refurbished port area towards the city, it was very much like a film set, all crowned off with a very inviting Jacuzzi nestling at the far end. There was a large marble topped table laid for three, but Jorge wouldn't divulge any further information as to the extra guest, who was due to arrive at any moment. I was just happy to be there, and would have settled for a night of domination by him alone and his colossal cock of course. As he was pouring us another drink his video entry system announced the guests arrival and he buzzed them in. I was most fascinated as to who would appear at his door; well what arrived took my breath away. Through the entrance stepped a very tall, striking looking brunette with a perfect figure, enhanced with a pair of what I can only describe as "porno" model breasts. She was a head taller than me, and dressed in a long figure hugging dress and simply looked quite spectacular.

Jorge introduced her as Isabela, and briefly explained they'd met several years previously whilst on holiday in Mexico. She was currently living down the coast in Marbella, not much else was forthcoming so I began telling her about me, and with much laughter how I'd come meet Jorge (although I felt she already knew the story). Something clicked once I offered her a St Moritz and we both visibly relaxed. She was very touchy feely, and throughout the conversation took every opportunity to stroke my thighs and face, overtly sexual behaviour and Jorge looked on approvingly. Shortly the intercom buzzed again to which Jorge loudly exclaimed "dinner". I liked his style, he'd only gone and rung the beach restaurant that we could see from the terrace and ordered a whopping freshly cooked Paella, complete with salads, which was delivered by three waiters, as it took two just to carry the main dish. It smelt divine but tasted even better, fresh and loaded with seafood, and zizzed up with a few squeezes of fresh lime. Absolutely hit all the right spots on the way down. The tropical salad was a taste explosion with bits of exotic fruits liberally scattered on top. The conversation flowed as we devoured the food, degenerating to tales of a sexual nature, my Parisian escapades and a few choice stories of some wild evening frolics at Cabopino from Jorge. Isabela was intrigued by my stories involving my much loved poppers, and when I told her I had a fresh unopened bottle with me she got very excited, insisting that we make good use of them. I could tell that Jorge was getting aroused, as there was a massive tell tale bulge in his shorts. It wasn't long after that it was decided that we'd have a brandy or in my case a large Jack Daniels and retire to savour them in the Jacuzzi.

I stripped of there, and then as Jorge showed Isabela to a room where she could disrobe and hang her dress. I'd already made it with my drink into the hot bubbling tub when Jorge appeared naked, proudly reintroducing me to his gargantuan semi aroused appendage. Once in he asked me how I liked our guest, to which I replied with great positivity, I immediately noticed he was grinning wildly, and then suddenly the penny dropped, and almost as if rehearsed a naked Isabela materialised, my eyes at first drawn to her large firm breasts and long bullet like chocolate nipples, then my jaw dropped fully into the water as I noticed she was also sporting what was a fully functioning cock of epic proportions. I was speechless as she stood there in all her/his glory flexing its awesome cock for my appraisal. I thought I'd seen it all, but this was right there in front of me larger-than-life in every sense of the word. Just phenomenal, she smiled very sensually and just said "surprise". Surprise didn't even begin to cover it, all I could think of was how the fuck was I going to explain this to Paul, where on earth would I start (thankfully I had my iPhone with me fully charged and Jorge captured some great photos throughout the evening). As she joined us in the bubbles she raised her brandy glass and toasted me saying, "tonight you are our personal little fuck toy". My first reaction is always the best one, and my "in for a penny in for a pound" attitude has always held me in good stead over the years. So I responded with "I'm yours to use as you choose", this produced a most approving and lecherous look from them both. After a while we decided to take the party indoors to the large lounge area with its huge sprawling sofas, not before I'd been instructed to get back into my heels.

Once inside Jorge took control instructing me to kneel in front of Isabela and service her with my mouth for a while, it was a very strange sensation having this large cock in my throat whilst locking eyes with the attractive owner, who also sported a phenomenal pair of breasts. I found myself getting massively aroused by the moment and my vagina began to open and throb in expectation. Jorge sat back occasionally stroking his erection whilst watching me drooling and salivating profusely over this most unexpected cock. This gorgeous creature knew how to feed a lady and was dominating my mouth with a mixture of ferocity and delicacy combined. It was a very different kind of experience, being instructed by a feminine voice as to how she liked her cock sucked, strange but highly erotic. Jorge soon joined us and at my request unsealed my little bottle of poppers, much to the excitement of Isabela, who was desperate to give it a try. She knelt down with me and watched intently as I took a big hit, I swiftly held them under her nose and encouraged her to sniff. For a first timer the effect is very swift and I could see her face flush as the warm tingling wave of pleasure began cursing through her veins, then her large cock jerked and flexed like a large snake, it was a ferocious sight, quite awesome. She gripped my shoulders to steady herself as Jorge offered us his colossal erection to suck on; we both used our tongues on him with aggressive passion, taking turns in having him deep in our throats. Eventually, we pushed him back on to the large sofa where I began to work on his balls with my tongue, whilst Isabela positioned herself behind me, lifting and spreading my bottom as she in turn went to work on my anus. Her tongue was amazing as it probed me deeply, weaving tantalising swirling circles over my sensitive rectum; all the while Jorge was keeping up a lewdly stimulating running commentary. It was a scene straight from ancient Roman times, total and utter depravity reigned throughout the evening. Isabela was fully into all things anal and spent a long period worshiping mine, and had me in all sorts of trouble as she used a chrome plug on me as she wanked my erect clitoris. Jorge fucked my mouth avidly as he looked down upon the scene. My orgasms were sharp and brutal, and Isabela absolutely adored it when I squatted over her face and squirted hot streams of my cum into her eager mouth, the sight of her huge smooth cock added to the depravity of the events. We were all pushing each other's boundaries to extreme levels of sexual decadence. The poppers were well used, and I thought my body was going to explode after one hit when Isabela began to penetrate me, deliciously stretching my engorged labia with her large tip whilst Jorge filled my mouth with his solid unyielding erection. The feeling of being fucked by her was very reminiscent of the times Sarah has used her mammoth strap on upon me whilst Paul and Mike looked on. Both my pussy and anus were well used over the course of the evening, pounded and drilled brutally by both of their monstrous cocks. My mouth was tested to the most extreme limits. The debauchery culminated as they both heavily lubricated my throat with profuse amounts of their hot seed, I called upon all my previous experiences to drink all I was given and not waste one precious drop of their offering. The beauty of it all was the afterglow and hot jetting water on my well-used body courtesy of the Jacuzzi, oh and a large Jack Daniels. It was certainly an evening to remember, let alone the rude awakening the following morning as they set about me again for some quick post breakfast filth before I had to scoot back to the cottage to get things sorted in readiness for my evening flight back to Paul with a few choice photos to show him.

Chapter Thirty-Six: Paul's Point Of View

This next segment is due to the feedback received in the many emails from readers and assorted Amazon reviews of "First Tango in Paris", where it was apparent that many of you wanted to know a little more about Paul and his experiences. With this in mind I set Paul a little mission of contributing a chapter to this "The Conclusion". I gave him a target of two to three thousand words written in own style, where he could put his viewpoint across. He ummed and ahed for a while, only agreeing when I promised to help him if he got stuck along the way. This little interlude in the process of writing the book really turned out to be a really fun refreshing time for us both, with Paul and I reliving some of our more memorable experiences over many evenings, accompanied by several bottles of fine wine and finally making a short list of what Paul felt were some of the finer moments. Eventually he had a clear direction in his mind as to how and what he was going to write. Armed with only his memories, a MacBook Pro and a blank Word document I left him to his task, which by this stage he was very enthused about. So at this point I hand you over to Paul, my most understanding and supportive husband and soul mate.

Well here goes, this isn't something that I ever thought I'd be doing, much preferring to relive certain magical memories purely in my mind, however, due to a vast amount of coaxing from "her who must be obeyed" I agreed to furnish you with a few thousand of my words of wisdom. So please bare with me, and have a little sympathy for my predicament as I sit in front of this keyboard pretty much devoid of any clue as how to proceed.

In my personal opinion fate dealt us a great hand all those years ago when we experienced first hand the delights of "swinging" in all its various guises during that first weekend in Paris. It has certainly broadened our horizons in nothing but a positive fashion. The people we have met along the way have been some of the kindest and genuine people you'd ever wish to meet in any walk of life, many of which have remained firm and trusted friends to this day. It has produced not only vast amounts of carnal pleasures, but also, especially for Emma several business opportunities which she threw herself into wholeheartedly and was rewarded by success and of course a whole lot of fun along the way. I can totally understand this kind of lifestyle and outlook is not suited to everyone, however, when both parties are in tune and on the same wavelength it can be highly rewarding. My advice when asked has always been to take things slowly at first, discuss the situation fully afterwards and proceed at your own pace. It is also imperative that your relationship is strong and has been built to include a high degree of trust on both sides.

There have been numerous unforgettable erotic liaisons over the years; however, one in particular deserves a special mention, as it was a direct result of Emma's initial book "First tango in Paris".

Early February 2014 Emma forwarded an email to me from a lady called Linda who lived on Long Island in New York State, in a small town called Syosett. She'd been gifted the book by a friend of hers, and had been totally overwhelmed by the honesty and forthright approach of the book and just wanted to express her admiration to both Emma and myself for having the courage to publish it as we did, no hiding behind pixelated faces or using exotic sounding pen names. She was particularly taken with the scenario Mike and myself had enjoyed with Antonia, whom at the time of our initial soiree was a time bomb waiting to explode. She empathised with Antonia and relished the idea of recreating a similar evening in a safe and private environment. After several emails and Emma chatting to her via Skype it was arranged for her and I to meet up for dinner the next time I was in New York on business, which at this time was pretty much every other week.

Linda turned out to be a very attractive brunette in her late thirties with a wickedly dry sense of humour. She was fresh out of a ten year marriage, which in her words was "soulless", they had drifted apart over the years as her ex husbands job in the financial sector had required a high level of schmoozing on the New York cocktail party circuit, something she didn't particularly enjoy. The inevitable had happened and she'd grown tired of overlooking his frequent indiscretions. She'd come away from the marriage financially very comfortable, and was actively planning the next phase in her life. Up near the top of her list was to find and unleash her inner sexual diva. She'd tried many of the clubs and bars of Manhattan, but said they were too false and could be very intimidating, and that she was looking for the elegance and sophistication that she said the book exuded. We parted upon a firm promise by myself that I' arrange a special evening for her the following month when she'd be in the U.K, using London as her base as she visited an old school friend, who was happily married and living in Bath.

After getting some much sought after input from Emma to get a female perspective I formulated an evening of elegant, sophisticated evening of sexual exploration for her. When confirming the evening Linda indicated that we should treat her like a "blank canvas" and to just ad layer upon layer until she was a near finished masterpiece. One that would allow her to visit a few select European clubs as a fully confident single lady.

Linda arrived on the Wednesday, and was staying for the first few nights in London at the opulent Mandarin Oriental Hotel in Knightsbridge prior to heading down to her friends in the West Country. We scheduled our little soiree for the Friday evening, giving her a period to acclimatise, and get her body clock adjusted to London time.

With a view to this evening I'd hooked up with Mike the previous week to discuss the ladies wishes, and we came to the conclusion that we should invite another male along to join the party. I thought that three of us could educate the lady without fear of overwhelming her. Mike suggested we should add a bit of colour to the proceedings, and invited a black gentleman, who'd been impressing Sarah recently after they'd met him at one of the Black Man Fan Club events that they now regularly attended. His real name is Charles, but is affectionately referred to as "The Dark Destroyer". Mike endorsed him highly, and as we'd known each other for a great many years I knew that his suggested third player would be of top quality in all the relevant areas.

We'd arranged to meet her at eight in the "Mandarin Bar" of the hotel, have an introductory drink before taking her for a pre event dinner at "Motcombs", just a few minutes away, whose basement dining area was most conducive to some decadent and flirtatious behaviour. As agreed, the three of us met up fully suited and booted for the occasion at seven thirty, so as I could have a few minutes to get to know Charles a little. It was the first time I'd been to this hotel since it's refurbishment and was completely blown away by the changes. The bar itself is centred around a rectangular marble-topped bar, designed to look like a catwalk, there are large brown leather armchairs and elegantly chic glass topped tables everywhere. The décor is luxurious to the maximum with glass cases lining the walls displaying a wide range of hand crafted cocktail glasses. Well worth popping in if you're ever in the area just to soak up the opulence of the space.

Linda arrived promptly, looking slightly nervous, but stunning in a full-length black silky evening dress, her heels added to the effect, as she appeared a lot taller than when we'd met a few weeks earlier in New York. Introductions were made and Linda's sense of humour immediately broke the ice, as when shaking Mike's hand she held it up exclaiming, "ah the legendary fingers, I'm most pleased to meet you at last, I look forward to getting to know you far more intimately." I'd taken the opportunity as soon as I'd arrived to have the barman put a bottle of Laurent Perrier Brut Rosé on ice, to be served when Linda arrived. Thankfully the conversation flowed with a natural ease and Charles really proved to be a real charmer, saying all the rights things, and generally ensuring the lady felt like the proverbial million dollars. Linda in turn was exuding class and style in buckets, let alone giving off a very powerful air of sexual desire. Any fears or slight reservations I'd had that she may freeze and clam up were immediately dispelled, and we were soon on to the diner segment of the evening. Suffice it to say the food was most appetising and fully in keeping with the restaurants reputation for exquisite cuisine. The dishes were accompanied by a large order of sexual seduction by the four hedonistic diners. By the time we left the restaurant everyone was in high spirits and anticipating a dessert of quite epic proportions.

Once back at the hotel we decided to take a brandy in the bar before retiring to Linda's room for the evening's main event. The tension definitely built to a crescendo of pure lust as everyone finished the drinks and we headed up to her room in the lift, in fact Linda was already looking a bit flushed, and was breathing quite heavily, it all bode well for a most mischievous hour or two.

As soon as we stepped into her room Mike went to the in house entertainment system and put some ambient background music on, whilst Charles and I began to seductively help Linda out of her gown. As she had insinuated on a number of occasions throughout the meal she was in fact panty less and stood before us naked, but resplendent in her heels. Her body was quite frankly magnificent, large firm breasts capped with the most edible perky brown nipples; her pussy had been waxed completely smooth, specifically for this encounter, it was also further adorned by two delicate gold labia rings. Linda had completely immersed herself into the scenario, urging us to get naked with her. She wasted no time in her desire to taste our erections, she was trembling when Charles offered her his exceptional endowment, her first black man, and he happened to be huge. She used her mouth and tongue with great aplomb, giving equal attention to each of us. Once she knew she had us all fully aroused she lay back into the large sofa and asked Mike to work his magic, as she wanted to feel what it was like to gush upon orgasm, something she'd never quite been able to achieve. Charles and I sat and observed as Mike began to use his skilled fingers on her, to begin with he expertly massaged each of her lips whilst instructing her to expose her clitoris to him, so as he could occasionally tweak it as her orgasm built. We encouraged her as Mike inserted two of his fingers and explored the inside was of her vagina until he found what he was seeking. His fingers worked feverishly, increasing and decreasing the tempo continually, she was getting wetter by the moment. The atmosphere was electric as he issued whispered instructions to her. I'd seen Mike in this situation on several occasions over the years, and could sense by both his body language, and by the ever increasing effect that this was having on Linda's body, her pupils had rolled up into her head and her thighs had gone into an uncontrollable series of spasms, jerking and flexing as if she was being electrocuted. Charles and I offered occasional lewd words of encouragement as Mike continued to bring her ever closer to her goal. The straw that broke this camels back was when Mike gently inserted his thumb delicately into her rectum, a deep gurgling mewling sound began to come from deep within Linda's chest until it exploded from her mouth as a high pitched scream, this was immediately accompanied by a huge torrent of fluid erupting from her. Mike kept up his intense finger work, which was now being supplemented by some clitoral slapping. Her eyes were rolling furiously as torrential spurts of her juices jetted from her, she was gurgling and crying with extreme pleasure as her ejaculate flowed profusely. As the outpouring subsided Mike and I held her open for Charles, who guided his large black cock into her very wet gaping vagina, she gasped in awe as he began to fuck her in a very forceful and vigorous fashion. Driving his cock into her with brutal and unrelenting power. She was one hundred per cent giving as much as she was received, meeting Charles's thrusts with her own, resulting in a continuous slapping of flesh on flesh, her rhythm was exceptional as she simultaneously offered her mouth to Mike and myself in turn. After several more drenching climaxes we had a break before continuing her education in multiple partner pleasure. She was an excellent pupil, eager to learn and most eager to please, offering herself fully to us to use as we wished. At one point (at her fervent request) Mike and I schooled her gradually into the art of double penetration, which she adored, especially as she had Charles's monstrous black cock to gorge on at the same time. She certainly matched us for stamina and had a prodigious skill at keeping three lust fuelled men satisfied. The three of us managed to stick to our task, and kept our own personal climax in check until we knew the time was right, at which point she greedily instructed us to shower her face with our semen, as in her own words she wanted a finish "just like in the porno films", that she'd seen over the years. Who were we to refuse the Lady her final request of this memorable and most gratifying soiree? Much to our amusement she wanted us to take a photo of our cocks laying on her cum covered face with her iPhone, so she could show "the girls back home", again we fulfilled her request, in fact we went one better and shot thirty seconds of video of her struggling to get all of Charles in her mouth. It was a wonderful and extraordinary evening of adult fun, and after a farewell drink Mike and I said our goodnights, leaving Linda in the more than capable hands of Charles, who by all accounts lavished more attention upon our American guest until dawn. Leaving her well and truly used, but more importantly satisfied.

    Well there you have it, I hope you enjoyed reading a snippet of what it's like from my point of view. As they say "don't knock it until you've tried it". So it's a big thank you from me for listening to me prattle on and maybe we will bump into one another at an event one day, you never know!

Chapter Thirty-Seven: The Exuberance Of Youth

Technology is a wonderful thing across all areas of living, and as mentioned earlier has been a major asset in the swinging arena, it has taken a vast amount of the leg work and dogged determination out of finding the hidden pleasures out there. In my opinion it has generally been a good thing, however, a lot has to be said about the pioneering spirit that we had back in the nineties, it gave everything a major sense of achievement, especially after you'd made great efforts in travelling to a place of possible interest on just word of mouth or a sentence in a magazine, many times we'd arrive at a destination to be let down for a variety of reasons. In this day and age everything is instant and available, things that back in the day would be near impossible are now just a mouse click away. One of the major benefits of this technological age has been the explosion in both the use and quality of Skype. I recently had an intriguing conversation with a couple that use this service frequently to live out their particular sexual fetish. They said it had injected another element to their sex lives that simply wouldn't have been possible ten years ago or even five. He frequently works away in Hong Kong and always arranges a different scenario for his wife whilst he's away. They had great pleasure in recounting several of the situations he's arranged, one in particular sounded quite debauched and well researched. Basically he'd contacted a group of gents via Fabswingers who call themselves "City Slickers", he'd arranged for five of them to pay his wife a home visit whilst he was abroad, he took his pleasure watching them enjoy his wife and her enjoying the attention of all the men whilst he directed the proceedings from his Laptop on the other side of the world. All in real time and high definition courtesy of Skype.

My particular enjoyment of Skype, Apples Facetime and other services of this type is the ability to instantly put a face to a voice or an email. It totally eliminates the "been had" element of things, as there's little chance of the handsome six foot two, thirty year old suddenly becoming a young spotty student with too much time on his hands. You still have to have your wits about you, but it certainly makes things simpler.

I digress, but my favourite Skype initiated encounter was when I received a private message on my personal blog site from a young chap who'd read the book, it simply said "loved the book, may I be this years Laurent?" along with his Skype address. I was momentarily transported back to that warm summer at the house in Kew, when upon a special request from his father (who at one stage was my cock of choice in Paris) I educated Laurent in the art of sexual pleasure. At the time he was eighteen and I was mid-thirties. It was a few weeks of self-indulgent pleasure, turning the young French boy into a man. Hence the message intrigued me, and awakened that little devil inside me, who does on occasion enjoy the attention of a younger man, but I was now in my early fifties and my sensible side quite firmly told me no, but the more I thought about it over the next few days the more excited I became by the idea. I talked about it with Sarah and Penny, both of whom urged me to pursue it, telling me to look upon it as a teacher and pupil arrangement. I was still unconvinced and had reservations, picturing myself in a sexual act with someone younger than my own children was foreboding. But the excitement remained and increased to a level where I had almost convinced myself I'd be doing a good deed. The decider came a few days later when another private message arrived from him that just said " ? You know you want to". That did it, I took the plunge and responded with a contact request to the Skype address he'd given. I must admit a fair bit of excitement ensued, and I avidly checked my Skype status regularly throughout the day. Eventually there was a message saying the request had been accepted and a personal message from him followed suggesting we have a video chat the following afternoon. He said he'd be online from around three, and perhaps I should do the same. I immediately replied saying that I looked forward to it.

    The only thing that I'd deduced was that he was quite probably young, as his original message suggested and he'd signed messages with the name Luke. That was the sum total of what I knew about him, intrigue, anticipation, trepidation, the whole spectrum of emotions ran through my mind. However, as explained before I felt safe in the knowledge that if it was anything other than what was expected I could just terminate the chat and block the person. In this respect it does give you a good feeling of security. I really needn't have worried as promptly at three o'clock my Skype chirped signalling an incoming call, taking a large sip of my Jack Daniels that I'd poured myself whilst putting on my game face and doing my hair I hit the green answer button. Connection made, and a few seconds later a very attractive young man with dark wavy hair appeared grinning on my screen. My immediate thought was "holy shit!" he was actually gorgeous beyond belief, exceptional by any standards.

Thankfully he wasn't backward at coming forward and launched immediately into telling me all about himself. Talk about confident, he exuded maturity beyond his years.

He was in fact called Luke, twenty two year old University student, currently two years into his law degree at Oxford. He lived in an apartment with two fellow students near the city centre. He was originally from Wimbledon, where his family still lived with his younger sister. He'd been intrigued by my book ever since listening two fellow female students discussing it, and basically raving about it and its honesty. I regarded this as a huge compliment; especially when he went on to tell me I was a bit of a legend amongst a certain group of his fellow students, both male and female. What was even more amusing was when he told me that during a weekend at home a few months ago he'd over heard his mother on the phone talking about the book to one of her friends, and promising to send her the Amazon link to buy it. After a good hour on Skype getting better acquainted we arranged to chat again a few days later and see if he was still intent on becoming "this years" Laurent. I'm glad to say he did, telling me that since our initial chat he'd reread the book and was more than ever up for a few intimate lessons from as he put it "a legendary cougar". I thought long and hard how to go about this, and eventually came up with a bit of a plan. Luckily for me Antonia was living in Paris but still had her apartment in Kensington, and after much ribbing from her she gracefully told me to use it whenever needed. She arranged with the property management company for me to pick up the spare keys anytime I was passing. During our next Skype call we arranged to meet the following Wednesday at lunchtime, and that I'd email him all the relevant details a day or two before.

I decided to give him the full Mrs Robinson experience, as so brilliantly portrayed in the famous seventies film "The Graduate". I got to the apartment mid morning with my outfit of choice and popped a nice bottle of Chablis in the fridge to chill. I'd booked a table for two at "*Côte Bistro*" in Kensington Court, which was very conveniently located close to the apartment. At midday armed with a small brandy from Antonia's drinks cabinet I soaked in her tub for a good half hour, accompanied by Ken Bruce droning on in the background on Radio 2. Then after coating myself with my regulation Chanel Body Velvet, and a dab of No.5 here and there, I dressed in my best "cougar" outfit, new lingerie bought just for this occasion from Rigby and Peller in Mayfair. A very elegant and sensual black Andres

Sarda Vitoria garter belt with matching thong and bra, La Perla seamed vintage stockings, topped with a crisp white shirt and navy two-piece fitted business suit by Max Mara, finished off with an elegant pair of black Kurt Geiger court shoes with a conservative (for me) four inch heel.

I arrived at the restaurant ten minutes early and was shown to a nice window table. I waited with a frisson of naughtiness cursing through me, playing various scenarios over and over in my mind. Shortly Luke came confidently through the door, waving as he approached, taller than I anticipated, but oh so eye catching, decked out in Ralph Lauren Oxford shirt with elegantly faded Levi 501 jeans and oxblood loafers. Most casual yet very classy and stylish. After a two-cheek kiss we ordered a bottle of house white wine whilst we chose from the well balanced menu. The food was excellent, I had the Cassoulet de Toulouse, whilst Luke had the Breton fish stew, very tasty and it gave off a very French ambience to the occasion. I have to admit the flirting over the food nearly got out of hand, with both of us getting more and more outrageous in the innuendo department. I had to talk in a bit of a whisper, as he had many questions regarding the book and the many places, people and experiences described therein.

He was very frank and open, telling me that he'd been sexually active since sixteen, and had always fantasised about older women ever since a family holiday in Italy when he was eighteen, and the wife of a family friend who was with them came on to him one evening after she'd had one two many glasses of red wine. He'd always regretted not taking full advantage of the situation, and had regularly thought about what might have been. He made me laugh when he said he settled for second best and slept with their daughter instead. He didn't have a steady girlfriend but was playing the field at university and keeping all his options open. Towards then end of lunch over the coffee I did up the anti a little by telling him I'd taken great care in dressing for the occasion, teasing him, making him guess as to whether it was stockings or hold ups, panties or no panties, the poor lad did become a bit flustered, especially when I revealed that the apartment was minutes away and he'd be most welcome in discovering what in fact I was or wasn't wearing for our illicit liaison. He held his composure together well, especially when I insisted on paying the bill, telling him that it's customary for any cougar worth her salt to pay for her cub on all occasions. This, I told him was the order of things and to get used to it, he did like this slightly bossy nature, something I nurtured over the following few weeks of his "education".

It was a strange but empowering feeling as we strolled back to Antonia's apartment, I saw people glancing at us, and I could only assume they saw us as a mother out shopping out with her son, little did they know!

We had two hours ahead of us until he had to leave to catch his train back to Oxford, as he had a student meeting to attend that evening. So I didn't was anytime, and asked him to open the chilled bottle of wine and pour us both a glass as I went to freshen up. I adored the feeling of being in complete control, and I became increasingly wet as I removed the suit and blouse, leaving me just in the elegant, sultry lingerie and heels. I stood for a moment and freshened my lipstick before returning to the sitting room. His reaction was the one that every woman hopes for, his jaw dropped and he just said, "holy fuck, you look awesome" and handed me my wine. I was elated and did a little twirl for him as he stood transfixed to the spot, his eyes flashing up and down my body. He tentatively stepped forward and very courteously asked "may I ?" as he leant in to kiss me, a kiss that was long deep and probing, making my abdomen flutter with the first crescendo of those furiously flapping butterfly wings, totally exquisite. If the quality of his kissing was anything to go by this young man was going to be a very good pupil, a quick learner who'd relish all his future lessons. I soon settled back into the sofa with my legs spread as he knelt in front of me staring longingly at my crotch area, which was still tantalisingly hidden by the lacy fabric of the thong. I told him that for the next thirty minutes he was to please me with his fingers and tongue, and I'd be issuing instructions and advice along the way. I fully stressed the importance for him and men in general to know their way around a woman's vagina, as I pulled the material to one side, exposing my wetness to him. I told him it was now his time to begin to explore me intimately. He set about his task with great enthusiasm, taking instruction well, after a while peeling off my thong to fully reveal my open pussy, inviting him to enjoy my taste. His tongue worked furiously on me, gently nibbling on my exposed clitoris with a deftness of a much more experienced man, he soon had me on that plateau where I could produce a successive series of squirting orgasms. He sensed this as my thighs began to quiver in his hands, and with a series of bone shaking spasms I let rip a huge stream of my sweet warm juices, filling his enthusiastic open mouth, splashing abundantly off his chin as he struggled to cope with the continual deluge. He continued undeterred, lapping at my pussy with an eagerness found only in a true connoisseur of the female vagina. We were rapidly coming towards the end of our first tutorial, and as we'd discussed there would be no full penetration, as this was going to be a slow and detailed approach, however, not wishing for him to make his way home unfulfilled with a raging erection straining at his jeans I instructed him to sit back and bring himself to orgasm whilst watching me play. He did exactly as told and took out a very solid and impressive looking manhood. Lifting his shirt he began to stroke it to climax, which didn't take long at all, understandable given his situation, an area to be worked on over the coming weeks. His eyes were solidly locked onto my gaping, drenched pussy as he began to powerfully unload his semen over his smooth muscular chest and abdomen, a seriously heavy load was ejaculated, much to my pleasure. He grinned when I said, "Here endeth the first lesson" and sent him to shower and get himself sorted out for his journey back to Oxford.

    Our second meeting took place exactly a week later, and lunch was taken in the same restaurant, a routine was being established, one that met with both our full approval. This governess – student two-hour lesson involved me teaching him the art of self control. Again I dressed for the occasion, however, this time telling him to get fully naked whilst I freshened up. I returned to the room in just a pair of sheer black hold ups and high platform court shoes, accentuating the length of my legs. It had an immediate effect on him, his erection jerked and flexed, veins pulsing, it took on a life of its own. The sole purpose was to teach him willpower, instilling in him a high level of discipline, simply not crossing the line and giving in to his penis and its desperate need to ejaculate. I set a time limit of one full hour, during which I worked on him with my mouth, letting my tongue glide all over his rock solid cock, firmly gripping the base when I sensed him getting too close to that point of no return, relaxing with a sip or two of wine whilst his urges subsided to a degree where he could once again control his cock. We worked together as a team for the full sixty minutes until he just couldn't take any more, and was literally pleading with me to allow him to cum. He begged me too let him stand and fuck my mouth, something he'd told me he'd been dreaming of doing since our first Skype call, when he'd fallen in lust with my techno pink lip gloss. I told him to briefly hold that thought and scurried off to the bathroom and quickly applied a fresh coat to my lips. I shouted from the bathroom, telling him to stand up, and as I entered the room I dropped to my knees, pouting my newly glossed lips and crawled seductively towards him and his fully loaded erection. Licking my lips in a full on porno style I began to lick and suck his smooth shaven scrotum, slowly working my tongue onto the base of his heavily veined shaft, lewdly telling him to feed me his cum. After several minutes of this intense tongue work he couldn't endure it anymore and began to violently ejaculate huge warm salty streams of his milk, pumping load after load into my hungry mouth, I was in heaven as my own tumultuous climax hit me as I was feverishly devouring all his colossal outpouring. I adored the feeling of the warmth of his semen as it filled my mouth and cascaded down my chin, big chunks of it splashing down on to my thighs. I came so hard as I was also imagining Laurent being there slut fucking me from behind at the same time. Before leaving I told him that his homework was simply to practice what we'd achieved until we met up the following week for more of this most enjoyable intensive tuition.

Our intimate afternoon liaisons continued in a similar vein, increasing in intensity each time. Together we honed his technique, his self-control and his overall confidence in giving pleasure to a woman, whatever age she may be. He achieved such a high level of skill in all areas that after a few more delightful meetings I decided he was ready to be released into the wild and unleashed on the general female population. With this in mind I arranged what was going to be our final afternoon for a while (as he was heading off on a family holiday) to be a little special, I wanted to put the young buck through his paces and see if he could put all that I'd taught him in to practice!

That particular Wednesday afternoon was memorable in so many ways, starting off with the complete look of shock and disbelief on Luke's face as he walked into the restaurant to be greeted not only by me, but also Sarah, who had embraced the idea with her usual enthusiastic exuberance. There was a dull thud as his jaw firmly hit the deck as the realisation of who this "other" lady of a certain age was dawned on him. His voice went up an octave and he shook a little as I made the introductions. His expression was a sight to behold. Once he'd pulled himself together and took a sip of his wine we began to tease and flirt with him unmercifully, he did a good job in giving back as good as he got in the verbal jousting, but the occasional trembling hand was a sure giveaway. It was even more electric as the attractive young waitress had definitely worked out the situation and gave me a very knowing grin at one stage. She looked about Luke's age, and they would have made a lovely looking couple, but sadly for her he was all ours for the afternoon. Sarah was playing the role of elder cougar with total commitment, really teasing Luke, with many of her comments verging on the obscene. However, in fairness he handled it all with complete aplomb.

The minx of a waitress winked at me as we were leaving, both of us leading him arm in arm from the restaurant towards the apartment. Once we were inside and drinks were poured Sarah and I went and undressed leaving just our lingerie in place, and much to our surprise and complete delight when we returned to the sitting room Luke was already naked, reclined on the sofa stroking his solid cock, which was already oozing copious amounts of his pre-cum fluid, making his erection glisten and shimmer invitingly. Sarah and I took immediate advantage of him and began taking him in our mouths in turn, nibbling his throbbing shaft, each suckling on a testicle, deftly working on his pristine anus with our fingers and tongues, we had him in all sorts of trouble from the very beginning. After a serious bout of this tongue treatment wee backed off for a moment, to take a drink and let this overwhelmed twenty two year old regain his composure and reign in his cock, mind over matter ruled, as his brain overrode the thoughts his erection was having. We then enjoyed some role reversal, with both Sarah and I lying back on the sofa, our legs open invitingly for him to eat our wet pussies, whilst tonguing one he'd deliciously finger the other. Sarah loved it as I issued instructions to him, reminding him with little hints at some of the things I taught him. This inspired him to new heights, his tongue seemingly to be able reach new hidden depths in both of us, we both reached our personal peaks where we would climax at will, he drank us both with relish as we shared his mouth, taking turns to fill it with our ejaculate, for a long period his face was shining with our excess vaginal fluids. We lewdly licked each other's juices off his face, and then we gave him every boys dream scenario as our mouths eagerly sought out each other's vagina. He watched intently as we lapped at each other with a complete lack of inhibition. We went at each other like two cats on heat, urging each other to even more lascivious tongue work, it was a very wet but incredibly pleasurable interlude.

After a reenergising with a five-minute break and a much needed glass of wine we both went at Luke again, in a way that would make every milf, cougar and aspiring cougar most proud. We took turns in riding him, milking him with our vastly experienced and well trained vaginas, on occasion he took control and dominated us in turn, instructing us to get on all fours in front of him and open ourselves up to accept a pounding from his rock-solid weapon. He was doing me proud and was putting everything I'd taught him into action, drilling into Sarah with powerful unyielding thrusts. He'd crossed the psychological barrier, and he had now most certainly developed a complete control of his penis, it performed, as he wanted it to perform, and not allow it to branch out and do its own thing. In my opinion, and more so my experience, is that it's a rare thing to find in a man who maintains a total unselfish control and unyielding focus on the females pleasure. If you find a man with such qualities keep hold of him, or at the very least get his contact details, you'll never know when he may come in handy.

    Luke was at this stage goading us with his new found prowess, and was using it to maximum effect, pounding into us relentlessly, making us climax time and time again until eventually we just had to turn the tables on him. I stood him up and firmly held his arms behind his back as Sarah knelt down and began to administer her famous cock sucking technique, salivating heavily over his flexing tool, teasing the tip with her teeth and tongue. I reached around from behind and took his erection into my firm grip and began to stroke him in to Sarah's hungry, open mouth, thankfully we were back in control and soon had him whimpering as he unleashed a tumultuous torrent of his warm sticky cum into the eager willing mouth before him, stream after stream pumped from him as his thighs tightened under the strain of this overdue release. Sarah was gurgling away, straining as she endeavoured to capture every last drop. She's never been a wasteful person! I joined Sarah in cleaning him with our tongues before we crashed in a spent heap on the sofa for a few minutes before showering and getting dressed. By which point young Luke was hard once more, but time had beaten us, I was proud of him and envisaged some lucky student being on the receiving end of one seriously hard fucking later that evening. He'd more than earned his stripes, and both Sarah and I wished him happy hunting on his family holiday and to keep an eye out for the older ladies, we are positively the best, and we do enjoy being taken by a young buck given half a chance.

Chapter Thirty-Eight: Paris v London

Since the publication of "First Tango in Paris" in 2013 I've received many emails, and had many face-to-face conversations with people, and there is one question that crops up time and time again, "London or Paris?" I obviously am very biased towards Paris, as this was where it all started for me and still continues to this day to draw me in to its delights and ever evolving "Swing Scene". However, it is a complex question, and one that deserves more than a simple and glib one-line answer. So I'll try and explain it best I can from my point of view, and the reasons why. And then I'll leave it up to you the individual to make your own decision, at least one that you can make on a relatively well-informed basis.

Many people often say to me "surely a club or party is only as good as the people who attend?" Well maybe at a small dinner party yes, however not in larger event, this old often quoted adage simply doesn't stack up.

To me, in my humble opinion an evening in a "Swinging" environment is far more than simply about sex, it's the whole ambience of the occasion from start to finish, the pre event build up can be a highly exciting hour or two in itself, especially if it occurs in a foreign country where the different language and culture can produce a feeling of complete anonymity, an aura of being detached from the reality of their normal daily life and environment, and give rise to a huge loosening of ones inhibitions. It becomes an exciting adventure, rather than a mundane night out in familiar surroundings. A high degree of sexual pleasure comes not only from the act itself, but also from your mind, those thoughts that can and do occur at anytime, but more so the closer you get to the evening in question.

As I've written earlier, in recent years (post New of The World) the club and party scene in London and the United Kingdom as a whole has exploded, whereas in Paris it has just evolved naturally over time, which in itself creates a huge difference in quality of events and venues. One massive advantage that Paris has over London is that every single club in Paris is licensed, and you simply arrive as you would any regular nightclub and order your drink of choice from the vast array on offer, where in the U.K there are virtually no clubs that are allowed to function like this. That creates a big problem in my opinion, to me it is very off putting having to turn up with a supermarket or off licence carrier bag with your evening's drinks inside, to me that is totally naff. It completely destroys the entire lead up to an evening of hedonistic delights. The idea of queuing up in an "Oddbins or Threshers" in a slinky LBD and Louboutins is a full on passion killer. Another key area where Paris and the French clubs in general come out firmly on top is the food. As I comprehensively describe in book one, the quality of the dining experience in many of the Parisian clubs is comparable to the finest found in its top class restaurants. Sadly many of the London clubs are still stuck in a bit of a time warp, with buffet food that still features sausage rolls and processed ham sarnies etc, not very appetising. Even the basic Parisian venue will have tasty and elegant finger food, but this is typically French.

Many people really find the anonymity aspect a great turn on in itself, and again being in an environment where the majority are speaking a foreign language is somehow adds to the decadence of it all, however, many of the London events can recreate this to a degree, with many holding "Masquerade" evenings. I personally find being naked amongst a group of men who are all wearing elegant Venetian masks is massively arousing and gets the juices flowing …so to speak!

At the end of the day what it all boils down to is personal taste, every couple or individual is very different in their needs, and what they are looking for from any occasion differs widely for each individual.

Both cities offer a broad spectrum of choice, and you'll find something somewhere that caters to most niches and fetishes. London has always had a thriving fetish scene, which has operated for many years, whereas Paris seems to mainly cater to regular mainstream swinging, but does have its share of fetish venues. One mentioned in the previous book, but well worth noting again here is Le Château des Lys, this has it all in buckets for the S & M lovers out there. A truly superb establishment, with outstanding facilities, from its top restaurant, to its magnificently equipped play areas. Take a look at what they offer on their website, I think it may tempt many of you, also it's open seven nights a week. If you are looking for something similar closer to home try the world renowned "Torture Garden", however their events are held at various locations, not in a specific club and the events are only held monthly.

For people who enjoy the impulsive side of swinging London can be very frustrating, especially if you're looking to play during the daytime, apart from the aforementioned Kestrel Hydro there is precious little else that caters to the "afternoon delight" crowd, and even then they are out on the fringes of Central London. Paris on the other hand is a whole different ballgame, with at least a dozen or so regular clubs and spa's that open specifically for this purpose, and the majority are all located centrally. They all also cater for singles as well as couples who enjoy daytime liaisons.

    So in conclusion, I would have to say that Paris is still absolutely streets ahead of London in all areas of the swinging lifestyle, but London and the rest of the U.K has most definitely made great advances over recent years, and is slowly catching up, however it has a long way to go, but I'm sure it will eventually be right up there alongside Paris within a few years. If the progress from London 2006 to London 2016 is anything to go by we may even surpass our French cousins at some stage. But I wouldn't hold your breath!

Chapter Thirty-Nine: A Late Entry

During the latter stages in the proof reading and editing of this book an email accompanied by a photograph from a thirty three year old single lady called Stephanie pinged into my inbox. It was so well written and just begged a response from me. Even though I've not met her yet I have agreed to meet her shortly with a view to arranging a unique event to help her realise her fantasy. Below is a copy of her mail.

"Dear Emma

Firstly thank you for bringing some much needed pleasure into my world with your books First Tango in Paris and Distracted, I read both over a two week period shortly after coming out of a long term relationship, the eventual separation was not a pleasant six months of my life. The books gave me a real positive hope that the next stage of my life would be more fun filled and free of baggage. I read them with a sense of admiration and a huge feeling of envy at your experiences (especially the Firemen in Paris). By the way I'm Stephanie and I'm thirty three years old, living in Fulham with only my cat for company. I have attached to recent photos of me and have included my direct phone number should you be inclined to help me achieve my fantasy. To explain, since my early twenties I have had an overwhelming love of anything "penis" (This is where I feel we have a lot of common ground). I have never really had the opportunity to translate my love of cock into reality. I cannot look at a man without imagining how his penis would look, feel, taste etc. I see oral sex as an art form and to me cock sucking is beyond sex. My eyes and mouth worship the cock, the veins, the balls, the shaft, the head, the hot semen. Every movement of my tongue, every shift of my head translates into a perfected state of communion between me and the man with whom I'm connecting. It may be that not a single syllable is uttered, but the level of communication transcends any language.

Because I love cock. I love how it looks, how it feels, how it tastes. I love it hard and I love it soft. I love to fondle it and make it hard. I love to take it into my mouth and bring it to orgasm and flood my mouth with hot spunk.

Because I love serving hot horny guys. I love to be on my knees for their pleasure. I love to bring them to shattering orgasm. I love to look up at them, their dick in my mouth, and see them smiling down at me, while I pleasure them.

Because I love how sucking cock makes me feel, and for that moment where I belong, doing what I should do, want to do, need to do, love to do, have to do. When a hard dick slides into my mouth and I begin to suck it, I feel something unique that I can experience in no other way. It is compounded by pleasure for both my feeder and myself, in me being a cocksucker, and gratitude for my feeder's generosity in sharing his cock with me and allowing me to serve him and nourish myself with his sexual power and his warm, rich cum.

I suck dick because I'm a natural born cocksucker.

Now I've got that off my chest I just hope you feel that you may be able to help and guide me in achieving my pent up inner fantasy of serving on my knee's for a select group of attractive well endowed men.

Thank you in advance for taking the time to read this and please feel free to call, text or email me if you can steer me on the correct course. Maybe we could meet for a drink and discuss?

Again many thanks and do let me know as and when your next book is available.

Kind regards

Steph xx "

There you have it; you can see why I was drawn to this particular email. I look forward to meeting up with her and seeing if I can arrange something suitable to fulfil her wishes. I'm pretty sure that it won't be a problem; if the resultant situation pans out like it should it could be the basis for a future novella, let's wait and see. It's always exciting to have little gems like this to look forward to.

Chapter Forty: In Summary

Finally I thought it might be a nice idea to conclude the book with a section that details some of the finer clubs out there that are worthy of a mention. I've included brief details regarding each venue that I have taken verbatim directly from the club/events web pages or reviews on various swinger sites. The ones listed here have either been visited by Paul and myself or come highly recommended by close friends and acquaintances that have. It just serves to give you the reader a quick reference point from where to start or in the majority of cases continue your sexual adventures. As Dermot O'Leary would say they are "listed in no particular order".

Kestrel Hydro

Kestrel Hydro is a mixed gender Naturist Spa that is located near Heathrow Airport. The Hydro, which has a warm, friendly and relaxed atmosphere, is a Naturist spa for those who prefer not to wear clothes whilst allowing them to enjoy the full benefits and pleasures of a sauna, a heated swimming pool, an outdoor and indoor hot-tub, relaxing rooms, a sunbathing area and so much more. As described earlier you'll see this venue gets a huge thumbs up from me.

Black Man Fan Club

Parties specifically organised for ladies and couples who appreciate the extras that Black Guys bring, and for the Black Guys that enjoy being appreciated.

Currently we have 6 Adult parties organised every month in various venues across the London Area and we have recently expanded to venues in the NORTH WEST of England too.

Strict NO PRESSURE policy so ideal for newbies and guests of all experience.

Great emphasis put on sourcing the best DJ's and well-designed venues.

We manage the guest list and ensure that the ratio of guys to females is no more than 2:1 - so all guests are assured of there being NO CATTLE market scenario

Our main aim is delivering Value For Money

Admission is by guest list only!

Party dates and Venues

1st SATURDAY of every month @ AROUSALS, Dunstable, Luton

2nd FRIDAY of every month @ XTASIA, West Bromwich, Birmingham

3rd SATURDAY of every month @ RADLETT, Hertfordshire

4th FRIDAY of every month @ THE NO3 CLUB, Chorley, Manchester

4th SATURDAY of every month @ FUNTIME Crystal Palace, South London

We also arrange BMFC Parties at EUREKA, Kent on a sporadic basis (check our website for exact dates)

Whilst admission to a BMFC party would never be refused based on the colour of someone's skin, guests must realise and accept that the ladies who attend our parties do so, because they are mainly into Black Guys!

More info? - www.blackmansfanclub.co.uk (where you will find a comprehensive FAQ page, advice galore and LOADS of tips and hints to ensure your BMFC experience is a FANTASTIC one!!).

The above is featured courtesy of our good friends Mike and Sarah amongst many others who attend regularly and can't speak highly enough of both the evens and their host and founder Helen, her attention to detail is legendary.

Radlett Parties Hertfordshire

We try to keep the format simple and fun. You don't need to join a club, pay membership, send photographs or give your life history. The devaluation of our home by parties is well into six figures, so we do look for a contribution to pool maintenance, damage, etc. from those who haven't had us to a recent uncharged party. We throw parties while we enjoy them, not as a business. While revellers defray the costs of parties we can throw more of them. Parties start from 21:30 and stop when the last person leaves.

To assist those who feel torn between eating out or frolicking, we ease the burden by feeding you to a fair standard. There are usually provisions for those who stay over to have breakfast etc. the following morning.

The facilities include a 50 foot long covered pool, 30 foot dance room with dance pole, sauna, hot tub, 3 secluded acres for summer evening revelry and a 500 square foot dungeon with winchable body hoist, and stocks. Between two and five bedrooms are made available for associative therapy. Go and explore their website www.radlettparties.net

Le Boudoir Club London

Le Boudoir is the UK's newest private members club and it is right in the heart of London.

Friendly, decadent and sexy, it is a bespoke venue for the whole LGBT, lifestyle and fetish communities, particularly those liberated ladies who want to enjoy their sexual freedom in a safe and stylish environment.

As a Private Members Club. Membership applications must be received and approved no less than 48hrs prior to your first planned visit. I am afraid that no membership means no entry.

Be seduced by Le Boudoir's cosy corners, seductive vaults and sexy, playful themes. Our regular Tantric events may just leave you breathless.... On my to visit list. www.leboudoir.net

The Townhouse: The Wirral

With Vicky and Jimmy at the helm, Townhouse has enjoyed swinging success since 2005 and is going through a full refurbishment; the club is looking amazing, with a classy makeover, moving away from the stereotypical black an red!!!

The club is spotlessly clean with a warm and friendly atmosphere. We enjoy a relaxed approach to swinging which is ideal for new swingers as well as established swingers who feel intimidated by the 'full on' expectancy from other venues. We do not expect a 'dress down' on arrival and in the bar areas, members can wear whatever they wish. Dress down is appreciated in the play rooms after 11pm.

The venue has a licence to sell alcohol but if you want to keep costs down then you are welcome to bring your own alcohol.

However our bar is highly subsidised i.e. a shot of Smirnoff vodka is £1.00. We offer towels and condoms free off charge and have showers/ toilets on 3 floors and a large changing room with lockers.

We have a fabulous refurbished hot tub and sauna area which is cleaned every night; it has it's own showers and toilet. For our smokers we have a heated outdoor smoking area with tables and chairs and dressing gowns are provided for your comfort; this area is on our plans for refurbished in 2016.

We are open 8:30pm to 3am Weds – Sat and 4pm to 10pm on a Sunday. Some events have different opening times, but these will be detailed on Fab listings and on our website

Facilities include:- Large, secure car parking, Bar and social lounge area Dance floor, pole Lounge with large stage for shows/bands, Changing/locker room, 3 separate showers, 8 playrooms including a refurbished orgy room (which is huge!), 2 private rooms, Jail/grope box/glory hole 2 x dungeon rooms with kneeling bench, bondage bed, A-frame and medical bed. We have cages, a St Andrews cross, several suspension points for rope work, queening stool, stocks and spanking horse in other parts of the club. We also have an authentic cellar dungeon with jail cells and a padded cell; this is one of the few cellar dungeons outside of London!

You will always receive a warm welcome at Townhouse and our reviews speak for themselves. We are a club owned and run by experienced swingers; our bar staff and managers are established members and understand the scene...you are in very safe hands! We are now one of the most talked about clubs in the North! Come and find out why! www.townhouseswingers.co.uk

If you look them up on Fabswingers you'll see the plethora of rave reviews they've been receiving. I might just take a trip and visit their "MILF Monday" which is held from10.30am-3.30pm on the 1st Monday of the Month for all the horny ladies out there.

Eureka Parties: Kent

As mentioned earlier in the book, this is well worth checking out, especially if the weather is set fair a daytime visit could be fun.

The South Easts Premier Adult Night Out and with over 200 people attending every Saturday and over 100 on Friday nights probably one of the busiest!

We are set in over 23 acres of land so parking isn't a problem and with two Jacuzzis, a sauna, steam room, showers, four themed play rooms, a stunningly refurbished couples room and a dance area with seating for 180, you should find plenty to do.

We hold parties every Wednesday, Friday and Saturday as well as themed nights most Thursdays.

We do not sell alcohol but you are welcome to bring your own and if you want to stay over we have thirteen cabins available for hire, please book well in advance for Saturdays as they go quickly.

If it's your first visit please let us know when you sign in and we will give you a tour of our facilities. Something for everyone at this long standing venue www.eurekaparties.co.uk

Xtasia: West Midlands

In the heart of the Midlands, Xtasia is located within half a mile of Junction 1 of the M5, and 2 miles from Junction 8 of the M6. Voted the UK's number 1 club in 2014 by its peers, its found within 50 yards of The Premier Inn on West Bromwich High Street.

The Xtasia complex provides a welcoming cosy bar called "Flirts", serving alcohol and food from 6pm to 10pm Wednesday to Saturday. The main club opens at 8pm, Wednesday to Saturday, and comprises of a main reception and cloak area, a massive dance area, fully licenced bar, pole dance areas, heated smoking area, playrooms of all descriptions including a dungeon, a chill out lounge, a dogging area with genuine car bonnets, a Jacuzzi, showers and cinema.

Wednesday to Friday is open to all members; Saturday night is Ladies and Couples only. Predominantly a nightclub feel, with the added benefit of being able to keep it sexy, Xtasia music is provided by a range of excellent DJ's bringing you nights of modern dance, classic hits, and various genre evenings throughout the year. Xtasia also runs numerous niche fetish events for the more adventurous, normally in its private Purgatory dungeon area www.xtstasia.co.uk

Spice Swingers Resort: Lanzarote

This deserves a special mention as Antonia and her new love interest have recently returned from a week at this all inclusive Swingers resort and have been raving about it, so much so Paul and I are going to book a week there later in the year. It does look absolutely gorgeous.

Spice is Europe's first all-inclusive, clothing optional, lifestyle friendly resort for couples in Lanzarote. With an ideal climate all year and within 4 hours of most European destinations, Spice is what until now, you could only have dreamed of.

An entire resort dedicated to providing open-minded, liberated couples a haven where they can feel at ease being themselves, explore and live out their fantasies.

67 typically Canarian white-washed suites set in sophisticated secluded surroundings, sun terrace, feature pool sunk below ground level, All-Inclusive restaurant serving some of the best international cuisine on the island, nightclub and bars with top brand drinks available 24 hours a day. Relax in dedicated chill out zones and indulge the ultimate experience in the purpose built hot tub known to take at least 50 people with sensual waterfall and swim up bar (and yes, you really can swim in it!).

Relax and take in the sunshine, meet couples from all around the world, join in the fun with our resident Animator or take in the stunning sites of the many wonderful places to visit on Lanzarote including numerous naturist beaches. It's all here, just for you and it's right on your doorstep.

So come taste the Spice for a long weekend, mid-week break or even a week or so and then the only other thing for you to decide is "How Hot Do You Want It?"

Become our friend &/or join our community to be sure of hearing about amazing special offers and great events first.

We look forward to welcoming you to Indulge the Spice Lifestyle! www.spicelifestyle.com

Finally in this section is one that I know absolutely nothing at all about but looks very different and interesting. Maybe worth pursuing, does anyone know more? Check their profile at Fabswingers.

Wonderland U.K

WELCOME TO WONDERLAND

Your Naughty Home From Home!

Join us in an exciting exclusive and curious adventure weekend away like no other experience you will have ever had. Our venues are selected for Seclusion, Luxury and Atmosphere.

Just www.follow-the-whiterabbit.co.uk to a magical world of erotic play and imagination where you can be free to be yourself, free to explore and embrace all this lifestyle has to offer in a safe secure luxurious environment with the best facilities.

Swinging meets fantasy meets fetish all rolled into one Mad Hatters Tea Party.

We are a non-profit organisation all the proceeds are re invested into the venues and parties.

In a moment of madness our crew of six people decided we should create a fantasy party for real people a sexual and sensual journey with a little of our own erotic fetish twist.

All of us bring something to the table at Wonderland from fantasy costumes Submission and domination, Shabari rope work and pure eroticism for liberated swinging adults. It's the party you should never miss.

For the curious swinger's amongst you our entertainment demonstrations and workshops will intrigue and introduce you to our wonderful world of mystery and intrigue.

With years of experience between us it helps to make our events all over the UK very special and unique. Please read our verification's.

THE WONDERLAND CREW.

Alice Fab Profile sated pleasure your main booking contact.

The White Rabbit Fab Profile follows the white rabbit Master of ceremonies.

The Red Queen Fab Profile follow the white rabbit The Boss.

Cheshire cat Fab Profile Party People Head of Marketing.

Mad Hatter Fab Profile submissivesexylady Tea party specialist & Hostess.

The White Queen Fab Profile sugar muffin Kink Hostess.

We cater for all tastes from Tea parties Grand Balls Masquerades and lots of debauchery but above all an opportunity to spend memorable time meet and make new fantastic lasting friendships with like minded people in stunning locations.

WHAT A WAY TO SPEND A WEEKEND!

The Wonderland crew will take care of your every need you will want for nothing. Our priority is you.

Wonderland may not be every body's cup of tea but if you have an open mind and want to embrace and challenge your own experiences The Party Never ends you will never want to leave!

Take a leap head first into the Rabbit Hole like Alice.

www.Follow-the-whiterabbit.co.uk

Don't be late book your tickets to our next event.

Limited places at our parties.

For information email registration & Bookings chat to Alice fab profile wonderland sated pleasure.

These are just a very small selection of what is available to enhance your pleasures, I suggest you take some time to search the internet and find exactly what you are looking for as it's all available to you at the click of a mouse, unlike when we initially delved into the lifestyle when it was all on a bit of a wing and prayer, how things have progressed with technology. I can't begin to imagine what it will be like five years from now!

Chapter Forty-One: And In Conclusion

There you have it, I sincerely hope you've enjoyed the read as much as I've enjoyed doing the research! This brings "First Tango In Paris" right up to present day. As always I value your feedback both good and bad, and if you feel so inclined please take a moment to leave a review at Amazon. For your information the hardest part in writing the book is doing the proof reads and trying to correct all the spelling mistakes that the keyboard makes when you're not looking!

So the rest is up to you, go and enjoy yourselves and feel free to use both books to guide you. Also if any of you find any new and exciting clubs or destinations please do let me know. Thank you for reading. Emma xx